W9-AVR-489

NEW STORIES
FROM THE SOUTH

The Year's Best, 1990

edited by
Shannon Ravenel

NEW STORIES
FROM THE SOUTH

The Year's Best, 1990

Algonquin Books of Chapel Hill

published by
Algonquin Books of Chapel Hill
Post Office Box 2225, Chapel Hill, North Carolina 27515–2225
a division of Workman Publishing Company, Inc.
708 Broadway, New York, New York 10003

Copyright © 1990 by Algonquin Books of Chapel Hill. All rights reserved.
Printed in the United States of America.

No part of this work may be reproduced or transmitted in any form or by any means, electronic or mechanical, including photocopying and recording, or by any information storage or retrieval system without the prior written permission of the copyright owner unless such copying is expressly permitted by federal copyright law. With the exception of nonprofit transcription in Braille, Algonquin Books of Chapel Hill is not authorized to grant permission for further uses of copyrighted selections reprinted in this book without the permission of their owners. Permission must be obtained from individual copyright owners as identified herein. Address requests for permission to make copies of Algonquin material to Permissions, Algonquin Books of Chapel Hill, Post Office Box 2225, Chapel Hill, North Carolina 27515-2225.

ISSN 0897-9073
ISBN 0-945575-52-1

"Crow Man" by Tom Bailey. First published in *The Greensboro Review*. Copyright © 1989 by Tom Bailey. Reprinted by permission of the author.

"The History of Rodney" by Rick Bass. First published in *Ploughshares*. Copyright © 1989 by Rick Bass. Reprinted by permission of the author.

"Letter to the Lady of the House" by Richard Bausch. First published in *The New Yorker*. Copyright © 1989 by Richard Bausch. Reprinted by permission of the author.

"Sleep" by Larry Brown. First published in *The Carolina Quarterly*. Copyright © 1989 by Larry Brown. Reprinted in *Big Bad Love* by Larry Brown. Reprinted by permission of Algonquin Books of Chapel Hill.

"Just Outside the B.T." by Moira Crone. First published in *The Southern Review*. Copyright © 1989 by Moira Crone. Reprinted by permission of the author.

"Changing Names" by Clyde Edgerton. First published in *The Southern Review*. Copyright © 1989 by Clyde Edgerton. Reprinted by permission of the author.

"Boarder" by Greg Johnson. First published in *The Southern Review*. Copyright © 1989 by Greg Johnson. Reprinted by permission of the author.

"Spittin' Image of a Baptist Boy" by Nanci Kincaid. First published in *The Carolina Quarterly*. Copyright © 1989 by Nanci Kincaid. Reprinted by permission of the author.

"The Kind of Light That Shines on Texas" by Reginald McKnight. First published in *The Kenyon Review*. Copyright © 1989 by Reginald McKnight. Reprinted by permission of the author.

"The Cellar of Runt Conroy" by Lewis Nordan. First published in *The Southern Review*. Copyright © 1989 by Lewis Nordan. Reprinted by permission of the author.

"Family" by Lance Olsen. First published in *The Iowa Review*. Copyright © 1989 by Lance Olsen. Reprinted by permission of the author.

"Feast of the Earth, Ransom of the Clay" by Mark Richard. First published in *Antaeus*. Copyright © 1989 by Mark Richard. Reprinted by permission of the author.

"Where We Land" by Ron Robinson. First published in *Phoenix*. Copyright © 1989 by Ron Robinson. Reprinted by permission of the author.

"Les Femmes Creoles" by Bob Shacochis. First published in *Hayden's Ferry Review*. Copyright © 1989 by Bob Shacochis. From *The Next New World* by Bob Shacochis. Reprinted by permission of Crown Publishers, Inc.

"Zoe" by Molly Best Tinsley. First published in *Shenandoah*. Copyright © 1989 by Molly Best Tinsley. Reprinted by permission of the author.

"Fishbone" by Donna Trussell. First published in *TriQuarterly*. Copyright © by Donna Trussell. Reprinted by permission of the author.

CONTENTS

PREFACE   VII

Nanci Kincaid, SPITTIN' IMAGE OF A BAPTIST BOY   I
From *The Carolina Quarterly*

Lewis Nordan, THE CELLAR OF RUNT CONROY   15
From *The Southern Review*

Lance Olsen, FAMILY   35
From *The Iowa Review*

Mark Richard, FEAST OF THE EARTH, RANSOM OF
   THE CLAY   47
From *Antaeus*

Moira Crone, JUST OUTSIDE THE B.T.   55
From *The Southern Review*

Reginald McKnight, THE KIND OF LIGHT THAT SHINES
   ON TEXAS   63
From *The Kenyon Review*

Richard Bausch, LETTER TO THE LADY OF THE HOUSE   79
From *The New Yorker*

Greg Johnson, THE BOARDER   89
From *The Southern Review*

Tom Bailey, CROW MAN   113
From *The Greensboro Review*

Clyde Edgerton, CHANGING NAMES   127
From *The Southern Review*

Bob Shacochis, LES FEMMES CREOLES   135
From *Hayden's Ferry Review*

Molly Best Tinsley, ZOE   161
From *Shenandoah*

Ron Robinson, WHERE WE LAND   179
From *Phoenix*

Larry Brown, SLEEP   191
From *The Carolina Quarterly*

Donna Trussell, FISHBONE   197
From *TriQuarterly*

Rick Bass, THE HISTORY OF RODNEY   211
From *Ploughshares*

BIOGRAPHICAL NOTES   227

PREFACE

The "Southernness" in Southern literature might be said to be like the "sex" in sex appeal—we know it's there, and we know how to respond to it, but frequently there is no explaining why it works the way it does or precisely how it achieves its effect.

—LOUIS D. RUBIN, JR., "From Combray to Ithaca; Or, the 'Southernness' of Southern Literature," *The Southern Review*, Winter 1990

For the past five years I have been trying—and failing—to come up with an all-encompassing definition for those deceptively simple words, "the South." Given the title of this annual gathering of short fiction, I've felt obligated. And, too, though I know I probably ought not admit this, I'm a person who likes rules and curfews and limits, so it makes me nervous not to have a nice firm definition in hand as I read each year's crop of stories. Life would be so much easier if I could say, "Well, I like that story and (but) its setting meets (doesn't meet) the criteria for 'South'."

A firm definition of "the South" might make my life easier, but it wouldn't be good either for my character or for Southern literature. In any event, I don't believe anybody really wants exact boundaries on the South, for most people are born wary of sharp lines. I have had to struggle against my nature to finally figure out that drawing such lines around the South would mean having to decide if Washington, D.C., should be inside or out. (Sometimes it is inside and sometimes it isn't. In "Zoe," it's very much inside a South of undying chivalry.) It would also mean having to decide whether to include Southern waters and Southwestern lands. For this anthology, then, we might have had to rule out an unnamed sea island south of Florida and a town in East Texas. We'd have missed some quite Southern stories that way. See, for example, "Les Femmes Creoles" and "Fishbone."

And anyway, real life is not meant to be simplified. Even if I could determine the South's two-dimensional shape, complications of third (and even fourth) dimensions would immediately set in. There are too many neo-geographical aspects with which to tangle the lines. What if a story has no setting (like Larry Brown's "Sleep")? Can it be enough that an author's birthplace is located inside the "South's" boundary lines? Or, what if the setting meets the criteria, but the author wasn't born in the "South" though he's long lived there? How long is long enough? Egad! Richard Bausch's "Letter to the Lady of the House" might not qualify.

See what happens? And once my consideration of from-the-South eligibility wanders beyond the confines of hypothetical geographic boundaries, I am in danger of bogging down even more hopelessly. If I find it so difficult to pin down "Southernness" when I'm talking latitude and history, what am I to do when I start talking literature? For when linked with literature, that "Southernness" is rendered, I think, pretty close to the magical. A tone. A feeling. A spell.

Not that I don't know how to conjure up a little conventional wisdom on the subject. That part's easy: Double, double, toil, and trouble. What makes fire burn and cauldron bubble—to cook us all a batch of Southern Literary Brew?

A quick chorus of answers wafts back through the steam: A strong narrative voice. A pervasive sense of humor even in the face of tragedy. Deep involvement in place, in family bonds, and in local tradition. A sense of impending loss. Celebration of eccentricity. Themes of racial guilt and of human endurance.

There are stories in this collection that illustrate the power of those very elements, singly and in concert—"The Boarder," "The Cellar of Runt Conroy," "The Kind of Light That Shines on Texas," "Spittin' Image of a Baptist Boy," "Family," "Crow Man," "Feast of the Earth, Ransom of the Clay," and "The History of Rodney." All of these are stories in which familiar traits of Southern fiction motivate new and startlingly original interpretations of the Southern experience.

But the Southern experience, like all human experience, is evolving with time and in history. Multigenerational ties to specific locales are loosening as natives move away and strangers move in. Neighborhoods are changing. And so is the concept and nature of marriage and family make-up. All this is going on in the South just as it is going on everywhere else in America. And the literature of the region reflects it. For proof, read Moira Crone's "Just Outside the B.T.," Ron Robinson's "Where We Land," and Clyde Edgerton's "Changing Names."

The point I'm trying to make is not so much that I'm incapable of giving myself a Southern grid against which to measure and select stories for this anthology as that I don't want to. I am, it turns out, incapable, but I don't mind. As Louis Rubin has also so wisely noted: "What makes literature a unique form of knowledge is its complex ordering of human experience into images." Human experience tends to lap over edges and a Southern grid might very well lop off something important. I wouldn't have wanted to risk lopping off any images gathered here. I believe you'll agree.

Shannon Ravenel

PUBLISHER'S NOTE

The stories reprinted in *New Stories from the South, The Year's Best, 1990* were selected from American short stories published in magazines issued between January and December 1989. Shannon Ravenel annually consults a list of more than 175 nationally-distributed American periodicals and makes her choices for this anthology based on criteria that include original publication first-serially in magazine form and publication as short stories. Direct submissions are not considered.

Nanci Kincaid

SPITTIN' IMAGE OF A BAPTIST BOY

(from *The Carolina Quarterly*)

I do not look one thing like Mother. Maybe just have some of her face. How her cheeks sit out there like little round biscuits of flesh that got put on last, as an afterthought, after the rest of the face was finished. My cheeks did like that too. Sat out there all by themselves, looking added on. And my hands and feet were like Mother's. Very square and neat. No fat-looking fingers or toes. Trim and square. We could pick up most anything as good with our toes as with our fingers. A marble. A thumbtack. Mother could be holding two arms full of grocery sacks and pick up the car keys off the ground with her toes, bend up her knee and hand them to Roy. It was a natural thing. Walter said it was amazing and that Mother must have some monkey in her. But I could do it too.

I had some of Mother's ways, but not much of her looks. It was Roy that had those. Brown Roy with his black, shiny, almost wavy hair. Roy, who could have dirt all over his hands and face and it wouldn't even be noticeable hardly. Not on his brown self.

It was funny how we were. Roy brown like Mother. Me golden like our real daddy, which is not what somebody said, but I just saw that. How he had this straight yellow hair like me. And we had those blue eyes and those white eyebrows that go away, invisible, all summer long and come back some in the fall and winter. And then Benny looks like Walter. Kind of, he really does. He's like me and our real daddy about his white hair and skin and all. But like Walter in his build, which is big. Thick. Husky. And like Walter in his quietish ways. And it was not unusual at all for folks to say, "Lord, that boy takes after his daddy." Meaning Walter. People that didn't know would say that. "You sure can't be denying that child, Walter Sheppard!" People could see it. Even Mother could.

When folks got to telling Walter how Benny was exactly like him, just him made over, Walter would smile and say, "That's one lucky boy there. Damn lucky." And he'd wink at Mother. And it was just generally recognized how Benny was Walter's spittin' image.

Walter's people lived in Valdosta. That's in Georgia, not too far off. There's a bunch of Sheppards there, a slew of them. Walter said he has more cousins than you could shake a stick at. Walter said every other person you'd meet on the street in Valdosta was a Sheppard, or married to one, or lived next door to one. He said there is such a thing as too much of a good thing. He said that's why he came down to Tallahassee. That, and because he had a a chance at a right good job with the highway department.

None of us ever laid eyes on any of Walter's people. Not a one. He never did say that much about any of them. Just his brother Hugh. Hugh Henry Sheppard. He was Walter's little brother, grown and all now. Walter liked the heck out of ole Hugh. But that was about all.

Mrs. Sheppard, Walter's mother, was very disappointed that Walter didn't make a better marriage. She called Mother 'the divorcee.' When Walter was fixing to marry Mother and he called Mrs. Sheppard to tell her about the wedding to see if she could come or not, she could not. Mrs. Sheppard couldn't come because it plum broke her heart, Walter marrying a divorcee. And

one with kids. She said Walter deserved his own flesh and blood
kids. And here he was going to be bringing his hard-earned pay-
check home to somebody else's leftover wife and another man's
kids. And it plum broke her heart. And there wasn't any need
in her coming clear down to Tallahassee to cry her eyes out at a
terrible mistake of a wedding like that. She wasn't up to it. Walter was just gon have to understand that. So Mrs. Sheppard had
never even seen Mother, or any of us. We didn't think she ever
wanted to. Walter said we were not missing one thing. He said
he'd seen enough of the woman for all of us.

And then one day out of the blue she calls up Walter and says
she is coming to visit. She's taking a Trailways bus down to Tallahassee and can he pick her up down there at the bus station.
She says her conscience cannot rest until she sees Walter, meets
his divorcee wife and all. She just has to come because she can't
rest until she does. Walter was married to Mother almost a year
by then—and his poor mother can't rest.

Mother went into a frenzy over the idea. Not mad exactly, just
a nervous wreck, worrying about what to fix for dinner. Does
your mama like this or that? Does she like biscuits better than
cornbread? Does she like sweet pickles in her potato salad? And
then Mother wished we could go on and paint my bedroom. It
had been needing it so she wished we could paint it. She wanted
Walter to mow the grass, and wash the car and his highway truck,
and fix the tear in the screen door. She wanted Roy and Benny
to get them a haircut. She wanted to clip our fingernails—and
our toenails. She did speeches on us acting nice, stuff about not
just yes ma'am, no ma'am, please and thank-you. But also about
chew with your mouth closed, put your napkin in your lap. Do
not pick your nose. Keep quiet. Don't scratch. Say excuse me.
Be polite. No fighting and yelling. No slamming the screen door.
No grabbing food. Smile. Say nice-to-meet-you. Walter's mother
coming was not one thing like when our granddaddy came.

We kind of had the feeling we were in a contest to see if we
could be nice enough to win Mrs. Sheppard so she might want to

be like our grandmother or something. Like she was the Grand Prize if we won the niceness contest. If we could be good enough.

Walter tried to calm Mother down because she was about to wear herself out, and us too. And Walter said it wasn't the queen of England coming, just his mother, Emma Jean Sheppard. And there wasn't no sense in trying so hard to please her. No sense at all. But you couldn't tell Mother that. On the day Mrs. Sheppard was coming, Mother changed clothes a half a dozen times. Brushed the curl right out of her hair. Got all the rest of us nervous too. She burned the first batch of homemade dinner rolls she put in the oven. Walter told me to go on up to Melvina's and get her. Mother did not know one thing about dinner rolls. He said to get Melvina in the kitchen before it was too late. So Mother went on in the bathroom and brushed her hair some more. Melvina got in the kitchen mumbling all kinds of this and that.

When Mrs. Sheppard finally came walking in the house with Walter one step behind her carrying her suitcase, she was not exactly what we were expecting because we didn't know what we were expecting. Walter standing there behind his Grand Prize Mother. Everybody, including Melvina, gathered up around her and stared like she was some outer-space creature or something. Mrs. Sheppard in her little pillbox hat with the flowers on it, with her silver-blue curled hair and her seashell earbobs. She was a pretty regular grandmother type we thought. She didn't look so bad.

Walter said, "Mama, I want you to meet Sarah here. My wife, Sarah."

Mother reached out her hand and said, "Mighty glad to meet you, Mrs. Sheppard. Walter has told me an awful lot about you."

Mrs. Sheppard did not go to shake hands with Mother, but just looked her over some. Just stood there with her hands folded across her stomach and let her eyes fix on Mother. "You are a pretty thing. I'll say so. Walter, she is a pretty thing. How is it a pretty girl like you come to be a divorcee?"

"Mrs. Sheppard, meet the children," Mother said, putting her arms around us. "This here is Lucy . . . and Roy . . . and little Benny. . . ." She didn't add that at that moment we were the three squeakiest clean children in Tallahassee. But she could have. She did not say, "Look here, Mrs. Sheppard, look behind these kids' ears, clean as a whistle. See that?" She did not make us show our teeth, how toothpaste-white they were, or make us hold out our hands for Mrs. Sheppard to check how our fingernails were clipped so nice and all. She didn't do it, but she could have.

We said, "Glad to meet you." Then Mrs. Sheppard told Walter she sure was tired and thought she would like to lie down and rest some. No howdy-do or nothing. And that was how the visit started. And it never got better.

Mrs. Sheppard was a right peculiar woman. She went and laid down on the bed in my room—with her flower hat still on her head and all. She laid on her back with her hands still folded over her stomach, her shoes still on her feet. She looked like somebody waiting to get buried in a grave.

Mother went and put on a Tennessee Ernie Ford religious record on the record player. She thought some music would help Mrs. Sheppard rest better, and it would drown out any noise me and Roy and Benny made, which wasn't much. Mother told Melvina she could go on home, since supper was under control and everything. But Melvina didn't want to. She said she ain't come clear down here for nothing and she's gon wait till after we eat supper. That was because if there was something good left over from this company dinner she was gon take it home with her. She always did like that. Fix her a big plate and take it up to her house. Meanwhile she was gon sit in the kitchen with a flyswatter in her hand and wait.

Most of the afternoon passed with Mrs. Sheppard laying up in my bed. Finally Walter went in there and woke her up to come eat supper. Mother made him do it because she didn't know how much longer the three of us could keep up with being so good. It was like she was afraid our good behavior was going to run out just about the time Mrs. Sheppard woke up and we sat down to eat, and Roy and me would go to chewing with our mouths open and grabbing food. And Benny would start crying and rub Jello in his hair. She wanted to get supper over with before our goodness ran completely out.

When we were all seated at the table, Benny in his highchair by Mother and all, then we bowed our heads and Mother asked the blessing, like she always did. Sometimes she would let me or Roy ask the blessing, but on an occasion like this with Mrs. Sheppard eating with us, then Mother said it herself. And she meant every word of it, you could tell.

We started up passing the food around in a quiet way, and Mrs. Sheppard looked at Mother and said, "What church do you go to?"

Walter made this noise in his throat.

"Well," Mother said, "I was raised Methodist, and I'm raising the children Methodist."

"What is the name of your Methodist church?"

"It's right in downtown Tallahassee," she said. "A big ole church. Trinity Methodist. It's a very nice church."

"Walter was raised a Baptist," Mrs. Sheppard said. "Been a Baptist all his life. My boys were raised Baptist. I saw to that."

Walter kept on eating.

"Walter never missed a day of Sunday school or church growing up. Did you, Walter? If the doors were open the Sheppard family was there. Walter's daddy was a deacon, rest his soul. Walter's been a Baptist all his life."

"There's not too much difference between Methodist and Baptist," Mother said. "They're pretty close."

"World of difference," Mrs. Sheppard said, putting spoonsful of sugar in her already sweetened tea. "World of difference. I know because I've been a Baptist my whole life and raised my boys Baptist. If it was good enough for John the Baptist, then it is good enough for me. Baptizing is. Real baptizing, like the Bible says. Dunking yourself clean underwater, head and all, washing away those sins, being reborn right on the spot. Wet as a newborn baby. Baptized and reborn."

"Mama," Walter said, in his please-don't-get-started-with-this voice. The same one he used on Mother sometimes.

"It's so," she said. "It is so. Methodists might think sprinkling a little dab of water on their heads is baptizing. But they're wrong. The Bible says that. Sprinkling is not baptizing. It is sprinkling. God does not care one thing about a few drops of water on your head—not even enough to mess up your hair. He wants wet. He wants hold-your-breath, underwater, soaking wet. That's baptizing. Nobody ever got born again over a little sprinkle of water on their heads. There's a world of difference."

Mother acted like she needed to be cutting up Benny's pork chop for him and wiping off his mouth with a napkin and all. We could just tell she was biting her tongue.

"Walter is baptized proper. Aren't you, Walter? Didn't I take you and Hugh Henry and get y'all baptized? I certainly did. Because if the Bible says it, then I believe it."

Mother was looking at Walter eat. Her eyes were beating on him. If her legs could have reached him, she would have kicked the daylights out of him as a signal for him to say something. It looked like she was chewing her food, but really she was biting her tongue. And beating on Walter with her eyes.

We all ate quietly for a few minutes. Me and Roy had not said one word. And we had not spilled our milk or dropped food in our laps. Since we did not know much about grandmothers, we just sat there watching Mrs. Sheppard. She was our first close-up look at a real grandmother.

"So," she said to Mother, "where is your first husband?" Mrs. Sheppard was mashing her Jello square with the back of her fork. That Jello was shaking like crazy. "Your first husband. Where is he?"

Mother darted her eyes at Walter, and then said, "Mrs. Sheppard, we ought not to talk about this at the dinner table with the children and all." Mother looked at Walter again.

"Sarah don't have a first husband and a second husband, Mama. All she's got is one husband, and that's me."

"I am just asking a harmless question, Walter. It is normal for a mother to have some curiosity about her boy's wife. It's perfectly normal."

"We're not gon talk about this now, Mama."

It was quiet a long time, us sitting at the table eating. Us using nice manners. Sometimes somebody said pass this or that and somebody would do it. Sometimes Walter cleared his throat. All there was was knives scraping across plates and forks tapping, and ice cubes melting some and clanking in the glass. And sometimes somebody said pass the butter please. Then Mother started saying did anybody want some dessert? Me and Roy did. Everybody did. So Mother starts fussing around the table, moving the plates and all.

Mrs. Sheppard put her hand on Walter's arm. "Son, it's normal for a mother to have some curiosity about her boy's wife. It's normal."

"Don't the Bible say something about curiosity, Mama? It's bound to say something on the subject."

Mrs. Sheppard looked at Walter in a mean way. "Well, I'll tell you one thing, Walter Sheppard, the Bible says plenty about a divorced woman. It says submit unto your husband, which means your one and only husband. It doesn't say one thing about trade this one in for that one."

Mother went carrying the dinner plates into the kitchen, they were all piled up with forks poking out between them and they rattled when she walked, like skeleton bones banging together. She closed the door with her foot.

Walter pushed back his chair from the table, and it made this loud scraping noise. Walter made some loud scraping noises of his own saying, "Let me tell you what!" He was about to speak to his mother, but then looked at me and Roy with our wide-open eyes and Benny, with Jello in his hair, and he stopped. "Lucy, you and Roy take Benny on out in the yard a while. You'll get your dessert later on."

We didn't like the idea.

"Right now I said!" And we could tell Walter meant it. So we got Benny out of his highchair and went on outside. We got up under the dining-room window as quiet as we could be—like we did when Melvina came to see Mother cause old Alfonso beat her up. We got up there by the window because we wanted to hear.

"Let me tell you something, Mama," Walter started. "This here is my house. You're in my house. And Sarah is my wife. This can be any kind of house I want it to be and I want it to be a Methodist house. You hear me? And if you and John the Baptist don't like it, it's plain too bad!"

We could hear Mrs. Sheppard sniffling. We wanted to look in the window so bad and see if Walter was making her cry. "And another thing, Mama. You cannot come in my house acting like it is your house. You cannot be talking that divorced woman trash to Sarah. Do you hear me?"

"Walter"—Mrs. Sheppard was crying her words—"you never used to talk to me like this . . . not before you married her."

"For Lord's sake, Mama!" It was Walter's maddest voice.

Mrs. Sheppard kept up the crying. "I just want what's best for you, Walter. That's all. That's all I ever wanted. For you a Christian home with a wife of your own and kids of your own. You can't blame a mother for that. I just want you to have a good wife that appreciates you."

"Mama," Walter said in a calm way, "I'm gon be picking out my wife, not you. And I picked Sarah. And she ain't making me into a Methodist any more than you made a Baptist out of me."

Mrs. Sheppard blew her nose.

"You don't know one thing about Sarah, Mama. Not one thing she's been through. And you ain't never gon know because it ain't your damn business."

"Walter . . ." she cried, "you never used to talk like that."

Then it got quiet. Just Walter sitting there and his mama crying into her paper napkin. Minutes passed with her sniffling and sobbing. "Do you think I'm blind? Do you Walter?" Mrs. Sheppard said. "Do you think I was born yesterday?"

"Mama, what are you talking about?"

"When I got here this afternoon and your wife said meet the children—and I saw that baby. Walter, I cannot tell you. I can't tell you what it did to me."

"What the . . ."

"It was like you standing there, Walter. Why, he couldn't be any more yours if you named him Walter Sheppard Junior. Did you think I wasn't gon notice that? That little baby looking like your spitting image."

Walter sort of chuckled.

"Don't Mama me. I'm no fool, Walter. I wasn't born yesterday. It just come to me this afternoon, standing there seeing that little baby—you made over. It come to me."

"What did?"

"Why you married that divorcee."

"Mama . . ."

"Don't deny it. I know you, Walter. I know you like a book. You're an honorable man about a thing like that. And then I just laid in yonder on that bed there, thinking how it was me that raised you that way. Honorable and all. You from a good Baptist home. Some men would be long gone when a divorcee comes up expecting a baby. But not you, Walter. Not one of my honorable boys."

Me and Roy were in the flower bed up under the window. We did not know what to think about crazy Mrs. Sheppard.

"You're dead wrong, Mama. Do you hear me? Dead wrong. This is my house and I'm saying you're dead wrong."

Mother opened up the kitchen door. Her and Melvina had been listening to every word said. They were listening in the kitchen same as we were listening in the flower bed. And so here comes Mother carrying Walter and Mrs. Sheppard plates of pound cake and ice cream. She set Walter's down in front of him, and when she went to set Mrs. Sheppard's down, Mrs. Sheppard said, "I'm sorry but, I do not believe I can eat this. I have just lost my appetite. I think I'll just go back in yonder and lay down a while. Excuse me." And she got up with her balled-up paper napkin pressed against her nose and went in my room and laid on the bed. Again.

Mother sat down at the table with Walter, who was eating his dessert like on any ordinary day. Putting a spoonful of ice cream in his mouth and letting it sit there and slowly melt. "Is she all right?" Mother asked.

"She's okay."

"Should we do something?"

"Nope."

"It seems like we should do something, Walter."

"Like what?"

"I don't know, go in there and talk to her or something. Get this thing straight."

Walter was eating his pound cake and ice cream slow, like he was enjoying the heck out of it. Like it was one million times more important than his mother laying like a corpse, crying like she had come down with some fatal truth.

"Well, we can't have her go around thinking Benny is yours, and I tricked you. Walter, I don't want her to think that. I'm no tramp. And it bothers me, Walter. It does."

"Look on the good side," Walter said. "It's not you being a tramp so much as it is her Baptist boy being one hell of a lover."

"Walter . . ." Mother smiled at him like she did when he would not take a serious thing serious. Like it could be the end of the world and Walter would sit and eat a plate of cake and ice cream, slow and relaxed. Like bombs were going off and Walter would sit still and feel good about himself.

In a minute he got up from the table and walked by Mother, patting her shoulder. "Good supper," he said. "Good supper for a Methodist divorcee." He walked on into the living room and sat in his regular chair over by the picture window.

When me and Roy and Benny came back in for our dessert we saw that Mother was crying, with her hands over her face, and Melvina patting her like Mother was a child. She turned her face from us when we came into the room and then hurried down the hall to her bedroom. Mother back in her room crying and crying, and Mrs. Sheppard laying in my bed doing the same. Some people would probably say that Walter didn't have much of a way with women.

Nothing can take away a child's appetite like a mother crying her eyes out. Me and Roy sat at the table sort of jabbing at our cake, but not eating any of it. Melvina came in and stood by us, saying very quietly, "Y'all allow your mama to be sad, now, you hear? Don't she allow you to be sad when you need to?"

We looked at Melvina, and she reached out both hands and took our serious faces in them. Her hands were soft and warm and wrapped most nearly from ear to ear under our chins. "God wouldn't have give folks no teardrops if he hadn't of meant for them to cry some. Now would he?"

We nodded our heads no.

"And Melvina wouldn't of give y'all no dessert if she didn't expect y'all to eat it." We half smiled at her. She smiled too, and gave our faces a squeeze. "See can you eat your ice cream fore it melts all over the table."

The next day Walter took his mother back to the Trailways bus so she could get on home to Valdosta. We said good-bye and nice to meet you like Mother told us to say. We felt disappointed for Mother because she wanted us a grandmother so bad and could not get us one no matter what. Me and Roy tried to tell Mother we did not need a grandmother. Not some blue-haired woman who just sleeps all the time with her shoes on. It was sort of like when you enter into a contest and try your absolute hardest to win, and then find out that the prize is something you never have wanted in your life. Just some contraption that's gon stay broken and tore up, and don't work good when it's fixed. We told Mother never mind about Mrs. Sheppard, but seems like that made her sadder than ever.

Later on when Walter saw how funeralish we were acting, he said his mother would not know a good kid if one bit her. In fact, he said, if she ever came back that's what me and Roy should do. Bite her. Bite her right on the leg. Me and Roy laughed our heads off. Walter is so funny.

Lewis Nordan

THE CELLAR OF RUNT CONROY

(from *The Southern Review*)

The only house in the Mississippi Delta with a full basement was a rambling many-roomed tarpaper shack owned by a white-trash gentleman named Runt Conroy. Runt was weaselly and drawn and he worked, when he was sober enough, as a backhoe driver, digging sewers and graves and ditches for pipelines. It was his own hands that had dug the basement of the Conroy shanty.

There was a passel of Conroy children, all red-haired and sunken-cheeked. I was never really sure how many. There were the twin girls, Cloyce and Joyce, children who spoke in unison. There was a misfit child named Jeff Davis, who believed his pillow was on fire. There was a boy my age, eleven, named Roy Dale, and a very young child, about four, named Douglas, whose only ambition when he grew up was to become an apple. There were others who were grown and had moved away.

Mrs. Conroy, the mother, was an angry woman. She seemed especially angry at Douglas, the child of low ambition. She berated him for it. She encouraged him to want to be something finer than an apple. She threatened to beat him if he did not change his mind. "You will always be white trash," she said to this four-year-old child. "You will never amount to anything. Do you want to be a doctor?" "Apple," Douglas replied. "Do you want to be a policeman? A fireman? A cowboy? A secretary?" "Apple," he replied each time. With enough effort she could wear Douglas down. With enough nagging he would change. Once he upgraded his ambition to a level that almost satisfied her. "Do you want to be a bootlegger? A pimp? A computer scientist?" "All right," Douglas said at last. "I don't want to be an apple." Mrs. Conroy was happy, she was a new woman, she was elated. She said, "I knew it! I was right after all, my darling boy, my own true son! You are not like the rest of the Conroys, you are not white trash. You are a wonderful child, the hope of our family." Douglas said, "I want to grow up to be a dog." It didn't matter. Mrs. Conroy was not dejected. Dog was not good, but it was progress. Dog was better than apple. Other days were less joyous. Other days Douglas would slip backwards. Once he wanted to be a cork. That night his mother cried herself to sleep while Runt sat lovingly beside her bed and wrung his hands and said, "He could do worse, darling, he could do a lot worse."

Most of the Conroy children were filthy and ragged and had sores on their legs and skin like alligator hide. One of them was different, Dora Ethel, a teenaged girl in perfect health who wore immaculate clothes and Woolworth makeup and made good grades in school, the freak of the family. She went out on dates.

My own family was poor, but this did not keep us from looking down on the Conroys and sneering when they took canned goods from the Episcopal charity box at Christmas.

Mrs. Conroy—Fortunata was her name—was a teacher's aide in an elementary school some ten miles away. She was not an attractive woman. She had a horsey face and buck teeth and a voice like sheet metal. Most of the children she taught were poor blacks, scared little first-graders with no telling what kind of homes in the swamp. She was gentle but not warm to them. In the middle of a reading lesson, when any person on earth might least expect it, let alone a small peasant child faced with reading

a language scarcely his own, Fortunata Conroy would suddenly
look up at the small quivering sea of little black faces and she
would say in her impossible voice, "God has denied me two gifts,
beauty and a pleasing voice," and without another word would
turn back to the struggle of sounding out the meaningless words
of the stories the children were pretending to read. Fortunata
was jealous and believed that every other woman in town was
sexually attracted to her weaselly husband, Runt.

I had been inside the Conroy home a few times, but only
briefly and never to take a meal or to spend a night. Roy Dale
never invited me to sleep over. He had a million excuses—the
small space, the lack of hot water and meals, his meddlesome sisters, the single bathroom, even the possibility of rats. Neither
Roy Dale nor I ever mentioned the real concern, that Roy Dale
was ashamed of his family.

Finally I wore him down. When you can manipulate a person
with nothing else, you give him your secrets. I told Roy Dale
that my father drank and was often depressed and maybe even
suicidal. Roy Dale did not believe me but he had sense enough
to know that such an admission, even if it were false, required
reciprocation.

"My daddy wants to die," I said.

"Want to sleep over?" he replied.

The Conroy home was a shack, but it was not small. There
was one impossible room after another. The floors were covered
with yellow linoleum, some of the rooms were papered with
newspaper. There were dangerous-looking space heaters in many
rooms. The pictures on the walls were of Blue Boy and of a wolf
standing on a snowy hillside looking at a house. They had been
cut out of a magazine and stuck in cheap frames. I pretended to
love the wolf picture. For effect I said, "Sometimes that's the way
I feel." Roy Dale gave me a look, but he didn't accuse me of lying.

The real reason I wanted to visit here was that I was interested
in the Conroys' cellar. I had never seen a cellar before. The word

itself impressed me. Cellar, root cellar, storm cellar. The cellar was the one detail of the Conroys' lives that almost rescued them, in my mind at least, from the charge of white trash.

Fortunata Conroy, Roy Dale's mother, did not agree. She hated the cellar. It reminded her of Runt. Runt had dug it. It was a sewer, it was a ditch, it was a grave. It was an underground monument to white trashery. Nobody should have a cellar. Having a cellar was proof positive to Fortunata Conroy that their genes and chromosomes were tainted. A billion dollars, a college education, and new teeth would not save a family from white-trash chromosomes if they were the only family in the Mississippi Delta with a cellar. Cellars stunk. Cats pissed in cellars. Potatoes rotted in them. Cellars were homes for rats.

Each day when Fortunata came home from work she walked into the house in search of evidence against herself and Runt. Her nose twitched, her entire face vibrated with accusation. And each day when she arrived home she said the same thing: "This place stinks!"

It was partly true. The incredible sea-level cellar could not be expected to hold out moisture. There was mildew built into the architecture. And the Conroys also had an old cat who sometimes peed in the basement, and especially on damp days a smell of urine could be detected in the air. "This place stinks!" Fortunata would say, and the cat and Runt and the whole gaggle and pride of viral and damaged children would leap for cover. At one time the Conroys had a parrot that could speak not a word but could make a sound like a cash register. It lived in the cellar until its feathers changed color and fell out. That, however, is another story.

The effluvium of the cellar was not really related to mildew or the cat; it was an accusation of Runt for his alcoholism, his birthright, his genes, his occupation, his adulteries real or imagined, his very breath. "This place stinks!" The house rang with the bad music of that refrain. "This place stinks!" The smell, real or imagined, was Runt's fault. Runt believed this as thoroughly as Fortunata.

He sniffed the cellar daily for the place where the cat was doing her evil business.

It was a day in April that I came to spend the night with Roy Dale and his family. It was this same day that Runt put forth his best effort to correct the smell in the basement.

He filled a yellow plastic bucket with hot water from the laundry tub and poured in a dollop of Parson's pine-scented ammonia. Roy Dale and I sat on the cellar steps and watched Runt the way normal children watch television. Runt swished the foamy water around with his hand and breathed the chemical fragrance into his nostrils. He began his search for cat piss.

He sniffed the fabric of a discarded chair near the useless hot water heater. He poked through a sad heap of linoleum scraps and cardboard boxes and cheap suitcases and round hatboxes containing veiled remnants of Fortunata's millinery past—and through newspapers and cinder blocks and a cracked mirror and the rags-and-tags of children's clothing, looking for the smell. He found nothing unusual, no cat piss, but he was not discouraged.

He tilted the yellow bucket so that the chemical water flowed over the basement floor. He had a new brush with yellow plastic bristles.

When he was finished, his undershirt was sweaty and his knees were wet. He wiped sweat from his forehead with his scrawny scaly forearm. He looked satisfied.

Roy Dale had said nothing at all during the whole time Runt had been working. Suddenly now he said, "It stinks!" He meant the pine-scented ammonia cleanser.

Runt looked up. He forced a pained smile. He said, "It smells kind of refreshing though, don't it? Kind of pine forest clean?"

Roy Dale said, "It stinks! Ugh! It stinks!" Then he jumped up and ran up the stairs holding his nose in an extravagant way. I leaped up and followed him. I held my nose also and said, "Ugh! Gag! It stinks!" I understood that there is something about seeing a wounded man that makes you want to hurt him.

For that reason it is hard for me to think of Fortunata Conroy, for all her meanness, as an evil woman. In fact, I believe she loved Runt and all her strange children. I think her intentions were always better than her actions.

Now when I look back on this day I think of Fortunata getting off work that afternoon at the elementary school in Leflore. I imagine that her classroom is neat and orderly, unlike her out-of-control tarpaper house and life. I imagine that the chalkboards are washed and the erasers are clean. I imagine that she puts an extra thumbtack in a colorful poster on the bulletin board. There are health charts and dental hygiene reminders and smiling Dr. Seuss monsters with good advice. *Stop Look Listen. Be A Friend. Don't Talk To Strangers*. I imagine Fortunata grading the last of the first-grade writing papers. She brings the hump of an *f* up to the top of a line; she extends the tail of a *g* to the line below. She checks the pregnant hamster for babies, she grieves the dying gila monster in the terrarium.

I imagine Fortunata driving home through the incredible flatscape of the Delta. She drives an ancient explosive Pinto beneath wide blue Mississippi skies. She smells the fragrance of cotton flowers on the breeze, she breathes the sweet swamp water of the rice paddies, she passes bean fields shrouded in dragonflies, a pasture with a white mule, the town dump where the rats are as big as collies, past a herd of deer in cornstalks, a dead armadillo on the berm, a flash and sudden clattering of swamp elves through the brush and across a high water bridge. The explosive Pinto is a spiritual thing. She is in love with her husband. Her children are normal children. She passes the local stick-fighting team, the high school arrow-catching team on a farther field. She watches Old Mr. O'Kelly carve soap on his front porch, and she sees the ventriloquist's dummy named Joseph of Arimethea that poor Mr. O'Kelly believes is his grandson. Mavis Mitchum, a neighbor woman, sucks her skirt. Hydro Conroy, Roy Dale's cousin, chases cars. Mr. Love's goat walks across the mantelpiece in praise. Parrots ring out a wealth of good news. Fortunata is beautiful, her voice is a melody, and she is coming home to the man she loves.

And then she pulls into her driveway and remembers that Runt is probably drunk, has probably already betrayed her today with another woman, or several, that Jeff Davis is trying to extinguish his pillow, and Douglas is a child of low ambition. Before she has set the emergency brake of the car, she can already smell the cellar. The cellar stinks.

These are her first words as she enters the house. "This place stinks!" she says, as if the cotton flowers and the tidy schoolroom had never existed. "This place stinks to high heaven!" she says. Her voice is the wheels of a braking freight train, metal on metal, alarm and dangerous discord. God has denied Fortunata two gifts, and Fortunata is here to prove it.

Runt was already defeated. Even Fortunata's voice and angry manner could not have made this more clear. Today of all days it was impossible to deny that the house stunk. It stunk worse than cat piss. It stunk worse than architectural mildew. It stunk as if an ammonia bomb had been exploded in a pine tree.

"This place stinks!" Fortunata said once again for emphasis.

She dropped her plastic briefcase onto a chair where the guiltless cat lay sleeping. The cat shot off the chair and down the cellar stairs, for what reason only God knows. Fortunata glared at Runt. Runt was responsible for the cat. It was a white-trash cat. This is what Fortunata's look told me.

Runt was glum. He said, "I scrubbed the basement floor." It was an apology and an admission of guilt.

Fortunata said, "My God, what did you *use*!"

Runt was hidden inside his own head. His eyes peered out of a skull. He looked like a rat in a soup can.

I was frightened of what might happen next. I said to Roy Dale, "Want to go outside?"

I could hear Jeff Davis far away in his room. "Fire!" he called out. "Man the hoses!" Jeff Davis was a madman, but he was also a practical joker. It was never clear to me when he was in psychosis and when he was a comedian. Runt knew, though. Runt, even in terror of Fortunata's wrath, could laugh a sweet and fatherly laugh at this dark joke of a little boy. Runt said with sincerity, "We are a lucky family."

Fortunata was having none of it. She said again, "What did you *use*?"—speaking of the ammonia bomb.

Jeff Davis called out, "Bucket brigade!"

Fortunata said, "What did you use to make this house stink?"

Runt said, "A good deal of time and energy."

I could look into Fortunata Conroy's eyes and know that she hated herself for this scene. I knew that she heard the impossibly harsh, hard metallic grating of her voice. I knew that she believed it was scenes such as this that gave her this voice, not genetics or even bad luck but only bitterness and a heart too long hardened by fear and rage and outrage. She knew how thoroughly out of line with her vision of marriage and joy and hope this scene fell and also that she was responsible for it. And yet she could not stop. In her mind swamp elves bolted from cover and crossed a glen into the trees and cane.

"Gallop the horses! Hook and ladders!" called Jeff Davis from his room.

Fortunata did not hold back on account of me. This open fighting told me that she was white trash to the core. A family of higher quality would have died before allowing me, an outsider, to witness their anger and pain. She said to Runt, "You worthless failure. You stinking drunk. You impotent pig."

I heard a voice say, "I like the way it smells."

It was Roy Dale. We were standing together in the room, practically clinging to each other. There were framed pictures of the entire white-trash family on the mantel above the living room space heater. Generations of rednecks in black and white and sepia and even in color. Aunts and uncles and cousins, nephews and nieces, foundlings and mulattoes, Ku Kluxers and gentle parsons. There were rednecks behind the traces of a mule, rednecks beneath false bowers at the senior prom, rednecks at weddings, rednecks in academic regalia at Ole Miss, rednecks in flannel shirts and fake pearls and with stethoscopes around their necks. There was enough money in professional photography of rednecks to fill in the miserable basement with dirt and bury Runt and the cat in the bargain.

When Roy Dale said, "I like the way it smells," all the rest of the people in the room, including myself, looked at him as if he were a man from Mars.

Nothing could stop Fortunata Conroy, or so I believed. She said, "I'll tell you why this house stinks."

Runt said, "Shut your ugly mouth."

Fortunata was momentarily stopped. She said, "What did . . ."

Runt said, "Your voice is like eating ground glass."

Fortunata said, "Don't you dare . . ."

Runt said, "Your breath is like Gary, Indiana."

Fortunata said, "If you ever . . ."

Runt said, "Your tongue is a snake that swallowed a frog."

Then Roy Dale's voice again: he said, "It smells like pine trees to me."

Runt said, "Your gums are raw liver."

Roy Dale said, "I sincerely like the smell of pine trees."

Jeff Davis was silent.

Fortunata said, "You low-life drunk."

Runt said, "You stooge."

Fortunata said, "You sexless lump, you eunuch."

Runt said, "You bitch."

Fortunata said, "Hit me! That's what you want to do! Hit me! It would be a relief!"

Runt said, "You sick slut."

Fortunata was screaming now. She said, "Get out! Go away! I don't want you near these children! Go to a mental hospital!"

Runt said, "Then I would be near your entire family."

Jeff Davis remained quiet. Even Jeff Davis could not be in a good mood all the time.

Runt went away from the house then. We heard the front screen door slap shut and then the Pinto started up. There was no explosion. Roy Dale led me out of the living room and down a dark hall to the room where he usually slept. Douglas, the child who wanted to be an apple, was sitting on an army cot, crying.

Roy Dale said, "What's your problem?"

Douglas said, "I don't know."

Roy Dale said, "Me and Sugar want to be alone."

Douglas said, "Ask me what I want to be when I grow up."

Roy Dale said, "I'll ask you tomorrow."

Douglas said, "Ask me now."

Roy Dale said, "What do you want to be when you grow up?"

Douglas stopped crying. He was about four and had a round moonlike face, streaked with dirt. He said, "Apple."

This was a joke the two of them seemed to share.

Roy Dale smiled and said, "Okay now, take off."

Douglas said, "Ask me the next part."

Roy Dale sighed. He said, "Do you want to be a cowboy?"

Douglas said, "No. Apple."

Roy Dale said, "A fireman?"

Douglas was giggling now. He said, "Apple."

Roy Dale said, "Astronaut?"

Douglas said, "Apple. Now say the best part."

Roy Dale said, "You've got no ambition."

Douglas said, "Say the next part. Say it right." Douglas was laughing now, really hard. He lay down on the cot and kicked his feet while he laughed.

Roy Dale said, "You'll always be white trash."

Even Roy Dale was laughing now. Both of them were cracking up. Douglas laughed so hard he got the hiccups and Roy Dale had to say, "Boo!"

Douglas said "Okay, okay, I don't want to be an apple any-more." Both of them were tickled but they were holding back.

This was their favorite part. Roy Dale perfectly imitated his mother's metallic voice: "My darling ambitious child!" he mugged. "My sweetest, most normal, most non-white-trash little angel!" he said in his mother's voice. "What *do* you want to be when you grow up?"

Now both of them were rolling on the army cot. They were pounding each other on the back. They fell on the floor. They were hysterical. Douglas tried several times and was too tickled to speak. At last he blurted it out: "I want to be a dog!" They hooted, they screamed, they guffawed, they chortled and lost their breath.

And then Douglas dried his eyes and got up off the floor. He was finished with the laughter. Roy Dale watched him, looking for something, I'm not sure what.

Douglas said, "That was a bad one." He meant the fight between Runt and Fortunata.

Roy Dale said, "Your tongue is the snake that swallowed a frog."

Douglas did not laugh. He said, "Yeah. Right." And then went on to bed in another room.

It was a good night for me to spend the night away from home. A steady rain had begun to fall and the clouds were dark and as low as the cottonwood trees in the bare grassless yard. Roy Dale and I sat alone in his room and played cards with a greasy deck of Bicycles and listened to the rain in the trees and on the roof and heard it puddle up in the yard. Life in the Conroy family went on and rarely touched the two of us. Supper was never mentioned, and my stomach gnawed on its own emptiness. It felt good to be hungry and to expect no food to relieve the hunger. It was easy to pay the small price of a night's hunger for the sweet isolation that Roy Dale and I were allowed to share. It frightened me to enjoy these moments with a white-trash child who, until now, I had believed was put upon earth only for my manipulation.

A few times family members stopped by our door and looked in. The twins who spoke in unison stopped for a moment and said nothing. Cloyce and Joyce.

At last Roy Dale said, "You can't come in here."

In unison they said, "We know that." They shared their mother's nasality, but in them it was sweet beyond belief.

Roy Dale said, "Sugar is my friend, not yours."

In one voice they said, "We know that."

Roy Dale said, "You're not really talking at the same time. Cloyce is talking first and Joyce is talking right behind."

In perfect duet they said, "You think you are so smart, Mr. Smarty pants." Then they went away.

Roy Dale said, "Just be lucky you don't have sisters."

Later Dora Ethel, the freak sister who wore makeup and got good grades, stopped at Roy Dale's door. She said, "Hey, Sugar" —talking to me.

Dora Ethel was very pretty and I was surprised to find myself speechless and in love. I said, "Huh, huh, huh." She said, "You're cute." The rain was drumming on the house. It was a tropical rain, a jungle rain. There was a prophet's voice in the rain. It said: *You will grow up to marry a white-trash girl*. Water stains were broadening across the ceiling.

Dora Ethel really wanted to speak to Roy Dale, though.

She said, "I'm going out."

Roy Dale said, "So?"

Dora Ethel said, "So look, I'm taking Daddy's pistol, okay? Don't tell, all right, but that's where it is."

Roy Dale said, "Got a date?"

Dora Ethel took the pistol out of her skirt pocket and twirled it on her finger in a funny little sexy way. She said, "Ask me no questions, I'll tell you no lies." Dora Ethel was by far the cutest white-trash person I had ever seen.

When she was gone I said, "She takes a pistol on a date?"

Roy Dale said, "She goes with Sweet Hodges. They shoot rats at the dump."

I said, "That's what she does on a date?"

Roy Dale said, "When it rains like this, yeah."

I said, "Shoots rats on a date? That's what she does?"

Roy Dale was not defensive. He said, "Her and Sweet. It's something they like to do together."

I said, "Sweet Hodges?"

Roy Dale let it drop. My heart ached with jealousy. I would never be old enough to leave the house beneath an apple-green night sky in a tropical storm, never old enough to love a girl who twirled a pistol on her finger, or to shoot rats at the dump for love. My genes had become infected with Conroy genes. I was terrified of the transformation, and I gloried in it.

No one came in later to tell us goodnight. One by one the children put themselves to bed. Lights went out. Runt's Pinto never returned, though Runt did, on foot. Maybe that was the night the Pinto exploded. Or maybe it only stalled out in the deep rainwater in the street. In any case, Runt came home, and there was no more fighting.

Roy Dale took off his clothes and lay on the bed naked, so I got naked too, and together we lay and listened to the drumming insistent rain. The yard outside our window was a lake. Douglas, who usually slept on the army cot, slept somewhere else tonight. We turned off the electric bulb hanging from a cord in the middle of the room and lay in the loud sounds of constant tons of falling water. Even Dora Ethel finally came in, dripping wet, and skulked through the house trying to replace Runt's pistol without being seen. The room was not entirely dark. There were streetlights far away, and the light from Red's All Night Bar at the end of the street. I could see Roy Dale place his hand between his legs, and so in a short time I placed my hand between my legs too, and we lay and breathed and did not speak.

It was very late now. So much time passed that I thought Roy Dale might be asleep. He said, "Runt has slept with two hundred and seventy different women."

I said, "Slept with them?"

He said, "I found a list of their names."

I was beginning to catch on to what "slept with them" meant.

I thought about this for a while. I said, "Can I see it?—the list?"

He said, "It's in the back of Runt's closet in a box."

I said, "My daddy hides a rock-and-roll suit in the back of his closet. It's black and it's got Rock-n-Roll Music spelled out on the back in little glittery things, sequins."

Roy Dale said, "Do you want a rubber? I stole some from Runt's drawer." He reached under his mattress and took out a few foil-wrapped packets.

I said, "Naw, thanks. Daddy's got plenty. I blow them up. Put water in them. You know."

Roy Dale said, "You ought to try jacking off in one some time. It adds a little something."

I said, "Hm."

We were silent again. The sound of the rain was without thunder. It was as constant as the feeling of loss that suddenly I felt inside me, that now I knew had been with me all along, a familiar part of me since the beginning of memory.

Roy Dale said, "Jeff Davis can pull a condom down over his head."

I turned and looked at Roy Dale in the weird green light of the storm sky. I said, "Get real."

He said, "No, really. All the way down over his face. Ears and everything."

I turned and looked up at the dripping ceiling. I said, "Caramba."

Roy Dale said, "He pretends he's robbing a 7-Eleven. Mama won't let him use one of her stockings."

I said, "That's really crazy, Roy Dale."

He said, "Right, I know. You can smother with a condom pulled over your head."

I said, "Caramba," again.

He said, "I know."

I said, "You would look pretty funny, you know, sticking up a store with a rubber over your head."

Roy Dale said, "It would be on the ten o'clock news. 'Two Caucasian males wearing condoms over their heads . . .'" We laughed pretty hard at this. We tried not to wake anybody up, but we were pretty tickled, I can tell you.

I said, "You wouldn't be able to talk. You couldn't say 'Stick 'em up.'"

Roy Dale said, "You'd have to go, 'Ump ump ump.'"

We laughed our damn heads off. We said, "Shh, shh!" And then we laughed some more.

There is not much more to tell. The storm outside was without wind and without lightning or thunder. The rain fell straight down and its falling did not diminish. The sound was constant, a pounding like heavy hammers that we could forget to hear. For a long time Roy Dale and I said nothing. He lay on his back, and I lay on my back. He did not touch himself and did not move. His breathing was soft and regular and I thought again he might be asleep. In the stillness a thought came to me like a friendly voice. The voice said: *We are all alone in this world.*

Just then Roy Dale said, "Your daddy has got a rock-and-roll suit?"

I turned my head in his direction and could see his body outlined in the green light of the storm-sky outside the window. I said, "In the back of his closet."

Roy Dale said, "So, like, what does he do?—like, puts it on and dances around, or what?"

I said, "I don't know. I don't think so. I think he just, you know, *has* it."

Roy Dale said, "Will you let me see it?"

I thought about this. No one had ever seen the rock-and-roll suit but me. I sneaked looks at it when no one else was in the house. Still I said, "I guess so."

Roy Dale said, "Great."

I said, "We wouldn't be, you know, like making fun of him or anything."

Roy Dale said, "No way. Uh-uh."

I said, "Well, okay, yeah, sure. I'll show it to you sometime."

Roy Dale said, "Tonight?"

I said, "Tonight?"

Roy Dale settled back on his pillow. He said, "You're right, it's a bad idea."

I said, "No, it's all right. We could do it tonight."

We did not go out that night, of course. We only lay in the dark and in the sound of the rain.

In a while Roy Dale said, "Come on," and the two of us stepped out of bed and moved quietly through the house and opened the cellar door. We were careful to wake no one. Jeff Davis might have called for the pumper trucks, the REO Speedwagon. Douglas might have wanted to be an apple. Cloyce and Joyce might have God-knows-what, in unison. Dora Ethel might have broken my heart. Roy Dale had a flashlight, which he shone into the darkness. At first I could see nothing, only the sturdy solid beam of light like a long pole. I followed behind Roy Dale, through the cellar door, down the steps, only two or three steps down before he stopped. He sat, and I sat beside him.

Roy Dale shone the light out into the basement and I understood for the first time what I was looking at, not mere blackness but deep water. The basement was four or five feet deep in rainwater. Roy Dale swept the light back and forth across it. I might as well have been Hernando DeSoto discovering the Father of Waters, the mighty Mississippi, for all my amazement at the sight. It was an interior sea, an indoor elementary mystery as dangerous and filled with evil meaning as any cavern, any water-filled cavity of the underworld.

Then on the face of the deep I thought I could see something else, some moving thing, or things. I imagined eyeless fish, I imagined mermaids, I heard their song. Roy Dale caught them in the beam of his flashlight. Earnest little faces and diamond-bright eyes, moving through the water, swimming for dear life, no doubt, but as if for pleasure. They were rats. A dozen or more of them. Large doglike barn rats, swimming quietly and without desperation along the black surface of this cellar sea.

Roy Dale said, "If Runt was awake he might let us shoot them with his pistol."

We took turns holding the flashlight on their sweet earnest evil little comical faces. I thought of the collie-sized rats at the town dump. They were burrowed deep in the garbage. They were waiting for the rain to end. I thought of that time a few hours from now, when this jungle storm would be finished. I thought of the Delta moon shining in the after-storm sky, with its ragged low moving clouds. I imagined the collie rats creeping from their hiding places in the rank waste pits of human misery and into the soft air. I saw them sit along riverbanks and scratch behind an ear or shake rainwater from their fur. I saw the collie-rats look up at the miraculous moon and howl and bay at its light. They barked and sang like mythical beasts and I heard the little town of Arrow-Catcher, Mississippi, fill up with their strange rodent harmony. I thought of the swamp elves, happy in their marshy cozy dens. The deer bedded down in cane, the muskrats and the beavers and the rope-whiskered catfish in the mud. One of us held the flashlight on the little swimmers while the other pointed a finger like a pistol and made pistol sounds—balooey, or ptoosh, or blammo!—and we passed the night in the belief that feeling love for each other and for this single incredible moment in time was all in the world that was important, and that it needed no acknowledgment, not even with a single word.

Later, when we had finished the game and only sat and shone the light onto the water, the old cat crept down the stairs and passed the two of us on the steps, first holding her tail up as she rubbed past, and then going all the way down to the last step visible above the surface of the waves. Roy Dale held the light on her, and we watched her test the water only once, briefly, one second, with one paw, before entering it in a kind of slow, mad cat-dive outwards, sploosh. The cat swam out into the cellar sea, holding her head high above the water and then relaxing some and swimming with confidence and ease. She was trying to corner one of the rats in the flood. Roy Dale and I cheered the cat. We shouted whispered directions—"this way!" and "behind you!"—and we tried to direct the cat to individual rats with the beam of the flashlight. It was no use. The cat was a good swimmer but no match for the experienced rats. This was their home, and there were frequent heavy rains in the Delta. Finally she gave up and left the water, back up the steps the way she had come, defeated and cranky and soaking wet, not even shaking herself to dry her fur. An apathetic, lazy, white-trash cat.

Roy Dale and I were finished. We were tired and sleepy. We turned off the flashlight and went back up the stairs. Roy Dale eased shut the cellar door so that no one heard. We went to bed then and snuggled close to each other. I felt his rough white-trash alligatory skin against my own softer skin and was comfortable and drowsy and I listened to the rain and I knew that it was falling more softly now, coming to an end, and that tomorrow everything that had been thrown underneath my own home a few blocks away—the empty whiskey bottles, the soup cans and empty paint buckets, a dead battery, a hairless doll, a slick tire, scraps of paper, indescribable garbage, the ice pick my father once stabbed himself in the chest with while I watched him, the towels he bled into as his face turned white while my mother closed the window shades so that no one else would see—all this would have been washed out from under our house by the jungle rain. It would lie in the yard and on the sidewalk and in the street for anyone to see. And then my mother would gather it all up again and toss it beneath the house again and again we would forget.

I moved my body close to Roy Dale. I reached in the darkness afraid even to open my eyes, afraid he would disappear, and I held him to me. I embraced him. I encircled him. We were like spoons together. We were like swamp elves. And in this way we went to sleep, bare-assed children, the two of us, and in my memory not blameworthy for any sin and not even victims of the sins of our sad fathers, but, only that moment, in love with what is and what has always been or what might forever be.

Lance Olsen

FAMILY

(from *The Iowa Review*)

Zach had been splitting wood most of the morning down by the shed when he first sniffed the familiar scent of his father who had died five years ago in a mining accident. It was early spring. Pale green buds fuzzed the birches along Amos Ridge and the ground was soggy and almost black with runoff. Zach straightened and let the axe swing down by his side. He sniffed the air again like a cat suddenly aware of chicken livers on the kitchen counter. The intimate aroma was hard to pin down. Some honey was in it. And some salt. Cinnamon was there. And maybe some sourdough and pine needles. Beyond that, precise words didn't work well. Something sweet. Something acrid. Something like rum and something gamy and musty and earthy and clean all at the same time. He hadn't smelled anything like it for half a decade but he knew it right away, down behind his stomach, down behind his knees. It didn't frighten him and it didn't gladden him. It was more interest that he felt.

He turned and squinted a little into the intense sunshine fanning through the branches around him and saw his father standing with his hands in his pockets in a misty golden nimbus of light near a wild dogwood. He looked just as he had on the day he left the cabin for the last time, wearing overalls and olive-green rubber tie-up boots and a stained undershirt and yesterday's beard. They stood there eyeing each other for several heartbeats. Then Zach nodded slightly in a gesture of acknowledgment and his father's ghost nodded back slightly in a gesture of acknowledgment and Zach turned and picked up his axe and picked up a foot-and-a-half pine log and set it upright on the stump before him and started splitting wood once more because there was still a good part of an hour left until lunchtime.

Strip mining had peaked outside of Frenchburg, Kentucky, in the late sixties and early seventies and then it began falling off. Houses went up for sale. Ken's Market, one of the two grocery stores in town, shut down. The lone car dealership burned to the ground one night and for nearly two years no one seemed to have enough money to clean up the charred remains. But Zach's father didn't have much else that he felt comfortable doing, so he decided to stick with mining as long as mining would stick with him. The company had brought in a mechanical monster called Little Egypt to make the job of digging more cost-efficient. Little Egypt was a machine the size of a small hotel. It was several stories tall and several stories wide and it was covered with gears the size of most men and it looked more like something people would use on Mars for space exploration than it did like something people would use in Menifee County for mining. Its sole purpose was to dig into the earth, slowly, cumbersomely, relentlessly, twenty-four hours a day, seven days a week, three-hundred sixty-five days a year, processing coal as it went, eating, gnawing, wheezing and clanking away with a deafening sound. Zach's father, who was fifty-seven at the time, was part of a team of men responsible for keeping the huge gears of Little Egypt clear from crushed stone and grit and keeping them oiled and running smoothly. One day in late summer during his lunch break Zach's father sampled a swig too much of shine a buddy of his offered him, turned tipsy, and tripped as he was shinnying among the intricate workings of the behemoth. Instantly he was pulled into the innards of the creaking, banging, raucous colossus, kicking and screaming, and was never seen in one piece again. Until, of course, that spring day.

At noon Zach's wife, Amelia, called him for lunch. She had made bean soup and black bread and apple cobbler. He washed his hands at the spigot outside and walked around his dark blue Ford pickup truck and went in and sat at the table near the stove and began to eat. Amelia told him how she was going to French-burg to pick up some things, and Zach told her how he was going to start patching the aluminum roof on the shed that had blown off during a big storm last November. Amelia told Zach how she had phoned Madge at the next farm over and how Madge and Opal's dog Mork had been bitten by the first copperhead of the season and how the dog's snout had grown a lump that made it appear as if it were raising a plum under the flesh. As Zach listened he became aware of another presence in the kitchen. He glanced up and saw his father standing by the refrigerator, hands in the pockets of his overalls, watching the couple talk and eat. Zach's father wasn't smiling and he wasn't frowning but his eyes seemed a little more yellowish than usual and they seemed infi-nitely sad. He didn't speak and he didn't move. He just looked on as Zach raised a forkful of apple cobbler to his mouth and then washed it down with a gulp of water. Amelia noticed Zach was staring hard and long at the refrigerator and turned to see what he was looking at.

"Your father's here," she said after a moment.

"Yep," Zach said, cutting himself another bite of cobbler. "I reckon he is."

And that's how it started. Zach's father just appeared one beau-tiful spring day in a misty golden nimbus of light and Zach and Amelia acknowledged his appearance and then they didn't say a whole bunch else about it. After all, they had a lot of other things to think about. The field down the road needed plowing and planting. The shed needed mending. The winter wood needed tending to. And if they knew anything about Zach's father they knew he could take care of himself.

In the beginning Zach had the impression his father had come to tell him something he didn't already know. Maybe some secret about life that fathers come back from the dead to tell their sons because it's so important. Maybe some word of wisdom that would suddenly illuminate the world for him and release some vise that had been clamping his head so he could see things in a way he had never seen them before. But Zach's father never spoke. In fact he never made any sort of sound, not even when he walked across the wooden kitchen floor in his olive-green rubber tie-up boots. Zach waited two weeks, thinking his father might be trying to find the right words in which to stick his wisdom. And when at the end of that time Zach figured maybe his father could use some coaxing, he prompted him one rainy night by asking, "So what do you have to say for yourself?"

His father had nothing to say for himself. His facial expression didn't change. His eyes continued to look more yellowish than usual and infinitely sad and they focused on Zach's moving lips and then on Zach's blue eyes and then it occurred to Zach that the problem was that his father couldn't hear a word he was saying. There must have been some kind of interference between this world and the next. So he went and got a slip of paper and a pencil and he came back and wrote down his question and tried to give it to his father but the paper just passed through his father's extended hand as though it were no more than colored air and it fluttered to the floor.

When Zach told this to his wife, she told him she was convinced his father had come back to visit them because death was such a lonely place.

"Death isn't a lonely place at all," Zach said. "Lots of people are dead. He should have lots of company where he's at."

"That's all you know, Zach Ingram," she said.

Amelia smiled a considerate smile at Zach's father as you might at any infirm elderly parent or parent-in-law and let him accompany her from room to room and when she went outside to hang clothes and clean the outhouse. The ghost followed her at a respectful distance and took what seemed an exquisite interest in the simple chores of daily life: baking muffins, boiling pot roast, frying potatoes, scrubbing the skillet, folding down the quilt on the bed, hanging the winter coats in the back of the closet until next fall. She set a place for him at dinner and even put scraps on his plate, although he couldn't sit at the table without falling through the chair and although when he bent down and tried to pick up a crumb with his tongue, the crumb passed right through his jaw. She lit a candle for him at night and put it on the kitchen table and bought a newspaper for him to read every Sunday when she headed into church even though she knew he wouldn't be able to hold it. Every night he stood in their bedroom door when they were ready to go to sleep until they said goodnight to him and turned off the lights and then he would wander into the living room and stand by the window and wait for the first gray glow of dawn. Sometimes Zach would come upon him standing at the end of Amos Ridge on Whippoorwill Point amid wild blueberry bushes and sassafras shrubs, looking out over the limestone cliffs and pines and cedars below, or kneeling by the thousands of large amazing jelly-bubble sacks of frog eggs in puddles that collected in ruts along the dirt road that lead up to the cabin.

They had no idea how good his presence made them feel until one morning in July Amelia went into the kitchen at six o'clock to grind some coffee and discovered he was gone. She thought he must be in the living room at the window watching the orange sun roll up behind the trees, but when she checked no one was there. She stuck her head into all the closets, and then she went outside and searched the shed and the outhouse and the area around the woodpile. She woke Zach and told him what had happened, and he immediately dressed and headed down to Whippoorwill Point and called out his father's name and when he didn't see him there he walked all the way to Madge and Opal's farm before understanding somewhere under his lungs that he had lost his father a second time. It hurt Zach terribly, like a hole in the heart hurts, like a hammer in the head hurts. He slowly walked back into the cabin and told Amelia what he hadn't found and then sat down in a fold-up chair on the porch and didn't get up for three weeks.

He sat there with his left ankle on his right knee and his hands in his lap, and he looked out over the ridge and waited for his father to return. The hot hazy sky purpled at twilight. Crickets chirruped. Stars blinked on in the sky. And after a while he put his chin on his chest and fell asleep. In the morning he didn't eat his breakfast. In the afternoon he didn't eat his lunch. In the evening he didn't eat his dinner. Gradually he became as quiet as his father had been. Amelia told him he was getting thinner and more pathetic every day, and when he didn't respond to her she began to eat his meals in addition to her own. First, it was simply a way not to let the food go to waste. Then it was a way to express her own grief, her own pain, her own sense of absence. She gained five pounds the first week. She gained eight pounds the second. She gained ten the third.

Late in August as Zach watched the burning ball of the sun dip behind the treeline, he noticed two figures walking up the road toward him. Through half-closed eyes he took them to be Madge and Opal coming over to check on them. But the closer the couple came the easier it was to tell they couldn't be Madge and Opal: the man was too old and the woman too short. Zach squinted and then he cocked his head to one side and then he shut one eye and then the other and then he opened both of them and then it struck him that he was looking at his parents, both of his parents, walking arm in arm up the road as they often did after dinner. His father was still wearing the same clothes he had on the day he fell into Little Egypt. His mother was still wearing the nightshirt she wore the day she said living without her husband was a stupid foolish thing and crawled into her bed and pulled up the quilt and turned her face to the wall. The couple mounted the porch and walked by Zach, and he rose and followed them and saw them halt in the bedroom door, watching Amelia, chubby, soft, round, and wide-eyed, watch them back from the bed.

Zach's parents were extremely considerate. They always stood in corners, out of the way, arm in arm, or, at night, by the window in the living room from which they could see the first gray glow of dawn. They never asked for anything, never offered advice, and never nagged. They took obvious delight in the wood-grain rippling through the kitchen table; the black-and-white patterns on the wings of the willet that magically appeared on the roof of the shed one cold autumn afternoon; the yellow-green leaves of tobacco ready for harvest in the field down the road; the five-inch-long acorn-brown lizard that perched every morning on the top step, head raised with dignity and alertness, reptilian grin frozen on its face; the short stubby ochre squiggle near the woodpile, looking at them with its black glassbead eyes. Sometimes at dusk they craned their heads slightly and closed their eyes and sniffed at the cool evening air filled with honeysuckle, jasmine, wet grass, endive, pine, moist soil, leafy mulch, a hint of cantaloupe rinds. Sometimes in the afternoon they bent over near a tall curl of wild grass and studied the shiny blue body of the dragonfly arched just above it.

Zach and Amelia barely noticed it when his mother disappeared for two nights, returning with cousin Virgil, who had died at thirty-one when his sleek black Toyota pickup skidded off Route 641 one rainy night in 1984 and smashed into a tree at eighty miles an hour. Or when Zach's father disappeared for nearly twenty-four hours, showing up cradling a baby in his arms, the Armstid's little girl, who had died last year when she was two weeks old because she had been born with some of her insides backwards. Amelia was startled to see her uncle Ferrell, who'd been killed in 1968 somewhere in Cambodia although the government had always said it had been in Vietnam, and her aunt Helen, who'd taken her own life in 1963 when she caught her husband, Tom, fooling around with that cheap blond Bobbie Ann Stills. Zach tried to shake hands with his nephew Billy, whose spine had snapped during an accident on his Honda three-wheeler RV in 1987, and he tried to hug his mother's friend, Mildred, who'd been bitten by a rattler while picking raspberries in 1956 on Madge and Opal's farm. Zeb, whose tractor engine fell on him two years ago while he was trying to tighten a bolt under it, showed up after all the leaves had dropped off the trees on Amos Ridge, and Abel, who choked on a chicken bone while watching the 1979 World's Series Game, appeared just as the skies turned the color of a field mouse's neck and the first light snow began to fall.

"House sure is gettin' mighty cramped," Zach said when he stayed in on Thanksgiving to watch the Macy's parade on television.

"Family's family," Amelia said.

Her voice was simple, kind, and firm.

Somewhere in his chest around where hope is kept, Zach knew she was right and didn't say anything else. He felt good. He felt complete. He felt a system of networks, harmonies, symmetries forming around him and had a tremendous sense of being somewhere, and knowing where that place was, and knowing what he should be doing and why and how. Only he had to confess at the same time that it was hard to see the TV set, what with little Dinamarie playing tag with Hazel and Gladys and Grace and Gary Bob and Johnny Jim in front of it and Angie smooching with George over at the kitchen table and Susie and Flinn bopping each other over the heads because Flinn had decided to appropriate Susie's favorite rhinestone pinky ring which he wouldn't give back and Aunt Beryl was trying unsuccessfully to bake and Uncle Gus was trying unsuccessfully to clean his 38-gauge shotgun on the living room floor.

Sleeping was difficult too because the children wanted to be in bed between Zach and Amelia and many of the adults felt the need to stretch out on the floor nearby. Zach couldn't turn over or get up to visit the outhouse, and he could never show his affection for Amelia, who had never stopped eating two portions of each meal every day and was now the size of a large flaccid dolphin. Little Ainsley and Harlan and Jake and Remus wanted to help with all the chores but they continually got under foot. More than once Zach bruised an ankle or knocked a knee, tripping because he didn't see one of the children waiting right behind him like a shadow. Amelia fared no better in the kitchen where her mother-in-law and aunts supervised all her cooking, which she now performed nearly fourteen hours a day. Although no one except Zach and herself could eat, Amelia felt it only courteous to make enough for everyone. Sometimes at three in the morning she would rise and begin cooking breakfast and sometimes after midnight she would still be cleaning dishes. Over time, she turned big as a baby elephant with wrinkled skin. She turned big as a bear whose stubby arms could no longer touch its sides. She turned big as a small whale which plowed through the cabin, shaking the foundation, moving ponderously yet carefully because she had lost sensation in her extremities and could no longer feel whether or not she might be bumping into things or people. Her neck disappeared, and she forgot what it was like to bend from the waist, and she only vaguely remembered what her once beautiful red-painted toenails had looked like.

By February the food supply had run down and Zach felt more tired than ever before in his life and Amelia could no longer walk. She could no longer fit through the bedroom door. Zach arranged pillows and blankets for her to lie in on the living room floor and he began feeding her through a funnel because she could no longer lift her hands to help herself. The voluminous flesh of her face tugged at her tiny miraculous brown eyes and made her look a little oriental. Fat from her arms and legs puddled near her on the rug and made it appear as though she were melting. All the ghosts were fascinated by her lying there gazing at the ceiling, unable to speak just as they were unable to speak, unable to partake of the world just as they were unable to partake of the world. They seemed to understand that Amelia was eating for all of them now, that her metabolism was lovingly digesting for the whole family. The adults solemnly kneeled by her. The children frolicked on her body as though it were an astonishingly soft playground. They burrowed under her breasts and they slid down the wonderful smoothness of her thighs and they curled by her massive head to nap.

Every day more relatives appeared: Samuella, who had fallen

down a well when she was three; Rachel, who had cooked up some bad mushrooms when she was twenty-seven; Ferris, who lived until he was ninety-four and would have lived until he was ninety-seven if he hadn't strained trying to pick up those logs in the autumn of 1934; Selby, who shot Seaton because Seaton had knifed Seldon because Seldon had got Leanne with child when she was fourteen. More relatives than Zach could count. More relatives than he could squeeze into the space of his imagination. More relatives than he could squeeze into the space of his cabin. They spilled out onto the porch and they spilled out into the shed and by the middle of March they were sleeping in the woods all the way down to Whippoorwill Point and Zach couldn't go anywhere without stumbling over them, being surprised by their faces, finding them staring back at him from around a corner or under a bush or behind a birch. He gave up all chores except feeding Amelia and he gave up all food except Amelia's food and he went out of the cabin less and less and he stayed in his bed more and more. The hot weather settled down and he realized he should have planted months ago. The cool weather came and he realized he had nothing more for Amelia to eat and nothing more to grow next year and no more firewood for next fall and winter.

In September as the sky blanched, Zach walked down to Madge and Opal's and borrowed some tools and supplies and began to construct a mobile pulley near his dark blue Ford pickup truck. At first the gizmo looked like an eight-foot-tall oil well. Then it looked like an eight-foot-tall oil well on a sturdy wooden base with wheels under it. When it was done, Zach removed the skeletal braces and rolled the contraption over to the sliding doors that led off the living room. He padded the sturdy wooden base with pillows and blankets and then went to the shed and got his snow shovel. He returned to the living room and gingerly navigated among the ghosts until he reached Amelia sprawled in the middle of the floor. He shoved his snow shovel under a lump of fat that he took to be her flank and heaved. Haltingly, falteringly, agonizingly, he began to roll his gigantic doughy wife across the floor. She could not move herself and she could not speak, but each time she found herself on her back she looked up at Zach with her exquisite brown oriental eyes, which were infinitely sad. Zach avoided her gaze and put his back into the work. He rolled her through the sliding doors and rolled her onto the porch and, having removed the banisters there, he rolled her over the edge and onto the padded mobile pulley, which groaned and wheezed and shook under Amelia's enormous weight. Then he struggled and pushed and heaved the mobile pulley around toward the front of the cabin.

Half an hour later Amelia flooded the back of his mud-spattered dark blue Ford pickup. Her rubbery arms and squelchy legs draped over the sides. Whitish flubber oozed all around her. She stared up at the trees above her. Zach climbed into the cab and turned on the engine and eased down the pedal. The shock absorbers creaked and swayed. The pickup lurched and began to crawl down the dirt road. When it tapped the first bump, the metal belly scraped sand and gravel. But Zach didn't pay any attention to the bump, and he didn't pay any attention to the sound. He already felt his heart expanding. He already felt a lightness entering his stomach. He blinked and smiled and looked up into the rearview mirror. All the dead people had collected outside the cabin behind him. They were watching the mud-spattered dark blue pickup creep down the driveway, winding its way toward Madge and Opal's and beyond. Zach saw them all raising their hands and waving goodbye. And, as he turned the corner, Zach caught a glimpse of them begin to follow.

Mark Richard

FEAST OF THE EARTH, RANSOM OF THE CLAY

(from *Antaeus*)

We bury our dead in the muscle of our town, in the shouldered hillock of clay once an island in a river finished flowing. The rest of town rests around its heart on the low relief of the alluvial plain, the sandy loam long yielded to the weathering ages of wear. From a folding chair on top of Cemetery Ridge you can sort the soil strata by the tops of the trees below, their foliage betraying their roots—the evergreen against the seasonal, roots suitable for the sand or for the loam but not for the clay. Nothing grows well on Cemetery Ridge. Nothing we plant here is ever expected to bloom.

Behind this ridge they laid bare the clay for the spur line of the railroad. Beneath this raw overhang beside the tracks, runoff from summer storms has carved out ragged ditches and hollowed out some caves. If you are a schoolboy in our town, you may be tempted to hole up here in ambush of the evening freight with your slingshot and your can of rocks, and sometimes some shanty-weary mongrel bitch will come sniffing around, sniffing out some place to lie in and squeeze out her litter. But in our town Mr. Leon lives in these caves behind Cemetery Ridge. He lives here the best he can, slathering his beard and his bald head, licking his alluvial walls, sucking the mud where it's wet.

Of the twice we always expect to see Mr. Leon, the first is in the evenings when he slips from the face of the cliffs on his way to our neighborhoods. Mr. Leon roams. Sometimes a dog will bark at his full-mudded appearance, a man a patchwork of crusty fractures in dried gray. Sometimes a child, seeing the city park statue stepped from its pedestal and coming down the street at dusk, will cry. But our dogs do not bite unless you are a thief or plan to be one, and someone will always come out to hush a child and Mr. Leon makes his way. Bark, you bastards, or, Cry, you little bastards, is all that he will say, shaking his fist in that way worn-out men will, pouring some kind of anointment into the air.

The other time we expect to see Mr. Leon is at the funerals of our dead—like today. In the middle of this cake-box spread of granite and marble atop Cemetery Ridge we wait for the out-of-town late arrivals and the tick-tock walk of Mr. Leon. The sun is bright off the worn, standing-around suits, mail-ordered and living-room tailored. And there are crisp glints of light in the hems of the dresses patched and passed around by the grocery bagful. There is no hurry on this side of the family. They have arrived early and will be the stragglers later along the alleyways of the marble-stoppered clay. While they wait, they break away weeds from around the low-humped inscribed rock, resettle the chipped glass baskets of plastic flowers, the paper pots of front-yard blooms. Little words. News, regret, respect. Within reach, these people smooth one another's arms through the worn clothing, then their hands return to the white that is working in their fingers, the worried twists of tissue, the thick, cupped curls of the hand-rolled smoke. The men's chins are held higher today, bolstered by the unaccustomed thick knots of the shoe-wide neckties they wear. This allows these men a proudness they do not possess, a skin-straightening effect in their faces for a few instants against years in the sun. Some of the women seem to notice this subtle flush of youth restored in their husbands here at the end of a life, and such women work up a little sob just for themselves.

The other side of the family arrives in unfamiliar out-of-town cars, shiny. Dark windshields. Music in the last of the caravan that scatters gravel past the paupers' square up the cart path past where the Beales and the Chessons and the Lamberts and the Warrens are all laid out, and then instantly, alarmingly, they park alongside the brass-railinged coffin of our most newly deceased.

Spiked heels and hand-stitched leather feel for footing, and there are belly-thrustings from the long ride, starch crackling. Chatter from the last caravaned car in the back. Singsong hand-bag indecision. Is it the addiction of tobacco or the obligation of tissue? To hell with it, leave it in the car, it will all be over with shortly.

The son of the deceased adjusts his entourage into seats adjoining what he calls over cocktails his previous administration. There are some missed looks, some coat and shawl tucks, spit whispers and lip-read warnings, but hands manage to cross divides from both sides and there is a quiet conference with the man in black with the book, the noddings to begin it, let's begin, okay Father.

Would that it were so simple in our town. Would that it were so simple to lay in this one old dead lady, to dismiss this bird-calling biddy who lived at the end of the road to Cemetery Ridge. The bird-calling biddy, flinging sometimes to her nearest neighbor, the cave-dwelling Mr. Leon, a nickel or a piece of pie wrapped in newspaper. The bird-calling biddy, night after night, year after year that phonograph record on her hi-fi turned so far up, her late husband's world-famous *Summerset Birdcalls of Enchantment*. Night after night, year after year, the whole neighborhood, the warbling, the trilling, the long deep swooning and the high-pitched chipping. Night after night, louder with her age and the wear on the phonograph record, and her not turning it all the way up to better hear her husband's calls, but to hear him draw his breath before them, like if you lived in our town before he died you could hear him do at every outdoor party with summer and gin, you could hear him draw his breath across the backyard barbecue over the sizzle of grease in the grill, over the rattle of ice in your glass, him drawing breath before setting off over the Eastern seaboard in search of mates, wooing them through the trees, purging the nests, warning the young. Would that it were so simple in our town to dismiss this old lady, the bird-calling biddy, quickly, the one who played that phonograph record over and over in the evenings so loud that it was something that you ceased to hear until it stopped and we knew that she was dead, the needle so grooved into the worn-out vinyl you heard just a long distorted rumble punctuated by squeaks, birds drowning in the surf of an ocean, echoing off the nearby cliff, the nighttime soundtrack for our landlocked streets.

Our quiet streets, her vacant house, this new funeral for our dead—and, of course, Mr. Leon. Just as we waited for the late arrivals from out-of-town we wait for Mr. Leon, because this evening the questions from the absent bedridden and from the indisposed will not be about you and how you dressed and how you fared. The whispers will be, Did Mr. Leon show up?

He did?

Did he . . . do anything?

Did he . . . *eat* anything?

A straggler appears on the opposing hill, canebrake stick raised in our direction, not so much as in greeting as in some self-directed indication of further, forward progress. This is a setback for the out-of-towners, those with the two-hour drives and the afternoon appointments. They settle back in impatient folding-chair slumps. A southeast breeze is all that is commencing. It brings up pine scent from the sand-floored forest. The soil spaded at our feet smells, its sugar attracting dime-sized shadows of wood spiders working their ways to the edge of the chiseled clay.

Mr. Leon spits a large wad of something among the paupers' places and sets toward us leaning heavily in a sideboard motion on his stick. He poles himself downstream the cart path afloat atop his shoes. From the folding chairs those who know know that Mr. Leon is wearing his finest—the homemade vest of domestic cat, tails adrip down the front, the head of a tom on each shoulder as the topoff to the horror-show epaulettes. Beard, bald head, bib overalls, the dull, slathered gray, the milky lusts of some mineral deficiency, Doc says, no doubt a freshly sliced chunk or two from Mr. Leon's alluvial walls in his pocket for a sit-down, sidewalk snack somewhere, maybe even in front of your house if you are a schoolboy and live in our town. Your father might look through the front blinds and then look at you and say, Why is Mr. Leon in front of our house tonight, and you will say, I don't know, even though you are one of the school-boys who pelts Mr. Leon with anything you might want to see him stop and bend over to pick up and lick. Rotten produce will do from behind the Belo Market, where you and your friends can sometimes find Mr. Leon in summer, perched on the broken crates and boxes of spoilage, Mr. Leon eating stick after stick of butter that has soured while you and your schoolboy friends scuff your bicycles closer and closer, taunting him for a curse, maybe even working up a spit to blow into whatever it is he is eating carefully cradled in his clay-caked fingers. But Mr. Leon even does better than curse you, he tells you something, something like, Pussy crackles when it's hot, you little bastards. And then he leaps down with his canebrake stick so that you pedal off, Flee, you little shits. If you are a schoolboy you go home and work out in your mind for days what he said. Crackling. And you, you little schoolboy, cannot hear the bacon cooking in your mother's skillet the same way ever again without suffering a secret thrill.

Mr. Leon poles himself along the cart path toward us, his backward-facing yellow tie swinging out from under one side of his domestic catskin vest to slip beneath the other, a pendulum marking time according to his own personal schedule of intent, until he sits, winded, on the tombstone of Mrs. Cannady. The police had come to the caves looking for her the day she disap-peared. Mr. Leon! they hollered up from the search party along the tracks. Mr. Leon! Have you seen Mrs. Cannady? And if you had been a schoolboy with them then you would have heard nothing until someone decided to start the climb up the cliff to the caves, and then you would have heard from deep in one of the gray, hollowed throats, sounding out, Drag the lake, you bastards! and you would have seen the men from the fire department fetch the rigging and the police would have shooed you home to supper so you would have cut through the woods around back and climbed the hunting stands high in the trees over the millpond where from up there, even in the deepening evening green of the pine forest and the algae dark around the water, you would have been the first to see the cold and green lovely glow of the alabaster body come rising to the surface on its hook; shoes and a note on the shore.

The out-of-town party is showing its restive eagerness now. Hems are kneecapped, furs reshouldered, fingers tap silk shirtsleeves that are timepieced beneath. Mr. Leon pries himself off Mrs. Cannady with his stick and tick-tocks toward us. He proceeds with his stick outstruck now and it wands back and forth like a water rod. Mr. Leon's shadow seeps upon us until he is so close the air is cool with the smell of wet clay. He stands before us, an eruption from the ground nearby, his eyelids so heavily crusted with clay that it is difficult to see where Mr. Leon's eyes are resting until you are sure they are resting on the mound of fresh fill from the grave. Mud forms in the corners of his mouth. The sharp teeth in the cat heads on his shoulders have bleached somewhat since his last appearance and the flesh has drawn drier back to lend the animals a fierceness in death they did not possess in life. A woman in the front row from out-of-town fans herself with one hand and has the other buried in the jacket pocket of the man beside her. There are many mansions in the house of the Lord, says the man in black with the book. Mr. Leon raises his canebrake stick for silence and climbs atop the mound of fresh grave fill.

He settles into a crouch upon the mound, shrouded with his catskin vest, his anointing fist in the air. Several people stand and step back. Air begins to blow through Mr. Leon's narrowing lips and he blows a fine mist of clayed spittle across the casket's pall. Mr. Leon draws another breath, and at once we hear the cooing of the mourning dove, a gentle fluttering touch of tongue that tapers into the chip of the lark cheated by spring. There is the whistling search for the sparrow's mate, the swallow in its field of straw, and the unanswered call of the bobwhite, unanswered, and unanswered again, the spiraling screech of the sea gull and the mimic of the mockingbird, taunting us with its screen door squeak, its cry of a cat, and then the cry of the crow, admonition, the call to fresh carrion, the feathering caw of flight.

Mr. Leon flaps his arms throwing mud and dust, still blowing the spittle from his foaming mouth, the worn vinyl sound of surf. Then he settles quietly into himself, hunkered on the mound of fill, a little last cooing, his eyes that are blind to us looking out at all of us who are there.

Thank you, you bastards, Mr. Leon says as he reaches down and eats from the lip of the grave.

Moira Crone

JUST OUTSIDE THE B.T.

(from *The Southern Review*)

This is about the last time I saw Steva Land before she disappeared. It was three and a half years ago, the August Claire entered kindergarten. I guess this is about Florida, too. I left Florida, but D.C. is exactly the same, I mean the people.

Steva was late that Saturday picking up her daughter, Rachel, who played with mine, but she didn't apologize. She said they were in the middle of a move to a place on Riperton Street: I had never heard of the neighborhood. When I first came to Jacksonville, Claire was just a baby, and I tried putting her into day care. But the nursery that took them that young was a nightmare. Religious cable in every room, nonstop. Steva was the only mother I knew who stayed home. She was a craftsperson then, she dyed things. So I asked her if she would watch my baby: I paid her. She did a good job for two years. She was very cooperative if I had to work late. In fact, nothing ever seemed to faze her.

Steva told me she had a new, half-time job, working on a video display terminal, so I said, "Good for you."

She said, "You bet. I'm going blind."

Steva usually wasn't like that. She was sweet, that was how I always described her. They needed the money from her job, I knew: her husband, Tony, had been trying to make it freelance. He had been laid off for about two months from the advertising firm where I worked. They picked me and some others to stay on and they didn't pick him. I tried to tell them they were wrong, but basically I didn't fight.

While Steva was still in my living room, I got a call about the job in Washington, where I eventually ended up. And Steva said, "Go ahead, I'll get Rachel together," and I thought she was being the way she usually was, effaced, you might call it. I remember I was hoping I could say all the right things to this lady on the phone, then maybe I could move, and that would solve all my problems.

But when I got off, I found Steva in my daughter's bedroom, tearing through the shelves, knocking things down, making a mess. She was looking for something. A wooden bunny and about six books hit the floor. This was not like Steva, you have to understand. In fact, I had never known anybody to come into my house and do that sort of thing, except one other person.

She turned and said, "What did you do with that monster book?" This went back to one day when Claire had a fit and wouldn't leave Steva's without taking home a library book of theirs, *Not Now Bernard*. I felt desperate. I tried to get her off the subject, but she started in on the beige slacks. Claire spilled some grape juice one day over there so Steva lent her a pair of slacks. That was nice. But it was at least a year ago, then. I didn't know where they were just that minute. I thought, what is wrong with me, an apology would just not be enough, so I started to wad things up in my hands, pull out drawers, make an effort.

"Your place is the regular B.T. when it comes to Rachel's stuff, huh," she said, with a scant laugh. B.T. was Tony's, he used it at the office when something disappeared, for Bermuda Triangle. Tony was a funny guy. He liked science fiction. The boss said he was too imaginative to be in our field, that was the indictment.

When I had first moved to Jacksonville four years before, I rented another place, small, but with a pool. I had just split from my husband a few months before and it was the opposite of amicable—not about the custody, but about the property. When I was still living in Lynchburg he would show up without calling, just to badger me about our old F.M. radio, or the exercise bike. That was what this scene with Steva reminded me of. I wanted a private life, and I got an offer in Florida, and I thought, well, palm trees, a pool, that would be the thing. Alone, at last, on my own. The dream.

Early on, Steva and Tony and little Rachel came over for a swim. I'd met Tony at work. He was new, too, a live wire. Our kids were around one, and our kids were what we had to talk about. Steva got into the water, then she slipped out and started to pick up their instamatic, not a complicated camera, put on the flash. He told me, "Steva's great but she's not too mechanical." They had a struggle over it and the camera ended up in the water. He was beside himself, maudlin. Later, he started holding on to Steva as if she were precious, they ate tons of barbecue. Steva didn't say another word, she just smiled and let Tony talk. She couldn't get angry, I didn't think. It was echoes of my marriage to me. Gave me the creeps.

That pool turned out to be a disaster. The second weekend I was there, four strangers came over at eight a.m. on a Sunday. I called the landlord. He said, in this "what's the problem?" voice, "They live two doors down, they like to use the pool." I was worried about this. I said to him, "But who is responsible if one of them drowns? Me? I'm renting this house with this pool. Should I watch them?" What he said then really knocked me back.

The pool filled with leaves, and the filter didn't work: mosquitoes were breeding, and the landlord was no help. He wouldn't drain it. He said if he did the concrete would buckle because the groundwater was so high. Sinkholes were a topic that year, the earth falling in on everybody. Cars disappearing in apartment parking lots, falling through the tar into the mushy sand below. Everybody had to look out. That was my introduction to the Sunshine State.

"Well, go through the drawers, anything," I said to Steva. I really didn't know what to say, with her standing in my daughter's bedroom, her fists full of stuffed dolls, My Little Ponies all over the floor. She started in on some Velcro sneakers. I didn't know anything about any Velcro sneakers.

I am talking about a woman who never once asked me for overtime. I got her out and into the front room again. I told her Rachel was good on the piano. She had been trying to play that afternoon. Anything but the sneakers. Our kids were still playing in the dining area, one of their pretend games, Superwoman or Cinderella. My Claire was usually the leader. Rachel was more delicate, but maybe smarter. It made me think of having another, almost, hearing them.

Then Steva said, "That's a nice tricycle out front, you just get it?"

I said, "It's too short, the front wheel is thirteen inches high, Claire has shot up this summer. Rachel can have it if she wants."

Steva said no, what did I think she was, then she asked me, out of the blue (although I think she read my mind), if I ever wanted to have another child.

And I said, "Oh, yeah, I do, but there's no man," and I shrugged. "Husband first, then a kid." I kept this to myself: the last thing on earth I wanted then was a husband.

She mentioned she was smoking again, what with the move and Tony home all day, so I offered her one. We burned through the last two Benson and Hedges I had in the house. "Oh, this is a nice room," she said, almost smiling. "So many windows. Riperton Street has lots of windows."

We talked a little about school. Rachel was going to be in another district, one with a lousy kindergarten. Then Steva said she didn't think Rachel would get anything out of it, no matter the quality of the school. Neither she nor Tony had much confidence in her anymore.

"She's wonderful over here," I said.

"She's hyper. I think she has attention deficit disorder," she said.

I said it was just a stage, Rachel was bright. I didn't know what to say.

She looked so morose, sitting there in her white shorts and her tank top, that I started to touch her hand. Instead, I said, "Come on, Steva."

"She could have smarts from her grandparents, I think. It skips. There's Tony's dad—"

Tony's father was a code cracker in WWII. A whiz. Moving is stressful. Steva was being so unlike herself, so critical. Rachel was just a miniature Steva, that's what was behind this. They shared the same paleness, the same lankiness, the same limp, dark hair. I guess you could say Steva was an underachiever in this world, whatever that means.

Then she sat up and said she didn't want to talk about Rachel's problems, end of subject.

I could hear our two daughters clattering around in the bedroom then, playing a game where one of them is sick, and they make it an emergency. They were like sisters, but with school and the move they wouldn't be seeing each other as much, I knew, but I didn't think this would be the last time they were together. I didn't anticipate that. I heard Rachel ringing the toy ambulance bell.

There was a big crack of thunder, gave us both a jump, then rain. It was the sort of sudden storm you sit and listen to. I remembered something I wanted to tell Steva about Tony.

Once, the March before, when we were coming to get Rachel and Steva to take them with us to a movie, I saw Tony out on the porch. Claire and I got out of our little silver car, and he said, "Hot enough for you, Marilyn?" He was a blond man, and he had a paunch back then, nothing so awful. Things were fatter all around. I heard Tony's voice that afternoon, though, really heard it. There was a little genius in that voice. He could do something with it, radio maybe. It sounded as if it came from far away. It was an intellectual voice. I got an idea what Steva could love about him, even if he was hard on her.

Later, that same day in March, something very strange happened. While we were in the theater, a hailstorm started, very rare for here, for anywhere, jawbreaker size or bigger. The racket inside the theater was amazing. Bang-bang-bang on the roof. Steva wanted to go outside and see, but I was sure it was the air conditioning breaking down. I guess the sky could have been falling in, but I insisted we sit there watching *Snow White*. That's how I always behaved in those days. I always sat tight.

When it was over the air outside was twenty degrees cooler and the hailstones were gone; holes in the leaves and traces were the only indication. When I took them back, Tony was still on the porch, with a beer this time, and he said, "Cool enough for you, Marilyn?" in almost the same way, but there was a real edge to it somehow. As if I were the cause of the weather, to be blamed. I was very scared of him all of a sudden. Not long after that Tony got canned.

As Steva was getting Rachel's sandals back on, fixing to leave, I offered her my umbrella. It was huge, a wood and canvas one. Steva said, "No, that's okay, it's ten steps to your parking lot."

I walked them to their car. It was the kind of downpour that comes in from the Atlantic in August and is so intense you think it will never stop, then it's over, and the streets just steam it away. After she snapped Rachel in the back, Steva looked up at me with her round gray eyes—pleading, maybe. "I'll hold it while you get in the front," I said. Claire was under the entry awning of our townhouse, calling for me. Steva's car was a real mess— newspapers, Slurpee cups, full ashtrays. This wasn't normal. She was very neat, she was careful in little ways.

Claire dashed up, held me by the waist to try to keep dry. She waved to Rachel, who was curling up quietly in the backseat, and said, "Bye-bye, see you soon." Then she tugged at me: "Mommy, Mommy, we got to go in, it is so wet." In twenty seconds out there, she was half drenched. Ever since we had that pool, she'd been terrified of water, even rain.

I said, "Look, I wish you luck, with your new place, with everything. And I'll look for that stuff, the book, the sneakers. I'll get them back. I am so sorry about them, I am." She stared at me, with this sad, half-angry, lost face.

I remembered what my landlord told me the second week I was in Florida: *if the neighbors drowned that was their business.*

"Come inside, please. Have a beer. Please don't drive until this is over," I said.

She agreed. I felt triumphant, I did, while I was leading them all back into the living room. I listened to her. I didn't interrupt. It all spilled out: Tony was riding her about working when he wasn't bringing in anything himself. She felt sorry for him, really, he didn't think he'd ever succeed. Riperton Street was a dump. He was trying to write again, sending stories out, and where was that going to lead.

The last thing she told me was, "Forget I was here, forget it. Forget you even saw me, I mean it."

But the next to last thing she said was Tony had upset her so much—he had told her something she felt was horrible: He'd finally figured out how other people operate. They all want to get to a point where nothing they do affects anybody, and nobody affects them. Everybody is trying to act as if nobody else were really there. And as if they were never even in a place, just alive, somehow, in a vacuum, getting what they need.

I told her no, that was crazy. What an absolutely crazy idea.

Before that, we really relaxed, and our daughters were kissing each other, and we even laughed when I said she saved Claire from the PTL fiends at that nursery. She never knew. I told her how smart I thought Tony was, everything else about what happened at the firm. I said she raised my baby, kept her safe, it was incredible how good she had been. I had paid her, but I had never thanked her before, that way.

When it was dark she and Rachel drove off, their Corolla spinning up the water, hydroplaning down the boulevard. I was busy, and when I got her new number it was disconnected. And then I tried the school Rachel was going to go to—they had never heard of her. Tony left, someone said, for Ohio or Maine, and Steva left him, I also heard.

Like I said, I've moved since I sat in my condo that August

listening to Steva describe the horrible ideas Tony had started to believe, telling her they were crazy, people don't act that way. But D.C. might even be worse than Jacksonville, it seems like it to me. My last response to Steva was that I would never forget her, of course not, and at least that part still holds, up until now.

Reginald McKnight

THE KIND OF LIGHT THAT SHINES ON TEXAS

(from *The Kenyon Review*)

I never liked Marvin Pruitt. Never liked him, never knew him, even though there were only three of us in the class. Three black kids. In our school there were fourteen classrooms of thirty-odd white kids (in '66, they considered Chicanos provisionally white) and three or four black kids. Primary school in primary colors. Neat division. Alphabetized. They didn't stick us in the back, or arrange us by degrees of hue, apartheidlike. This was real integration, a ten-to-one ratio as tidy as upper-class landscaping. If it all worked, you could have ten white kids all to yourself. They could talk to you, get the feel of you, scrutinize you bone deep if they wanted to. They seldom wanted to, and that was fine with me for two reasons. The first was that their scrutiny was irritating. How do you comb your hair—why do you comb your hair—may I please touch your hair—were the kinds of questions they asked. This is no way to feel at home. The second reason was Marvin. He embarrassed me. He smelled bad, was at least two grades behind, was hostile, dark skinned, homely, close-mouthed. I feared him for his size, pitied him for his dress, watched him all the time. Marveled at him, mystified, astonished, uneasy.

He had the habit of spitting on his right arm, juicing it down till it would glisten. He would start in immediately after taking his seat when we'd finished with the Pledge of Allegiance, "The Yellow Rose of Texas," "The Eyes of Texas Are upon You," and "Mistress Shady." Marvin would rub his spit-flecked arm with his left hand, rub and roll as if polishing an ebony pool cue. Then he would rest his head in the crook of his arm, sniffing, huffing deep like blackjacket boys huff bagsful of acrylics. After ten minutes or so, his eyes would close, heavy. He would sleep till recess. Mrs. Wickham would let him.

There was one other black kid in our class, a girl they called Ah-so. I never learned what she did to earn this name. There was nothing Asian about this big-shouldered girl. She was the tallest, heaviest kid in school. She was quiet, but I don't think any one of us was subtle or sophisticated enough to nickname our classmates according to any but physical attributes. Fat kids were called Porky or Butterball; skinny ones were called Stick or Ichabod. Ah-so was big, thick, and African. She would impassively sit, sullen, silent as Marvin. She wore the same dark blue pleated skirt every day, the same ruffled white blouse every day. Her skin always shone as if worked by Marvin's palms and fingers. I never spoke one word to her, nor she to me.

Of the three of us, Mrs. Wickham called only on Ah-so and me. Ah-so never answered one question, correctly or incorrectly, so far as I can recall. She wasn't stupid. When asked to read aloud she read well, seldom stumbling over long words, reading with humor and expression. But when Wickham asked her about Farmer Brown and how many cows, or the capital of Vermont, or the date of this war or that, Ah-so never spoke. Not one word. But you always felt she could have answered those questions if she'd wanted to. I sensed no tension, embarrassment, or anger in Ah-so's reticence. She simply refused to speak. There was something unshakable about her, some core so impenetrably solid, you got the feeling that if you stood too close to her she could eat your thoughts like a black star eats light. I didn't despise Ah-so as I despised Marvin. There was nothing malevolent about her.

She sat like a great icon in the back of the classroom, tranquil, guarded, sealed up, watchful. She was close to sixteen, and it was my guess she'd given up on school. Perhaps she was just obliging the wishes of her family, sticking it out till the law could no longer reach her.

There were at least half a dozen older kids in our class. Besides Marvin and Ah-so there was Oakley, who sat behind me, whispering threats into my ear; Varna Willard with the large breasts; Eddie Limon, who played bass for a high school rock band; and Lawrence Ridderbeck, who everyone said had a kid and a wife. You couldn't expect me to know anything about Texan educational practices of the 1960s, so I never knew why there were so many older kids in my sixth grade class. After all, I was just a boy and had transferred into the school around midyear. My father, an air force sergeant, had been sent to Viet Nam. The air force sent my mother, my sister Claire, and me to Connolly Air Force Base, which during the war housed "unaccompanied wives." I'd been to so many different schools in my short life that I ceased wondering about their differences. All I knew about the Texas schools is that they weren't afraid to flunk you.

Yet though I was only twelve then, I had a good idea why Wickham never once called on Marvin, why she let him snooze in the crook of his polished arm. I knew why she would press her lips together, and narrow her eyes at me whenever I correctly answered a question, rare as that was. I knew why she badgered Ah-so with questions everyone knew Ah-so would never even consider answering. Wickham didn't like us. She wasn't gross about it, but it was clear she didn't want us around. She would prove her dislike day after day with little stories and jokes. "I just want to share with you all," she would say, "a little riddle my daughter told me at the supper table th'other day. Now, where do you go when you injure your knee?" Then one, two, or all three of her pets would say for the rest of us, "We don't know, Miz Wickham," in that skin-chilling way suckasses speak, "where?" "Why, to Africa," Wickham would say, "where the knee grows."

The thirty-odd white kids would laugh, and I would look across the room at Marvin. He'd be asleep. I would glance back at Ah-so. She'd be sitting still as a projected image, staring down at her desk. I, myself, would smile at Wickham's stupid jokes, sometimes fake a laugh. I tried to show her that at least one of us was alive and alert, even though her jokes hurt. I sucked ass, too, I suppose. But I wanted her to understand more than anything that I was not like her other nigra children, that I was worthy of more than the nonattention and the negative attention she paid Marvin and Ah-so. I hated her, but never showed it. No one could safely contradict that woman. She knew all kinds of tricks to demean, control, and punish you. And she could swing her two-foot paddle as fluidly as a big league slugger swings a bat. You didn't speak in Wickham's class unless she spoke to you first. You didn't chew gum, or wear "hood" hair. You didn't drag your feet, curse, pass notes, hold hands with the opposite sex. Most especially, you didn't say anything bad about the Aggies, Governor Connolly, LBJ, Sam Houston, or Waco. You did the forbidden and she would get you. It was that simple.

She never got me, though. Never gave her reason to. But she could have invented reasons. She did a lot of that. I can't be sure, but I used to think she pitied me because my father was in Viet Nam and my uncle A.J. had recently died there. Whenever she would tell one of her racist jokes, she would always glance at me, preface the joke with, "Now don't you nigra children take offense. This is all in fun, you know. I just want to share with you all something Coach Gilchrest told me th'other day." She would tell her joke, and glance at me again. I'd giggle, feeling a little queasy. "I'm half Irish," she would chuckle, "and you should hear some of those Irish jokes." She never told any, and I never really expected her to. I just did my Tom-thing. I kept my shoes shined, my desk neat, answered her questions as best I could, never brought gum to school, never cursed, never slept in class. I wanted to show her we were not all the same.

I tried to show them all, all thirty-odd, that I was different.

It worked to some degree, but not very well. When some article was stolen from someone's locker or desk, Marvin, not I, was the first accused. I'd be second. Neither Marvin nor Ah-so nor I were ever chosen for certain classroom honors—"Pledge leader," "flag holder," "noise monitor," "paper passer outer"—but Mrs. Wickham once let me be "eraser duster." I was proud. I didn't even care about the cracks my fellow students made about my finally having turned the right color. I had done something that Marvin, in the deeps of his never-ending sleep, couldn't even dream of doing. Jack Preston, a kid who sat in front of me, asked me one day at recess whether I was embarrassed about Marvin. "Can you believe that guy?" I said. "He's like a pig or something. Makes me sick."

"Does it make you ashamed to be colored?"

"No," I said, but I meant yes. Yes, if you insist on thinking us all the same. Yes, if his faults are mine, his weaknesses inherent in me.

"I'd be," said Jack.

I made no reply. I was ashamed. Ashamed for not defending Marvin and ashamed that Marvin even existed. But if it had occurred to me, I would have asked Jack whether he was ashamed of being white because of Oakley. Oakley, "Oak Tree," Kelvin "Oak Tree" Oakley. He was sixteen and proud of it. He made it clear to everyone, including Wickham, that his life's ambition was to stay in school one more year, till he'd be old enough to enlist in the army. "Them slopes got my brother," he would say. "I'mna sign up and git me a few slopes. Gonna kill them bastards deader'n shit." Oakley, so far as anyone knew, was and always had been the oldest kid in his family. But no one contradicted him. He would, as anyone would tell you, "snap yer neck jest as soon as look at you." Not a boy in class, excepting Marvin and myself, had been able to avoid Oakley's pink bellies, Texas titty twisters, Moon Pie punches, or worse. He didn't bother Marvin, I suppose, because Marvin was closer to his size and age, and because Marvin spent five-sixths of the school day asleep. Marvin probably never crossed Oakley's mind. And to say that Oakley hadn't bothered me is not to say he had no intention of ever doing so. In fact, this haphazard sketch of hairy fingers, slash of eyebrow, explosion of acne, elbows, and crooked teeth, swore almost daily that he'd like to kill me.

Naturally, I feared him. Though we were about the same height, he outweighed me by no less than forty pounds. He talked, stood, smoked, and swore like a man. No one, except for Mrs. Wickham, the principal, and the coach, ever laid a finger on him. And even Wickham knew that the hot lines she laid on him merely amused him. He would smile out at the classroom, goofy and bashful, as she laid down the two, five, or maximum ten strokes on him. Often he would wink, or surreptitiously flash us the thumb as Wickham worked on him. When she was finished, Oakley would walk so cool back to his seat you'd think he was on wheels. He'd slide into his chair, sniff the air, and say, "Somethin's burnin. Do y'all smell smoke? I swanee, I smell smoke and fahr back here." If he had made these cracks and never threatened me, I might have grown to admire Oakley, even liked him a little. But he hated me, and took every opportunity during the six-hour school day to make me aware of this. "Some Sambo's gittin his ass broke open one of these days," he'd mumble. "I wanna fight somebody. Need to keep in shape till I git to Nam."

I never said anything to him for the longest time. I pretended not to hear him, pretended not to notice his sour breath on my neck and ear. "Yep," he'd whisper. "Coonies keep ya in good shape for slope killin." Day in, day out, that's the kind of thing I'd pretend not to hear. But one day when the rain dropped down like lead balls, and the cold air made your skin look plucked, Oakley whispered to me, "My brother tells me it rains like this in Nam. Maybe I oughta go out at recess and break your ass open today. Nice and cool so you don't sweat. Nice and wet to clean up the blood." I said nothing for at least half a minute, then I turned half right and said, "Thought you said your brother was dead." Oakley, silent himself, for a time, poked me in the back with his pencil and hissed, "*Yer* dead." Wickham cut her eyes our way, and it was over.

It was hardest avoiding him in gym class. Especially when we played murderball. Oakley always aimed his throws at me. He threw with unblinking intensity, his teeth gritting, his neck veining, his face flushing, his black hair sweeping over one eye. He could throw hard, but the balls were squishy and harmless. In fact, I found his misses more intimidating than his hits. The balls would whizz by, thunder against the folded bleachers. They rattled as though a locomotive were passing through them. I would duck, dodge, leap as if he were throwing grenades. But he always hit me, sooner or later. And after a while I noticed that the other boys would avoid throwing at me, as if I belonged to Oakley.

One day, however, I was surprised to see that Oakley was throwing at everyone else but me. He was uncommonly accurate, too; kids were falling like tin cans. Since no one was throwing at me, I spent most of the game watching Oakley cut this one and that one down. Finally, he and I were the only ones left on the court. Try as he would, he couldn't hit me, nor I him. Coach Gilchrest blew his whistle and told Oakley and me to bring the red rubber balls to the equipment locker. I was relieved I'd escaped Oakley's stinging throws for once. I was feeling triumphant, full of myself. As Oakley and I approached Gilchrest, I thought about saying something friendly to Oakley: Good game, Oak Tree, I would say. Before I could speak, though, Gilchrest said, "All right, boys, there's five minutes left in the period. Y'all are so good, looks like, you're gonna have to play like men. No boundaries, no catch outs, and you gotta hit your opponent three times in order to win. Got me?"

We nodded.

"And you're gonna use these," said Gilchrest, pointing to three volleyballs at his feet. "And you better believe they're pumped full. Oates, you start at the end of the court. Oak Tree, you're at th'other end. Just like usual, I'll set the balls at mid-court, and when I blow my whistle I want y'all to haul your cheeks to the middle and th'ow for all you're worth. Got me?" Gilchrest nodded at our nods, then added, "Remember, no boundaries, right?"

I at my end, Oakley at his, Gilchrest blew his whistle. I was faster than Oakley and scooped up a ball before he'd covered three quarters of his side. I aimed, threw, and popped him right on the knee. "One-zip!" I heard Gilchrest shout. The ball bounced off his knee and shot right back into my hands. I hurried my throw and missed. Oakley bent down, clutched the two remaining balls. I remember being amazed that he could palm each ball, run full out and throw left-handed or right-handed without a shade of awkwardness. I spun, ran, but one of Oakley's throws glanced off the back of my head. "One-one!" hollered Gilchrest. I fell and spun on my ass as the other ball came sailing at me. I caught it. "He's out!" I yelled. Gilchrest's voice boomed, "No catch outs. Three hits. Three hits." I leapt to my feet as Oakley scrambled across the floor for another ball. I chased him down, leapt, and heaved the ball hard as he drew himself erect. The ball hit him dead in the face, and he went down flat. He rolled around, cupping his hands over his nose. Gilchrest sped to his side, helped him to his feet, asked him whether he was OK. Blood flowed from Oakley's nose, dripped in startlingly bright spots on the floor, his shoes, Gilchrest's shirt. The coach removed Oakley's T-shirt and pressed it against the big kid's nose to stanch the bleeding. As they walked past me toward the office I mumbled an apology to Oakley, but couldn't catch his reply. "You watch your filthy mouth, boy," said Gilchrest to Oakley.

The locker room was unnaturally quiet as I stepped into its steamy atmosphere. Eyes clicked in my direction, looked away. After I was out of my shorts, had my towel wrapped around me, my shower kit in hand, Jack Preston and Brian Nailor approached me. Preston's hair was combed slick and plastic looking. Nailor's stood up like frozen flames. Nailor smiled at me with his big teeth and pale eyes. He poked my arm with a finger. "You fucked up," he said.

"I tried to apologize."

"Won't do you no good," said Preston.

"I swanee," said Nailor.

"It's part of the game," I said. "It was an accident. Wasn't my idea to use volleyballs."

"Don't matter," Preston said. "He's jest lookin for an excuse to fight you."

"I never done nothing to him."

"Don't matter," said Nailor. "He don't like you."

"Brian's right, Clint. He'd jest as soon kill you as look at you."

"I never done nothing to him."

"Look," said Preston, "I know him pretty good. And jest between you and me, it's cause you're a city boy—"

"Whadda you mean? I've never—"

"He don't like your clothes—"

"And he don't like the fancy way you talk in class."

"What fancy—"

"I'm tellin him, if you don't mind, Brian."

"Tell him then."

"He don't like the way you say 'tennis shoes' instead of sneakers. He don't like coloreds. A whole bunch a things, really."

"I never done nothing to him. He's got no reason—"

"*And,*" said Nailor, grinning, "*and,* he says you're a stuck-up rich kid." Nailor's eyes had crow's-feet, bags beneath them. They were a man's eyes.

"My dad's a sergeant," I said.

"You chicken to fight him?" said Nailor.

"Yeah, Clint, don't be chicken. Jest go on and git it over with. He's whupped pert near ever'body else in the class. It ain't so bad."

"Might as well, Oates."

"Yeah, yer pretty skinny, but yer jest about his height. Jest git im in a headlock and don't let go."

"Goddamn," I said, "he's got no reason to—"

Their eyes shot right and I looked over my shoulder. Oakley stood at his locker, turning its tumblers. From where I stood I could see that a piece of cotton was wedged up one of his nostrils, and he already had the makings of a good shiner. His acne burned red like a fresh abrasion. He snapped the locker open and kicked his shoes off without sitting. Then he pulled off his shorts, revealing two paddle stripes on his ass. They were fresh red bars speckled with white, the white speckles being the reverse impression of the paddle's suction holes. He must not have watched his filthy mouth while in Gilchrest's presence. Behind me, I heard Preston and Nailor pad to their lockers.

Oakley spoke without turning around. "Somebody's gonna git his skinny black ass kicked, right today, right after school." He said it softly. He slipped his jock off, turned around. I looked away. Out the corner of my eye I saw him stride off, his hairy nakedness a weapon clearing the younger boys from his path. Just before he rounded the corner of the shower stalls, I threw my toilet kit to the floor and stammered, "I—I never did nothing to you, Oakley." He stopped, turned, stepped closer to me, wrapping his towel around himself. Sweat streamed down my rib cage. It felt like ice water. "You wanna go at it right now, boy?"

"I never did nothing to you." I felt tears in my eyes. I couldn't stop them even though I was blinking like mad. "Never."

He laughed. "You busted my nose, asshole."

"What about before? What'd I ever do to you?"

"See you after school, Coonie." Then he turned away, flashing his acne-spotted back like a semaphore. "Why?" I shouted. "Why you wanna fight me?" Oakley stopped and turned, folded his arms, leaned against a toilet stall. "Why you wanna fight *me*, Oakley?" I stepped over the bench. "What'd I do? Why me?" And then unconsciously, as if scratching, as if breathing, I walked toward Marvin, who stood a few feet from Oakley, combing his hair at the mirror. "Why not him?" I said. "How come you're after *me* and not *him*?" The room froze. Froze for a moment that was both evanescent and eternal, somewhere between an eye blink and a week in hell. No one moved, nothing happened; there was no sound at all. And then it was as if all of us at the same moment looked at Marvin. He just stood there, combing away, the only body in motion, I think. He combed his hair and combed it, as if seeing only his image, hearing only his comb scraping his scalp. I knew he'd heard me. There's no way he could not have heard me. But all he did was slide the comb into his pocket and walk out the door.

"I got no quarrel with Marvin," I heard Oakley say. I turned toward his voice, but he was already in the shower.

I was able to avoid Oakley at the end of the school day. I made my escape by asking Mrs. Wickham if I could go to the restroom.

"'Restroom,'" Oakley mumbled. "It's a damn toilet, sissy."

"Clinton," said Mrs. Wickham. "Can you *not* wait till the bell rings? It's almost three o'clock."

"No, ma'am," I said. "I won't make it."

"Well, I should make you wait just to teach you to be more mindful about . . . hygiene . . . uh things." She sucked in her cheeks, squinted. "But I'm feeling charitable today. You may go." I immediately left the building, and got on the bus. "Ain't you a little early?" said the bus driver, swinging the door shut. "Just left the office," I said. The driver nodded, apparently not giving me a second thought. I had no idea why I'd told her I'd come from the office, or why she found it a satisfactory answer. Two minutes later the bus filled, rolled and shook its way to Connolly Air Base.

When I got home, my mother was sitting in the living room, smoking her Slims, watching her soap opera. She absently asked me how my day had gone and I told her fine. "Hear from Dad?" I said.

"No, but I'm sure he's fine." She always said that when we hadn't heard from him in a while. I suppose she thought I was worried about him, or that I felt vulnerable without him. It was neither. I just wanted to discuss something with my mother that we both cared about. If I spoke with her about things that happened at school, or on my weekends, she'd listen with half an ear, say something like, "Is that so?" or "You don't say?" I couldn't stand that sort of thing. But when I mentioned my father, she treated me a bit more like an adult, or at least someone who was worth listening to. I didn't want to feel like a boy that afternoon. As I turned from my mother and walked down the hall I thought about the day my father left for Viet Nam. Sharp in his uniform, sure behind his aviator specs, he slipped a cigar from his pocket and stuck it in mine. "Not till I get back," he said. "We'll have us one when we go fishing. Just you and me, out on the lake all day, smoking and casting and sitting. Don't let Mamma see it. Put it in y' back pocket." He hugged me, shook my hand, and told me I was the man of the house now. He told me he was depending on me to take good care of my mother and sister. "Don't you let me down, now, hear?" And he tapped his thick finger on my chest. "You almost as big as me. Boy, you something else." I believed him when he told me those things. My heart swelled big enough to swallow my father, my mother, Claire. I loved, feared, and respected myself, my manhood. That day I could have put all of Waco, Texas, in my heart. And it wasn't till about three months later that I discovered I really wasn't the man of the house, that my mother and sister, as they always had, were taking care of me.

For a brief moment I considered telling my mother about what had happened at school that day, but for one thing, she was deep down in the halls of "General Hospital," and never paid you much mind till it was over. For another thing, I just wasn't the kind of person—I'm still not, really—to discuss my problems with anyone. Like my father I kept things to myself, talked about my problems only in retrospect. Since my father wasn't around, I consciously wanted to be like him, doubly like him, I could say. I wanted to be the man of the house in some respect, even if it had to be in an inward way. I went to my room, changed my clothes, and laid out my homework. I couldn't focus on it. I thought about Marvin, what I'd said about him or done to him— I couldn't tell which. I'd done something to him, said something about him; said something about and done something to myself. *How come you're after* me *and not* him? I kept trying to tell myself I hadn't meant it that way. *That* way. I thought about approaching Marvin, telling him what I really meant was that he was more Oakley's age and weight than I. I would tell him I meant I was no match for Oakley. *See, Marvin, what I meant was that he wants to fight a colored guy, but is afraid to fight you cause you could beat him.* But try as I did, I couldn't for a moment convince myself that Marvin would believe me. I meant it *that* way and no other. Everybody heard. Everybody knew. That afternoon I forced myself to confront the notion that tomorrow I would probably have to fight both Oakley and Marvin. I'd have to be two men.

I rose from my desk and walked to the window. The light made my skin look orange, and I started thinking about what Wickham had told us once about light. She said that oranges and apples, leaves and flowers, the whole multicolored world, was not what it appeared to be. The colors we see, she said, look like they do only because of the light or ray that shines on them. "The color of the thing isn't what you see, but the light that's reflected off it." Then she shut out the lights and shone a white light lamp on a prism. We watched the pale splay of colors on the projector screen; some people ooohed and aaahed. Suddenly, she switched on a black light and the color of everything changed. The prism colors vanished, Wickham's arms were purple, the buttons of her dress were as orange as hot coals, rather than the blue they had been only seconds before. We were all very quiet. "Nothing," she said after a while, "is really what it appears to be." I didn't really understand then. But as I stood at the window, gazing at my orange skin, I wondered what kind of light I could shine on Marvin, Oakley, and me that would reveal us as the same.

I sat down and stared at my arms. They were dark brown again. I worked up a bit of saliva under my tongue and spat on my left arm. I spat again, then rubbed the spittle into it, polishing, working till my arm grew warm. As I spat, and rubbed, I wondered why Marvin did this weird, nasty thing to himself, day after day. Was he trying to rub away the black, or deepen it, doll it up? And if he did this weird nasty thing for a hundred years, would he spit-shine himself invisible, rolling away the eggplant skin, revealing the scarlet muscle, blue vein, pink and yellow tendon, white bone? Then disappear? Seen through, all colors, no colors. Spitting and rubbing. Is this the way you do it? I leaned forward, sniffed the arm. It smelled vaguely of mayonnaise. After an hour or so, I fell asleep.

I saw Oakley the second I stepped off the bus the next morning. He stood outside the gym in his usual black penny loafers, white socks, high-water jeans, T-shirt and black jacket. Nailor stood with him, his big teeth spread across his bottom lip like playing cards. If there was anyone I felt like fighting, that day, it was Nailor. But I wanted to put off fighting for as long as I could. I stepped toward the gymnasium, thinking that I shouldn't run, but if I hurried I could beat Oakley to the door and secure myself near Gilchrest's office. But the moment I stepped into the gym, I felt Oakley's broad palm clap down on my shoulder. "Might as well stay out here, Coonie," he said. "I need me a little target practice." I turned to face him and he slapped me, one-two, with the back, then the palm of his hand, as I'd seen Bogart do to Peter Lorre in *The Maltese Falcon*. My heart went wild. I could scarcely breathe. I couldn't swallow.

"Call me a nigger," I said. I have no idea what made me say this. All I know is that it kept me from crying. "Call me a nigger, Oakley."

"Fuck you, ya black ass slope." He slapped me again, scratching my eye. "I don't do what coonies tell me."

"Call me a nigger."

"Outside, Coonie."

"Call me one. Go ahead."

He lifted his hand to slap me again, but before his arm could swing my way, Marvin Pruitt came from behind me and calmly pushed me aside. "Git out my way, boy," he said. And he slugged Oakley on the side of his head. Oakley stumbled back, stiff-legged. His eyes were big. Marvin hit him twice more, once again to the side of the head, once to the nose. Oakley went down and stayed down. Though blood was drawn, whistles blowing, fingers pointing, kids hollering, Marvin just stood there, staring at me with cool eyes. He spat on the ground, licked his lips, and just stared at me, till Coach Gilchrest and Mr. Calderon tackled him and violently carried him away. He never struggled, never took his eyes off me.

Nailor and Mrs. Wickham helped Oakley to his feet. His already fattened nose bled and swelled so that I had to look away. He looked around, bemused, wall-eyed, maybe scared. It was apparent he had no idea how bad he was hurt. He didn't even touch his nose. He didn't look like he knew much of anything. He looked at me, looked me dead in the eye in fact, but didn't seem to recognize me.

That morning, like all other mornings, we said the Pledge of Allegiance, sang "The Yellow Rose of Texas," "The Eyes of Texas Are upon You," and "Mistress Shady." The room stood strangely empty without Oakley, and without Marvin, but at the same time you could feel their presence more intensely somehow. I felt like I did when I'd walk into my mother's room and could smell my father's cigars, or cologne. He was more palpable, in certain respects, than when there in actual flesh. For some reason, I turned to look at Ah-so, and just this once I let my eyes linger on her face. She had a very gentle-looking face, really. That surprised me. She must have felt my eyes on her because she glanced up at me for a second and smiled, white teeth, downcast eyes. Such a pretty smile. That surprised me too. She held it for a few seconds, then let it fade. She looked down at her desk, and sat still as a photograph.

Richard Bausch

LETTER TO THE LADY OF THE HOUSE

(from *The New Yorker*)

It's exactly twenty minutes to midnight, on this the eve of my seventieth birthday, and I've decided to address you, for a change, in writing—odd as that might seem. I'm perfectly aware of how many years we've been together, even if I haven't been very good about remembering to commemorate certain dates, certain days of the year. I'm also perfectly aware of how you're going to take the fact that I'm doing this at all, so late at night, with everybody due to arrive tomorrow, and the house still unready. I haven't spent almost five decades with you without learning a few things about you that I can predict and describe with some accuracy, though I admit that, as you put it, lately we've been more like strangers than husband and wife. Well, so if we are like strangers, perhaps there are some things I can tell you that you won't have already figured out about the way I feel.

Tonight, we had another one of those long, silent evenings after an argument (remember?) over pepper. We had been bickering all day, really, but at dinner I put pepper on my potatoes and you said that about how I shouldn't have pepper because it always upsets my stomach. I bothered to remark that I used to eat chili peppers for breakfast and if I wanted to put plain old ordinary black pepper on my potatoes, as I had been doing for more than sixty years, that was my privilege. Writing this now, it sounds far more testy than I meant it, but that isn't really the point.

In any case, you chose to overlook my tone. You simply said, "John, you were up all night the last time you had pepper with your dinner."

I said, "I was up all night because I ate green peppers. Not black pepper but green peppers."

"A pepper is a pepper, isn't it?" you said.

And then I started in on you. I got, as you call it, legal with you—pointing out that green peppers are not black pepper—and from there we moved on to an evening of mutual disregard for each other that ended with your decision to go to bed early. The grandchildren will make you tired, and there's still the house to do; you had every reason to want to get some rest, and yet I felt that you were also making a point of getting yourself out of proximity with me, leaving me to my displeasure, with another ridiculous argument settling between us like a fog.

So, after you went to bed, I got out the whiskey and started pouring drinks, and I had every intention of putting myself into a stupor. It was almost my birthday, after all, and—forgive this, it's the way I felt at the time—you had nagged me into an argument and then gone off to bed; the day had ended as so many of our days end now, and I felt, well, entitled. I had a few drinks, without any appreciable effect (though you might well see this letter as firm evidence to the contrary), and then I decided to do something to shake you up. I would leave. I'd make a lot of noise going out the door; I'd take a walk around the neighborhood and make you wonder where I could be. Perhaps I'd go check into a motel for the night. The thought even crossed my mind that I might leave you altogether. I admit that I entertained the thought, Marie. I saw our life together now as the day-to-day round of petty quarrelling and tension that it's mostly been over the past couple of years or so, and I wanted out as sincerely as I ever wanted anything.

My God, I wanted an end to it, and I got up from my seat in front of the television and walked back down the hall to the entrance of our room to look at you. I suppose I hoped you'd still be awake, so I could tell you of this momentous decision I felt I'd reached. And maybe you were awake: one of our oldest areas of contention being the feather-thin membrane of your sleep that I am always disturbing with my restlessness in the nights. All right. Assuming you were asleep, and don't know that I stood in the doorway of our room, I will say that I stood there for perhaps five minutes, just looking at you in the half-dark, the shape of your body under the blanket—you really did look like one of the girls when they were little and I used to stand in the doorway of their rooms; your illness last year made you so small again—and, as I said, I thought I had decided to leave you, for your peace as well as mine. I know you have gone to sleep crying, Marie. I know you've felt sorry about things, and wished we could find some way to stop irritating each other so much.

Well, of course, I didn't go anywhere. I came back to this room and drank more of the whiskey and watched television. It was like all the other nights. The shows came on and ended, and the whiskey began to wear off. There was a little rain shower. I had a moment of the shock of knowing I was seventy. After the rain ended, I did go outside for a few minutes. I stood on the sidewalk and looked at the house. The kids, with their kids, were on the road somewhere between their homes and here. I walked up to the end of the block and back, and a pleasant breeze blew and shook the drops out of the trees. My stomach was bothering me some, and maybe it was the pepper I'd put on my potatoes. It could just as well have been the whiskey. Anyway, as I came back to the house, I began to have the eerie feeling that I had reached the last night of my life. There was this small discomfort in my stomach, and no other physical pang or pain, and I am used to the small ills and side effects of my way of eating and drinking; yet I felt the sense of the end of things more strongly than I can describe. When I stood in the entrance of our room and looked at you again, wondering if I would make it through to the morning, I suddenly found myself trying to think what I would say to you if indeed this *was* the last time I would ever be able to speak to you. And I began to know I would write you this letter.

At least words in a letter aren't blurred by tone of voice, by the old aggravating sound of me talking to you. I began with this, and with the idea that, after months of thinking about it, I would at last try to say something to you that wasn't colored by our disaffections. What I have to tell you must be explained in a rather roundabout way.

I've been thinking about my cousin Louise and her husband. When he died, and she stayed with us last summer, something brought back to me what is really only the memory of a moment; yet it reached me, that moment, across more than fifty years. As you know, Louise is nine years older than I, and more like an older sister than a cousin. I must have told you at one time or another that I spent some weeks with her, back in 1933, when she was first married. The memory I'm talking about comes from that time, and what I have decided I have to tell you comes from that memory.

Father had been dead four years. We were all used to the fact that times were hard and that there was no man in the house, though I suppose I filled that role in some titular way. In any case, when Mother became ill there was the problem of us, her children. Though I was the oldest, I wasn't old enough to stay in the house alone, or to nurse her, either. My grandfather came up with the solution—and everybody went along with it—that I would go to Louise's for a time, and the two girls would go to stay with Grandfather. You'll remember that people did pretty much what that old man wanted them to do.

So we closed up the house, and I got on a train to Virginia. I was a few weeks shy of fourteen years old. I remember that I was not able to believe that anything truly bad would come of Mother's pleurisy, and was consequently glad of the opportunity

it afforded me to travel the hundred miles south to Charlottesville, where Cousin Louise had moved with her new husband
only a month earlier, after her wedding. Because *we* travelled so
much at the beginning, you never got to really know Charles
when he was young; in 1933, he was a very tall, imposing fellow,
with bright-red hair and a graceful way of moving that always
made me think of athletics, contests of skill. He had worked at
the Navy yard in Washington, and had been laid off in the first
months of Roosevelt's New Deal. Louise was teaching in a day
school in Charlottesville, so they could make ends meet, and
Charles was spending most of his time looking for work and fixing up the house. I had only met Charles once or twice before the
wedding, but already I admired him, and wanted to emulate him.
The prospect of spending time in his house, of perhaps going
fishing with him in the small streams of central Virginia, was all
I thought about on the way down. And I remember that we did
go fishing one weekend, that I wound up spending a lot of time
with Charles, helping to paint the house, and to run water lines
under it for indoor plumbing. Oh, I had time with Louise, too—
listening to her read from the books she wanted me to be interested in, walking with her around Charlottesville in the evenings
and looking at the city as it was then. Or sitting on her small
porch and talking about the family, Mother's stubborn illness,
the children Louise saw every day at school. But what I want to
tell you has to do with the very first day I was there.

I know you think I use far too much energy thinking about and
pining away for the past, and I therefore know that I'm taking a
risk by talking about this ancient history, and by trying to make
you see it. But this all has to do with you and me, my dear, and
our late inability to find ourselves in the same room together
without bitterness and pain.

That summer, 1933, was unusually warm in Virginia, and the
heat, along with my impatience to arrive, made the train almost
unbearable. I think it was just past noon when it pulled into the
station at Charlottesville, with me hanging out one of the win-

dows, looking for Louise or Charles. It was Charles who had come to meet me. He stood in a crisp-looking seersucker suit, with a straw boater cocked at just the angle you'd expect a young, newly married man to wear a straw boater, even in the middle of economic disaster. I waved at him and he waved back, and I might've jumped out the window if the train had slowed even a little more than it had before it stopped in the shade of the platform. I made my way out, carrying the cloth bag my grandfather had given me for the trip—Mother had said through her rheum that I looked like a carpetbagger—and when I stepped down to shake hands with Charles I noticed that what I thought was a new suit was tattered at the ends of the sleeves.

"Well," he said. "Young John."

I smiled at him. I was perceptive enough to see that his cheerfulness was not entirely effortless. He was a man out of work, after all, and so in spite of himself there was worry in his face, the slightest shadow in an otherwise glad and proud countenance. We walked through the station to the street, and on up the steep hill to the house, which was a small clapboard structure, a cottage, really, with a porch at the end of a short sidewalk lined with flowers—they were marigolds, I think—and here was Louise, coming out of the house, her arms already stretched wide to embrace me. "Lord," she said. "I swear you've grown since the wedding, John." Charles took my bag and went inside.

"Let me look at you, young man," Louise said.

I stood for inspection. And as she looked me over I saw that her hair was pulled back, that a few strands of it had come loose, that it was brilliantly auburn in the sun. I suppose I was a little in love with her. She was grown, and married now. She was a part of what seemed a great mystery to me, even as I was about to enter it, and of course you remember how that feels, Marie, when one is on the verge of things—nearly adult, nearly old enough to fall in love. I looked at Louise's happy, flushed face, and felt a deep ache as she ushered me into her house. I wanted so to be older.

Inside, Charles had poured lemonade for us, and was sitting in the easy chair by the fireplace, already sipping his. Louise wanted to show me the house, and the back yard—which she had tilled and turned into a small vegetable garden—but she must've sensed how thirsty I was, and so she asked me to sit down and have a cool drink before she showed me the upstairs. Now, of course, looking back on it, I remember that those rooms she was so anxious to show me were meagre indeed. They were not much bigger than closets, really, and the paint was faded and dull; the furniture she'd arranged so artfully was coming apart; the pictures she'd put on the walls were prints she'd cut out—magazine covers, mostly—and the curtains over the windows were the same ones that had hung in her childhood bedroom for twenty years. ("Recognize these?" she said with a deprecating smile.) Of course, the quality of her pride had nothing to do with the fineness—or lack of it—in these things but in the fact that they belonged to her, and that she was a married lady in her own house.

On this day in July, 1933, she and Charles were waiting for the delivery of a fan they had scrounged enough money to buy from Sears, through the catalogue. There were things they would rather have been doing, especially in this heat, and especially with me there. Monticello wasn't far away, the university was within walking distance, and without too much expense one could ride a taxi to one of the lakes nearby. They had hoped that the fan would arrive before I did, but since it hadn't, and since neither Louise nor Charles was willing to leave the other alone that day while traipsing off with me, there wasn't anything to do but wait around for it. Louise had opened the windows and drawn the shades, and we sat in her small living room and drank the lemonade, fanning ourselves with folded parts of Charles's newspaper. From time to time an anemic breath of air would move the shades slightly, but then everything grew still again. Louise sat on the arm of Charles's chair, and I sat on the sofa. We talked about pleurisy, and, I think, about the fact that Thomas Jefferson had invented the dumbwaiter, and how the plumbing at Monticello was at least a century ahead of its time. Charles remarked that it was the spirit of invention that would make a man's career in these days. "That's what I'm aiming for—to be inventive in a job. No matter what it winds up being."

When the lemonade ran out, Louise got up and went into the kitchen to make some more. Charles and I talked about taking a weekend to go fishing. He leaned back in his chair and put his hands behind his head, looking satisfied. In the kitchen, Louise was chipping ice for our glasses, and she began singing something low, for her own pleasure, a barely audible lilting, and Charles and I sat listening. It occurred to me that I was very happy. I had the sense that soon I would be embarked on my own life, as Charles was on his, and that an attractive woman like Louise would be there with me. Charles said, "God, listen to that. Doesn't Louise have the loveliest voice?"

And that's all I have from that day. I don't even know if the fan arrived later, and I have no clear memory of how we spent the rest of the afternoon and evening. I remember Louise singing a song, her husband leaning back in his chair, folding his hands behind his head, expressing his pleasure in his young wife's voice. I remember that I felt quite extraordinarily content just then. And that's all I remember.

But there are, of course, the things we both know: we know they moved to Colorado to be near Charles's parents; we know they never had any children; we know that Charles fell down a shaft at a construction site in the fall of 1957 and was hurt so badly that he never walked again. And I know that when she came to stay with us last summer she told me she'd learned to hate him, and not for what she'd had to help him do all those years. No, it started earlier and was deeper than that. She hadn't minded the care of him—the washing and feeding and all the numberless small tasks she had to perform each and every day, all day—she hadn't minded this. In fact, she thought there was something in her makeup that liked being needed so completely.

The trouble was simply that whatever she had once loved in him she had stopped loving, and for many, many years before he died she'd felt only suffocation when he was near enough to touch her, only irritation and anxiety when he spoke. She said all this, and then looked at me, her cousin, who had been fortunate enough to have children, and to be in love over time, and said, "John, how have you and Marie managed it?"

And what I wanted to tell you has to do with this fact—that while you and I had had one of our whispering arguments only moments before, I felt quite certain of the simple truth of the matter, which is that, whatever our complications, we *have* managed to be in love over time.

"Louise," I said.

"People start out with such high hopes," she said, as if I wasn't there. She looked at me. "Don't they?"

"Yes," I said.

She seemed to consider this a moment. Then she said, "I wonder how it happens."

I said, "You ought to get some rest." Or something equally pointless and admonitory.

As she moved away from me, I had an image of Charles standing on the station platform in Charlottesville that summer, the straw boater set at its cocky angle. It was an image I would see most of the rest of that night, and on many another night since.

I can almost hear your voice as you point out that once again I've managed to dwell too long on the memory of something that's past and gone. The difference is that I'm not grieving over the past now. I'm merely reporting a memory, so that you might understand what I'm about to say to you.

The fact is, we aren't the people we were even then, just a year ago. I know that. As I know things have been slowly eroding between us for a very long time; we are a little tired of each other, and there are annoyances and old scars that won't be obliterated with a letter—even a long one written in the middle of the night in desperate sincerity, under the influence, admittedly, of a considerable portion of bourbon whiskey, but nevertheless with the best intention and hope: that you may know how, over the course of this night, I came to the end of needing an explanation for our difficulty. We have reached this—place. Everything we say seems rather aggravatingly mindless and automatic, like something one stranger might say to another in any of the thousand circumstances where strangers are thrown together for a time and the silence begins to grow heavy on their minds and someone has to say something. Darling, we go so long these days without having anything at all to do with each other, and the children are arriving tomorrow, and once more we'll be in the position of making all the gestures that give them back their parents as they think their parents are, and what I wanted to say to you, what came to me as I thought about Louise and Charles on that day so long ago, when they were young and so obviously glad of each other, and I looked at them and knew it and was happy—what came to me was that even the harsh things that happened to them, even the years of anger and silence, even the disappointment and the bitterness and the wanting not to be in the same room anymore, even all that must have been worth it for such loveliness. At least I am here, at seventy years old, hoping so. Tonight, I went back to our room again and stood gazing at you asleep, dreaming whatever you were dreaming, and I had a moment of thinking how we were always friends, too. And what I wanted finally to say was that I remember well our own sweet times, our own old loveliness. I would like to think that even if at the very beginning of our lives together I had somehow been shown that we would end up here, with this longing to be away from each other, this feeling of being trapped together, of being tied to each other in a way that makes us wish for other times, some other place, I would have known enough to accept it all freely for the chance at that love. And if I could, I would do it all again, Marie. All of it, even the sorrow. My sweet, my dear adversary. For everything that I remember.

Greg Johnson

THE BOARDER

(from *The Southern Review*)

People enter your life in the oddest ways!—something I've often observed to Ralston, without his exactly agreeing. Ralston is my husband: fifty-five, soft-spoken, and solid as a brick building, but he isn't much for philosophical remarks or stepping back to consider the long view. He just plows right along, one day after another, and you've got to admire that. He likes most people, but doesn't have the easily piqued *curiosity* about them like I do, and so it's doubtful that he'd ever have met Professor Coates—in the odd way I met him, or any way at all—if I hadn't had what Ralston calls, dry-mouthed, one of my "bright ideas." In my opinion he'd also have missed a most profound and illuminating experience, though there's little chance of Ralston admitting to that.

My idea, to be plain, was that we take in Professor Coates as a boarder. He and I had met in the cleaners one day, the one I've patronized for twenty years or so, where I'd just gotten in line behind a small-framed youngish man in a tweed jacket. He stood quietly holding up a dress shirt on a hanger, the sleeves lifted up to show underarms that had been . . . well, pulverized, it looked like. In a snap I saw that they'd used much too strong a chemical for the underarm stains and that the young man should get a new shirt, but the clerk—a tiny, red-haired girl I'd never cared for—

stood there shaking her head. And then, out of the young man's mouth, came the most amazing words: "Oh, very well. I hope you don't mind my having asked." The girl blinked, half smiled in a smug way, and it was then I had one of my "impulses," as Ralston calls them. I just *had* to see that young man's face, so I stepped around and got on tiptoes (I'm a rather petite woman) to peer over the shoulder of the ruined shirt.

"I couldn't help overhearing," I began—and not to brag or go on about it, I had the manager out front within five minutes and a new twenty-dollar bill in Professor Coates's hand. The red-haired girl had left for her lunch break, in something of a huff.

Anyhow, that's how we met, and out on the sidewalk we got to talking. He interested me right away because he seemed so help-less and had such excellent manners. He spoke in this odd, kind of formal way, not off-putting or affected but like he hadn't yet got the knack of talking like ordinary people. For instance: "You were extremely kind to intercede for me like that." And a minute later: "Why, a cup of coffee at your house would be delightful. How hospitable of you." Now I found this way of talking most intriguing, especially since the man looked normal in every other respect. Professor Coates was about thirty-five, with dark hair neatly cut, and eyeglasses with thick rims tinted the same deep brown as his eyes, and slender clean hands—the nails *exquisitely* clean and well tended—and a generally shy and kind-hearted aura to him, the sort that's very appealing to a woman. And he looked at you so directly, with such friendliness and gratitude, that you couldn't help but love him right away ("love" is exactly the right word, but don't jump to conclusions: I'm old enough to be the professor's mom and besides, despite all the little digs, I'm nuts about Ralston). It's just that I found Professor Coates . . . well, so interesting, and also vulnerable somehow, undefended. An attractive trait in that rough-and-tumble world out there, so I was tickled pink when he accepted my invitation for coffee—after all, I told him, I lived just around the corner, and no, it wasn't any trouble at all.

So we went. And sat there talking. And having coffee, and later some lemonade, followed by a plateful of macaroons. And we talked some more. The experience, I tell you, was beyond anything I could have expected. Granted, I did most of the talking at first. I told him about Ralston and his work down at the tire store, and about our daughter Sarah, who had just flown off to college the month before, and about our sixteen-year-old spaniel, Lucky, who'd died in her sleep just a week before that. I said how upset Sarah had gotten, insisting that Lucky had somehow sensed that she was going to abandon her, how it was all her fault and now she wasn't going after all!—those few days had been terrible, probably the worst we'd ever lived through as a family. Ralston had spent a couple of hours up in Sarah's bedroom, talking in a gentle, persuasive voice, and when he came out he looked gray as ashes and said that Sarah had decided to leave a week *early* for college, she'd get there the day the dorms opened and try to busy herself with—But then I stopped myself; I'd felt a little catch in my throat. "Enough of that!" I said to Professor Coates, laughing it off. "I guess you're not interested in an old lady's troubles."

This wasn't completely honest, I suppose, since all the time I talked Professor Coates hadn't moved his damp brown eyes from mine. He sat very erect, every now and then taking a small sip of the coffee, looking concerned and thoughtful; his listening so closely made me a bit self-conscious.

"On the contrary," Professor Coates said, in his polite way. "Your story is very affecting. You must have a great deal of strength."

"Strength?" I said. I didn't understand.

"Inner strength," Professor Coates said.

No one had ever told me such a thing, and I felt that I'd earned the professor's respect without even trying. Certainly I'd earned his trust, since right away—and this is what I'd never have expected—he began talking about his own past life. Somehow I'd pegged him as a timid, withdrawn type, but actually he spoke in a frank, unhurried voice, the rhythms pleasant and convincing. As he talked, I imagined this as the same voice he used to teach his classes at the University. For that's what he talked about first —his one-year appointment in the history department, his heavy work load of preparing lectures and corresponding with other professors and writing a book (a long, complicated book, he said with a sigh) about Napoleon's last days. He'd moved to Atlanta in August, he said, but after two months he still didn't know much of anyone here, and he often thought that there wasn't much point—he had so much work to do, and he'd be moving somewhere else when the school year ended. The more Professor Coates talked, the more wistful he sounded. When I got up for the lemonade and cookies, I said, "Go on, go on," and by the time I sat down again he'd already started talking about his parents.

Something awful had happened, he said. He broke one of the macaroons neatly in half, but then put both halves back down on the plate. The previous year, he said, he hadn't done any teaching. His mother had become very ill and he'd returned to Boston last September to help take care of her. His father was retired but depressed—"severely depressed," Professor Coates said—and couldn't do much. Cancer, it was; a hopeless case. As the doctors had warned him, things went from bad to worse, and before Christmas she was gone. But that was only the beginning, in a way, because then he had to tend to his father, which was really much more taxing than his mother's care had been. In a slow, mournful voice Professor Coates told me that his father had died suddenly—that is, by his own hand. He didn't specify how, and of course I didn't ask. Big tears stood in my eyes; I took a swallow of lemonade to wash down the lump in my throat.

"That's—that's awful," I finally managed.

Professor Coates opened his long immaculate hands, palms up. "Thank you for listening," he said, his voice remarkably calm. "Over where I'm staying, it's pretty isolated. I really haven't made very many friends."

"Where *are* you staying?" I asked.

"Oh, just in the faculty quarters," Professor Coates said, shrugging. "Actually, it's quite a nice—"

"Why don't you move in here?"—the question and the idea came at the same moment, but I didn't regret my words. Ralston often says that I speak before I think, but what was there to think about, really? It was the perfect solution.

"You could stay in Sarah's bedroom," I said, talking faster now that Professor Coates was shaking his head. "I've often thought to myself, we should take in a boarder, we really should"—this was a white lie, I guess, but maybe I'd *felt* it, without really *thinking* it—"and since Mr. Parks and I sleep downstairs you'd have plenty of privacy, and your own bath. You could have dinner with us, too. I'm not a bad cook, and I—"

"Mrs. Parks, you're far too kind," and I could tell by his face that he was both alarmed and pleased by the invitation. The alarm I understood—it seemed too sudden, it was ridiculous when you thought that we'd only met a couple of hours ago. I've always had faith, however, in my woman's intuition—I have this knack for seeing to the heart of a situation, even Ralston will grant me that. Sometimes you have to proceed slowly, though; you have to bring people around.

"Well, at least come for dinner tonight," I said. "You can meet my husband, and we'll talk about it."

He paused, looking pleased despite himself. "I'd be delighted to come for dinner," he said, "but as for the other—" He stopped himself, reaching down and taking one of the macaroon halves.

We could discuss the matter, of course, but I knew that the thing was as good as done. I felt happy—completely, absurdly happy. So there was nothing left to do but reach across and take the other half of Professor Coates's macaroon. We sat there for a while, smiling, chewing happily. There was nothing more to say.

Granted, the idea of a boarder caused a little tiff between Ralston and me. I'd told Professor Coates to come for dinner

around seven, thinking I'd have a couple of hours to break the
news to Ralston, calm him down, win him over; but naturally he
picked that very evening to stop by his brother Ferris's house for
a beer, so that when he got home at six-thirty I had to explain
everything in a rush. We were in the dining room, where I kept
straightening and restraightening the three plates, the silverware.
I didn't much want to look at Ralston.

"Honey?" I said at last, adjusting a candle in the silver-plate
candelabrum we'd gotten for our twenty-fifth anniversary, from
Ferris and his wife, Julie. "Shouldn't you get cleaned up? I told
Professor Coates seven o'clock, and it's already—"

"No," Ralston said, from behind me.

I turned around. He looked clean enough in his work khakis,
his silver-white hair combed back neatly from his crown. Yet his
eyes had darkened; he looked tired and angry at once.

"Then at least change your clothes, OK?" I said, keeping my
voice light. "See what I'm wearing?" And I lifted my arms, turning smartly like one of those models on TV, showing off my
sky-blue linen with the gathered sleeves and hoping to get a smile
out of Ralston.

"I don't mean that," he said, the twin creases between his eyes
getting deeper. "I mean *no* to the whole idea. No, no, no."

He pulled out his chair at the head of the table, snapping the
cloth napkin onto his lap. "Let's eat."

"Ralston, I've invited the man for dinner. He's a very nice man,
and I want *you* to be nice, too."

Ralston put down the fork he'd been holding above his empty
plate, mockingly. The corners of his mouth drooped.

"For heaven's sake, Lily. Did you really ask the man to *live* with
us? Without discussing it with me?"

He was weakening. I hurried over and sat in my usual chair,
leaning close to Ralston and speaking in a near whisper. "It's only
for a few months, sweetie, only till the end of the school year.
Then Sarah will be coming home, but in the meantime won't it
be nice to have someone in the house? It's been so quiet around
here."

"*You* live here," Ralston said, but I saw the little glint in his eye that meant I'd won. "So it's never quiet."

I reached out and pinched his forearm. "Scalawag," I said.

"But a perfect stranger, Lily," Ralston said. By now, even his shoulders had drooped. "A man we don't even know—"

"He's a lonesome fellow, I think," I said quickly, bringing out the ammunition I'd stored in my head all during the afternoon, "and it's the Christian thing to do, isn't it? I'm sure that Father Dalton would approve. And it'll bring a little money in, of course, and maybe he can even help around the house—you know, small repairs and such, and on top of that—"

Ralston had lifted his palm, so I stopped.

"It'll depend," he said.

"Depend? Depend on what?"

He threw me a look that said, *Dumb question, Lily!* Experience had taught me not to react to this look, so then Ralston said: "On *him*."

The doorbell rang.

"Fine," I said, getting up, smoothing my dress. "You'll see that I'm right, then. You'll be forced to *admit* that I'm right."

And, of course, he did exactly that, for Professor Coates was a completely charming dinner guest. He brought flowers for me, a bottle of Chardonnay for Ralston; he remarked on my dress several times and didn't seem to notice Ralston's khakis. And if I say so myself, the meal was delicious. Swiss steak, new potatoes, Caesar salad; and my famous raspberry cheesecake for dessert. During the meal Professor Coates asked us a good many questions, but nothing personal or inappropriate; he asked about Ralston's work down at the store, he asked about our church after I'd mentioned something about Sunday Mass, saying that he'd been raised as a Catholic too, though unfortunately he had "lapsed" in recent years, and most of all he asked about Sarah, assuming that she was the favorite topic of conversation for both Ralston and me, which of course she was. This was the point, in fact, when the professor finally won my husband over. Ralston had been a bit reserved and stiffish up to now, but he leaned for-

ward and asked Professor Coates eagerly about the college Sarah
had chosen—was it really as well regarded as Sarah thought,
would it give her the best possible chance for getting into law
school, presuming she did well? Did most of Professor Coates's
students, especially his freshman students, seem *happy* in their
new lives, did they get over their homesickness quickly, did they
make new friends?—and for that matter, what was college like,
exactly? Professor Coates reassured him on all points, telling him
about the social activities, the counselors, the sheer excitement
of college life for most students. We shouldn't be alarmed at not
hearing from Sarah very often; that was a good sign, in fact; it
meant that she was just too busy to be homesick.

Ralston sat back from the table, satisfied. "How about some
brandy for Professor Coates, Lily?" he asked, to my great surprise. "We still have that bottle, don't we?"

He meant the bottle from our little anniversary party, eight
months before.

"Yes, of course," and as I poured brandy in the kitchen I heard
Ralston saying to Professor Coates that if he'd like to board with
us for the rest of the school year, that would be fine with him. For
reply, I could hear only the professor's polite murmuring, but I
felt sure that he would accept. During the dinner, it occurred to
me that we had found out very little about him, and of course I
didn't allude to the sad story about his parents. Having unbur-
dened himself, perhaps he now felt embarrassed; and I wondered
if his barrage of politely worded questions was a way, partly, to
avoid revealing more about himself. A very shy man, this Professor Coates! And how pleasant it was, to be able to help him!
Feeling a bit sly, I lifted one of the brandy glasses and made a
toast to myself, for having accomplished so much in one day. The
liquor burned in my throat and stomach, like the sweet glow of
charity itself. Then I refilled the glass, and went back to join my
husband and our new boarder.

For a long while, the arrangement worked perfectly. Professor
Coates kept to himself most of the time, but he took his meals

with us and occasionally joined us for an evening of TV in the den. What a polite, well-groomed man he always was!—never a hair out of place, always wearing one of his tweed jackets and his carefully polished shoes. (Ralston and Professor Coates had made a Sunday morning ritual of polishing their shoes together, the professor his Bass Weejuns and Ralston the chunky black wing tips he wears to church, the two looking for all the world like father and son as they worked and chatted.) Nor did he seem to mind our simple ways, commenting often on how "cozy" our house was, repeating every week or so how "eternally grateful" he felt to have lived here for a brief while, just like a member of the family. I noticed how often he mentioned his departure the following May, as though reminding himself that his "family member" status was temporary, or reminding us that he didn't intend to overstay his welcome. I'd feel a bit melancholy then, but with Sarah coming home for the summer I couldn't suggest that he stay any longer and decided to just enjoy him while I could.

So, everything chugged along perfectly during the fall. Only one thing bothered me, and that was how I kept feeling I didn't really *know* the professor very well, despite all the time we spent together. When I brought this up to Ralston, he said I was being silly: Professor Coates was a grown man, he needed his privacy; and there was an age difference, too. For that matter, Ralston said, in an irksome, commonsensical voice, what does he know about *us*, exactly? We're just an aging couple who watches TV on Saturday night and goes to Mass on Sunday morning. How many of *your* deep, dark secrets have you confided to the professor, Lily? I told Ralston that I wasn't talking about "deep, dark secrets," only about getting to know the man. What had his childhood been like, what made him happy or angry, what did he think about right before he went to sleep, what were his dreams about the future?—that kind of thing. You expect too much, Ralston said flatly, and then he added: Also, remember that he's not a southerner. He's from New England, right? From Boston or somewhere? That's a different kettle of fish, you know.

There was no point in arguing with Ralston, but the truth was that the longer Professor Coates lived with us, the more curious I got. I guess I should blush to admit this, but a few times, while doing the cleaning, I lingered in his room a bit longer than necessary, knowing that the professor wouldn't return until late afternoon. (Not that much cleaning was needed: he kept his closets neat as a pin, the jackets and slacks organized by color, dark things on the left, shading to tans and beiges on the right. That tickled me, somehow. His drawers were orderly too, the socks arranged in matching pairs, the jockey shorts folded and neatly stacked.) Externally the room was pretty barren: while Sarah had covered the walls with posters, lined her dresser with keepsakes and picture frames, and kept a menagerie of stuffed animals on her bed, the professor hadn't added any personal touches. He'd brought an ordinary bedspread of white chenille, and though I offered to do it, he made the bed himself every morning. He left the walls bare, and on the dresser there were only a few magazines, a small box of stationery, and a little brass tray holding spare change and some matchbooks. I knew that the professor didn't smoke, so I did examine the matchbooks. They were all from a place called "The Den" with a midtown address, and none of the matches had been torn. One had something written inside: the initials "D.J." with a phone number. Probably a colleague of his from the university, I thought; maybe "The Den" was a lunch place. Among the matchbooks I also found a small strip of paper with a neatly printed sentence: "History is no more than a lie agreed upon," followed by the initials "N.B." Another colleague, I guessed, though the message didn't make much sense to me. Anyhow, I didn't go further than that. In the back of his bottom drawer, under some knit shirts, there *was* a small packet of letters, but I wasn't that much of a snoop. I closed the drawer with a sigh, and never opened it again.

When Sarah came home at Thanksgiving and Christmas, the professor took off for Boston, so it happened that our daughter never met the man who'd begun inhabiting her room. The arrangement was "OK by me," she said, but she refused to stay in the room, sleeping instead on the lumpy sofa in the den. That hurt my feelings a bit, but Ralston said that Sarah was going through "a phase" and it was probably best to let her alone. Otherwise she seemed happy, though. She made all A's and B's her first semester, she had a boyfriend ("sort of," she qualified), also I noticed that her clothes had gotten deliberately sloppy and more colorful; and she'd started frizzing her hair, tying it together in a kind of pony tail perched on the very top of her head. For once, though, I did agree with Ralston: I wasn't worried about Sarah any longer, and when she left the day after New Year's the melancholy lasted only an hour or two. And besides, I was looking forward to the professor's return later that week.

He came back on a Saturday evening, but almost immediately went out again. I must admit, my feelings were hurt. I'd fixed him a nice dinner and put it in the refrigerator, wrapped in foil, but Professor Coates just said, "I ate on the plane, thank you. Quite a delicious meal." It was almost ten o'clock, but he rushed upstairs and took a quick shower, then changed into jeans and a sports shirt. During the fall he'd often gone out on weekend nights, by himself—for a movie, he said, or just for a walk around the neighborhood. Though I'd tried once or twice, I'd never managed to keep myself awake until he got home, so I knew he stayed out late. Now we were having a cold snap, though, and when I heard him move lightly down the stairs I came out from the den. "My, it's such a cold night!" I said, laughing. "Why don't you come on back, have some hot chocolate with Ralston and me? You can tell us about your trip." Professor Coates smiled politely, opening the hall closet and taking out a short leather jacket I hadn't seen before. A Christmas present, maybe, though I hesitated to ask. He looked tired; even the smile seemed a bit forced. (Now Lily, Ralston had said over the holidays, when I'd expressed curiosity about what the professor was doing that very moment, you've really got to let the man alone. He's an ideal boarder, but he isn't a—a personal *friend*. Now I didn't agree with this at all, but I said nothing. Didn't Ralston understand that the professor was lonely? That he needed someone to bring him out, get him to talk a little about himself?) He zipped up the jacket and said, "Thanks, but I'm meeting a friend of mine. I called—um, I called her from the airport, and—" He broke off, looking embarrassed. "Oh, well," I said, flustered myself, "then don't mind me! We'll talk tomorrow—have a good time!" And he was gone.

Now I'd better confess something: I felt jealous. But, to my credit, almost immediately after that I felt happy for Professor Coates. I remembered the matchbook and amused myself with a guessing game for the rest of that evening—that is, guessing what the "D" stood for. Diane? Darlene? Dorothy? It was a pointless game, of course—there were dozens of possibilities—and I didn't even mention to Ralston what the professor had said. I knew he would be irritated if I were even thinking about the professor's private life.

So, I had to keep my own counsel where the professor was concerned. There was a lot to think about, I must say, for if anything, the professor became more secretive that winter. He started missing dinner and arriving home later and later from the University, his briefcase bulging. He'd mentioned that he had a heavy teaching load this semester, and he was trying to finish his book by May, and there was so much new material on Napoleon, it seemed a new book was published every other day. . . . We'd stand talking at the foot of the stairs, the professor in his beige overcoat, his hands and nose reddened from the cold (though he owned a car, he walked the half-mile to the campus no matter how cold the weather, no matter how I chided him), his body dragged down on one side by the weight of the briefcase. But he wouldn't put down the briefcase; wouldn't let me take his coat and damp shoes and lead him into the kitchen for a nourishing dinner, or some hot chocolate, or hot tea and lemon to keep him from catching a cold. It was seven-thirty, it was eight o'clock, I *knew* he hadn't eaten a thing but still he'd back up the stairs, thanking me anyway, apologizing, touching his glasses between the eyes in an odd gesture he had (for the glasses hadn't slipped

out of place) and saying sorry, he had so much work to do, papers
to grade, and some reading, he was really very sorry. . . . And then
I'd be left standing there, my neck aching as I peered upward
into the dark.

Lose something, Lily? Ralston said smartly one night, passing by.

As the winter dragged on, the professor's company got scarcer,
and when he did show up for a meal—breakfast, usually—he
looked awful. Except for his red-rimmed nostrils he'd gotten
white as the tablecloth, that kind of dead white people get when
they don't sleep right or exercise or take any vitamins. His eyes
were dull and glazed, and he'd murmur that he hadn't slept well,
he knew he'd be fine if he could manage to get some rest. By now,
even Ralston was getting a bit concerned, and he jotted down
Dr. Hutter's name and phone number—that's our internist—in
case Professor Coates wanted a checkup, or maybe something to
help him sleep. The professor mumbled his thanks, folding the
slip of paper inside his wallet. "I really *do* regret," he said carefully,
his eyes not meeting Ralston's, "having been such poor company
of late."

"My goodness, don't apologize!" I broke out, before Ralston
could answer.

"You see," he began, "I've been troubled by—well, something
of a personal matter that I—"

"Professor Coates," I said, reaching out my hand and patting
his, "don't feel like you owe us any explanations—none whatever.
Your private life is your private life, and we understand that."

I glanced at Ralston, thinking he'd be pleased, but instead he
shot me a threatening look—a *scowl* it was—that made my heart
jump. Ralston isn't a big man, but he has a fleshy face, thick neck,
dark quick-moving eyes, and when he gets mad that combination
can be fearsome. The skin hardens, the neck thickens, and the
eyes have the effect of freezing you in place. You can't move, and
you can hardly speak.

"What—what I meant—" I stammered.

"Why don't you let Professor Coates finish?" Ralston said, in a polite voice that was curiously like the professor's but that Ralston used only when he was furious.

"I—I'm sorry, I—"

"Please, don't trouble yourself," the professor said, and I'd no idea what he meant. I looked back and forth between him and Ralston, but they were both looking down at their plates, embarrassed. Then the professor rose quickly, saying he'd better be off. I didn't say anything, even though I noticed that he'd forgotten to take the multiple vitamin I'd put beside his plate; he hadn't eaten his scrambled eggs either. No sooner was the professor out the door than Ralston left too, so I got up and started cleaning the breakfast dishes, feeling sadder and more bewildered than I'd ever felt in my life.

I stayed melancholy for a long while, feeling that I was in a kind of fog and that I didn't know what I was doing. I noticed the professor's exits and entrances—he left earlier and earlier in the morning, sometimes stayed gone until nine p.m. or later, and on weekends stayed out late at night and then slept until long after Ralston and I got back from ten o'clock Mass—but I no longer went out to greet him in the hallway, or tried to coax him into the kitchen for food or conversation. February passed, and March; we began making plans for Sarah's visit during Easter vacation, though we hadn't asked the professor about his own plans. I started worrying about what would happen if they both planned to be here—who would sleep where, would the situation be strained, et cetera. And something else troubled me: all during the fall, Professor Coates had called home frequently—at least, I assumed he was calling home, I knew he had a couple of brothers still in Boston—and I remember feeling gratified that he kept in such close touch with his family. At the end of each month, the professor would ask about the long distance charges—sometimes they were more than a hundred dollars—and would promptly write me a check. After the Christmas holidays, though, the calls abruptly stopped, and I wondered if his overwork or stress or whatever was bothering him had made him decide not to call home for a while, so that his family wouldn't worry. That would be just like him, I thought. So considerate of others, he always was. That's one thing about Professor Coates that never changed. No matter how much he kept to himself or how bad he obviously felt, he always took the time to compliment a new hairdo of mine, or a dress he thought was becoming; and every once in a while he'd repeat his thanks to us for having him as a boarder. These days, I didn't know how to respond, since his boarding with us had seemed to coincide with such a difficult period in his life, but nonetheless I appreciated his comments and wanted to say to Ralston—though I didn't dare—that I wouldn't have missed knowing Professor Coates for the world.

Despite what happened, I still feel that way. Now that the shock has worn off; now that enough time has passed that Ralston and I have talked the matter over, not only between ourselves but with Father Dalton down at church. It was Father Dalton, after all, who pointed out that we'd given Professor Coates a "room in the inn," so to speak, and tried to ease his way during a time of great suffering. Nonetheless, it wasn't ours to judge, Father said, in response to some complaint Ralston had made (in a low, surprisingly meek voice) about Professor Coates's having been dishonest, in a way; having lied "by omission," as Ralston put it. But no, it wasn't ours to judge. I couldn't have agreed more, and was happy that Father Dalton was so understanding and open-minded. Maybe it rubbed off on Ralston, for this time I didn't get the usual smart remarks—the "I told you so," the "See what you get" kind of talk. No snide references to my "impulsiveness," my "harebrained schemes." We've reached a kind of truce, it would seem, where our different views of the world and other people are concerned. Finally, after all this time, we're even.

The shock was the main thing, I think, for in the past it was always yours truly who ended up surprised, or disappointed, or hurt by people I tried to befriend. Ralston, on the other hand, tended to be smug, as though taking in stride the quirks of other people and the world at large; nothing surprised *him,* he'd have you believe. The incident with Professor Coates did surprise him, though–surprised the hell out of him, if you'll excuse my language. It goes to show, I guess, that something good can come out of even the most tragic circumstances, and to this day I believe that the whole experience *was* illuminating, *was* profound— though Ralston certainly would not agree.

It was just another Sunday morning, in early April. I'd had breakfast ready at eight-thirty, like always, and of course Professor Coates hadn't come downstairs; it had been weeks since he had risen before noon on a weekend day. Last night, though, I'd stayed up extra late—I was watching one of those old forties melodramas on TV that I love so much, this one with Loretta Young—and it had crossed my mind that maybe Professor Coates *would* come home before the movie ended at one a.m., and maybe we would have a little chat. But no. I turned off the set and even dawdled in the kitchen over some hot milk and graham crackers, but still no professor. I went on back to the bedroom, and by the time my head hit the pillow I was asleep.

At breakfast, Ralston and I were chatting about this and that, nothing special, and I was just about to go and change my dress for church, when we heard a sudden noise from upstairs. A crash, it sounded like, followed quickly by two or three more. Ralston had pricked his ears, his coffee cup suspended in midair. "What on earth—," he began, but then we heard other sounds—a series of muffled, heavy grunts, like you hear from boxers when they're fighting. Professor Coates's room was catty-corner on the other end of the house from where we sat, so the sounds were blurry, but nonetheless that was my first thought: fighting. Two men, fighting. But then I thought of soft-spoken Professor Coates and knew I must be imagining things. Though Ralston would often say, later, "Why did I just *sit* there?" I knew he had the same reaction. It sounded like one thing but had to be something else.

At such times, of course, thoughts race through your mind: maybe he's moving the furniture around? maybe he's exercising? maybe he bought himself a TV and is watching something noisy and violent? But then came a loud thud that made the walls tremble even downstairs, and Ralston and I looked at each other with our eyes opened wide. A door slammed, and we heard the loud, thumping footsteps coming down—making a racket, I knew, that Professor Coates had never made in his life. Then, at the doorway of the breakfast room, he appeared: a tall, mustached man wearing boots and blue jeans, and a very soiled light blue sweatshirt. He had dark bushy eyebrows, big red-knuckled hands. I noticed the hands because he thrust one arm forward, as if pointing or accusing, his finger shaking in our direction.

"Look, I need some money," he said. "Do you people have any money?"

Ralston said at once, "Just what's in my wallet."

The young man wriggled his fingers. "C'mon, hurry up." I saw how nervous he was, his eyes reddened, his body moving constantly in little jumps and spasms. His longish dark hair looked electrified, standing out in all directions. When Ralston held out the wad of bills, the young man snatched them the way Lucky used to snap her dog treats out of our fingers. He turned and ran out of the house.

Feeling limp, scarcely breathing, I followed Ralston to the front door, which the young man had left standing open, and we stood watching as he raced Professor Coates's little car—some kind of hatchback, I think—backward out of the driveway, then down the street with a loud squeal of the tires.

"My Lord . . . ," Ralston whispered.

At the same moment we turned, gazing up to the top of the stairs.

"Professor Coates? . . ." I said, but it came out as a croak and I knew he couldn't have heard.

Then Ralston squeezed my wrist, trying to pull himself together.

"Wait here," he said.

He climbed the stairs three at a time, and of course I wasn't far behind. At the bedroom doorway he said again, "My Lord . . . ," and gestured me back with his hand. For a moment, I obeyed. I heard my husband's low murmuring inside the room, as though he were comforting Professor Coates, or gently questioning him. Then I heard him talking in a louder, more businesslike voice: the one he uses on the phone.

I crept forward, just barely peeking my nose and eyes inside the doorway. This sounds cowardly, I know, but I was truly frightened; I believe that my teeth were actually chattering. And then I saw him. Lying on the bed, one arm splayed outward. His glasses had been knocked off: later they'd be found on the floor, underneath his desk. His face was pale, and there was a long streak of blood along one side of his mouth, like saliva. His eyes were open but dead-looking; glazed over. No, I thought, please God, please Mother Mary, no no *no.* . . . When Ralston finished ordering the ambulance, he dialed again and asked for the police. All the time I stared at Professor Coates's face: so pale, so dead white, except for the thread of blood out the side of his mouth. His T-shirt and the mussed white chenille bedspread were also streaked with blood, stray blots and wriggles of blood, random designs. I felt myself becoming sick.

I turned and hobbled down the hall, into the upstairs bathroom.

When the ambulance arrived, they loaded him quickly. The driver told Ralston not to worry, that he was in shock but would be fine; there seemed to be no serious internal injuries. A broken wrist, maybe a couple of broken ribs, but nothing to cause undue concern. . . . When the police arrived, they were amazingly callous; or so *I* thought. Later Ralston remarked philosophically that we led a sheltered life, that maybe we were to blame for being so shocked, so defenseless. . . . I didn't understand what my husband meant. The policeman who did the talking—a short, jowly man in his forties—said this wasn't unusual, not in Atlanta;

this happened all the time. He seemed rather pleased, somehow. I didn't know what he meant by "this," exactly, but a part of me was too angry to speak, part of me still too frightened. I kept glancing around the room at the bloodstained bed, the broken desk leg, the papers scattered everywhere; I was already picturing myself cleaning up the room, slowly and methodically. I clung to that.

For the next day or two, Ralston and I talked very little about what had happened. Occasionally we'd give each other the same wide-eyed look we'd exchanged at the breakfast table that morning, as though we were reliving the incident together; and yet we were apart, too, because we couldn't talk about it. We didn't have the words, it seemed to me. On Monday morning Ralston did go down to the hospital, but was told that Professor Coates couldn't have visitors except immediate family members; later that day, one of his brothers would be flying down from Boston. That night, I happened to answer the phone when it rang, and it was the brother, Jason; he said he would like to come over at once, if convenient, and clean out the professor's things. He called the professor "Jim," which sounded funny to my ears. After we hung up, I stood by the telephone table a long while, understanding that we would never see Professor Coates again. After a few minutes Ralston came up behind me. "Don't worry, Lily," was all he said.

Jason Coates turned out to be a slightly older, darker-complected version of the professor; and he looked fleshier, stronger. It took him and Ralston less than half an hour to load the professor's things into the man's rented car, and then we were all standing at the front door together, awkwardly saying good-bye. Mournful and slump-shouldered, Jason stood there a long while, as though there was something more he wanted to say. And then, looking chagrined, he brought out that the professor *had* been well enough to see visitors, but he felt too embarrassed, too ashamed. He never dreamed of our having to encounter that —that acquaintance of his, Jason said, dropping his voice even more. As for the money and the damage, he would send a check from Boston as soon as he was able; and above all, Jason said, the professor wanted us to know how grateful he was for our being so kind to him, during these past eight months.

"He says he's never known such fine people," Jason said, with a quick smile. "And as for myself, I'd like to thank you, too. For being so good to my brother."

"But," I began, "I still don't understand—"

"Hush, Lily," Ralston said. "We were glad to have him," he told Jason Coates. "And you tell him not to worry. We know it wasn't his fault."

Suddenly Jason looked anxious. "You know," he said, "he has had some personal problems. There was a—a person, someone he was involved with up in Boston, and it ended very abruptly last year. Jim has a knack, it would seem, for choosing people who aren't good for him, who don't have his best interests at heart. It amazes me, really, that he found you people." Jason smiled, ruefully.

"I found *him*," I said. "But I still don't—"

"Tell him we wish him well," Ralston said. "And God bless." I could hear in his voice—though Jason probably couldn't—that he wanted to end this conversation. As he held my wrist I could feel the tension in his fingers.

"I'll tell him, and don't worry about him, *please*," Jason said, and he was gone before I could even get his address or phone number. So I never found out how long it took Professor Coates to recover, or whether he went on to another teaching post the next fall, or whether he finished his book on Napoleon. Whenever I brought any of this up, Ralston would say shortly that it didn't matter if we knew these things or not.

Anyhow, despite Ralston, the incident never quite went away. For several weeks there was a change in the atmosphere somehow; when Ralston and I talked over dinner, or during the TV commercials in the den, we sounded awkward and a bit false, like people rehearsing their lines in a play. I suspect he was thinking, as I was, that everything would change when Sarah got home in mid-May, but actually the opposite happened: for Sarah, once as talkative and carefree as her mother, had become a different person in the last nine months. She moved all her things back into the professor's room—that is, *her* room—but not only had she gotten sloppy and a bit "wild" in her dress, as we knew from her visits home, but was quieter, moodier, spending long hours alone in her room, reading and listening to music, and writing letters that she rushed out of the house every morning to mail. (During her first week home, practically her only words were the daily request for stamps, her eyes not quite meeting mine. I'd stall for a moment, looking over this girl who had once been, people said, the spitting image of me, petite and auburn-haired and, if I may say so, very pretty. Delicate, pointed features; very fair skin. But she'd ruined all this with heavy eye-makeup and the frizzed hair and the bright loose-fitting clothes, and I hardly knew her. Soon enough, I began to think that Sarah—our new boarder— was as much of a stranger as Professor Coates had been.)

Finally, one Saturday morning after Sarah had taken off for the post office, I began crying over my scrambled eggs. I don't cry often, as you might guess, but when I do it's quite a sight. I can't hold back, you see. Great racking sobs, like hiccoughs. Tears running like a faucet. When Ralston said, "All right then, let's go see Father Dalton," I could only nod and let him lead me out to the car.

Mostly I've reported what Father Dalton said, but I did leave one part out, and that was about the letters. This part even surprised Ralston, I believe. You see, the day after Jason Coates's visit I was cleaning the professor's room yet another time when I saw that someone had thrown some papers into his wastebasket, and of course I recognized the letters I'd glimpsed in the back of the professor's drawer. Evidently Jason had thrown them away, and naturally I wondered about this. It seemed a callous thing to do, but maybe he knew more than I did? Were the letters somehow linked to whatever was troubling Professor Coates? Sitting in the little reception room at the rectory, I remembered that I'd recently glimpsed some letters of Sarah's, too, in the very same drawer; and of course I hadn't touched them either, much as my fingers itched. Anyhow, I told Father Dalton about retrieving the letters from the wastebasket, and noticing they had a Boston return address, but no name above the address. The handwriting was small, neat, precise; "Dr. Jim Coates" was how they were addressed. After telling him about the letters—there were five of them, all folded inside the same pale blue envelopes—I asked Father Dalton if it would be all right (if it wouldn't be "sinful," I suppose I meant) if I opened them.

Ralston jumped in his chair. "Lily, what on earth—"

But Father Dalton had raised his hand, shushing Ralston; *he* didn't seem surprised.

"Why would you want to do that, Mrs. Parks?"

"Because—because then it might make sense," I told him. "It's not idle curiosity, I'm not a snoop," I said quickly, "it's just that it's so hard, not being able to know people. Not feeling that you really *know* another person, even when he lives right under your own roof."

"Father, she's been very upset—," Ralston began.

"Even my own daughter, now that she's home. And even—"

"Lily!" Ralston said, his neck thickening. "You're not making sense."

Ah, my stern husband, my protector!—actually, I knew him very well.

Then, for a long while, Father Dalton spoke. Again he mentioned Christ, and how he taught forgiveness without explanations, without conditions. He suggested that just as Christ's life was a mystery, so is each of ours, and no matter how we might try, there's no getting to the genuine heart of another person. Not even when they live in our own house, he added gently. But knowing one another wasn't finally important, he insisted; it might even be considered a wasted effort. All of life, finally, was a mystery, Father Dalton said, but a mystery made bearable by Christ's unstinting love.

It was a very nice speech, I guess, but Father Dalton never did get around to answering my question. Months have passed, and I still have the letters, tucked into the back of my own dresser drawer. I haven't opened them, I think, because I'm afraid they *won't* tell me much, or at least not enough, and that certainly they won't ease the hollow feeling that has gradually settled in my heart, and that stays whether Ralston is nearby or not, whether I'm having a good day or a bad one. Though I try to stay cheerful, I'm no longer the person who'll just start talking to someone on the street, as I did to Professor Coates; and even with friends of ours, even at church, I'm aware that I'm not quite as friendly, don't laugh as much. She's getting older, people must say, if they notice at all. I'm fairly sure that Ralston hasn't noticed.

So, we go about our lives. Ralston is next in line for manager down at the tire store, then retirement and a good pension in six more years. Sarah's back at college, and I guess I understood too late that she was a separate person from myself, and that we've never really known each other. Maybe we'll become friends one day, close and confiding friends? . . . As for Professor Coates's letters, I'm sure that I'll never read them and also sure that I'll never throw them away. Whenever I remember them, though, I become thoughtful for a moment—it's like praying, almost—and my heart lies hollow and silent as that empty room upstairs.

Tom Bailey

CROW MAN

(from *The Greensboro Review*)

And Rarden then whining down over the border oaks, swooping down that stick, flapping rudders, to hop, skip, jump down over those trees and trailing poison out of his wings, six long thin streams over twelve rows of cotton, and him so low his wheels go to brushing the bolls, a *thup-thup-thup* sound like the queen of hearts stuck in the spokes of my now grandson's bike, and his great double-winged eagle shadow bunched down so small underneath or to either side depending on the time of the summer sun. Straight up and down noon when he would spray out the last of his load, shoot his wad, as he used to say, and buzz back to Legion Field and land and then throw me his goggles and leather helmet, which he wore but of course didn't have to, and jump in his truck and head for Nadine's.

Nadine's where Naomi was, who he called Felicity Jane, and him being from the North and her some breed of Chickasaw, Choctaw, probably Negro, mixed-up kind of blood, cheekbones high and silent, but with a strong questionable nose, and wider lips than maybe she had a right to as just an Indian, and a kink to her hair which was unexplainable any other way.

The truth of the whole thing being he, Rarden, scared the shit out of people whether he was looping and swoop-diving almost crash in that plane, an old barnstorming Jenny, or at Nadine's, drinking Dixie beer or any whiskey they had, and just after twelve noon too, or before even it didn't matter to him. There to see Naomi, saying *Good afternoon, Miss Felicity Jane,* like he was a cowboy or something and this in Mississippi, and, of course, her never saying nothing, and not even hardly raising her eyes.

But it was her that shot him. Nobody else had to do it. Killed him, I believe, like you would stomp the head off a wing-crippled mockingbird. And everybody always used to say there wasn't no need to shoot him even if there was a need to because the way he piloted that plane he was quick on his way to hell anyway. If you ever heard a boom of lightning-flash thunder, first you thought it was old Rarden done bought his ticket, done gone home, but then it never was, and he became a kind of legend like some nine-foot Jesus, gained a reputation, see, for being crazy and so for the most part people left him alone, just shook their heads and waited for him to die, which of course, he did, just not like they expected.

The water tower stood up like a silver head, winking in the sunlight, and as I yanked back the stick and bellied by it the ground dropped and became blue way up sky and away and then spinning under and back rotating blue, green, brown where it should be, and I could read where he'd painted her name, red, candy-apple red, FELICITY JANE, over the kid signs OLD MISS REBELS, CLASS OF '25, JOEY C. LOVES S.M., and older rain-streaked and year-faded loves and cheers. There for anybody who wanted to see. FELICITY JANE. Rolling that old Jenny over and spraying back through Mr. Sutton's fields close by my last tis-sue marker, and then empty-light and streaking straight back to Legion Field where Rarden would be looped and feeling high, ready to fly, *to be up,* after his whiskey lunch and beer and seeing Naomi. He'd tell me how fine she was. *Something.* And already wearing his leather helmet and goggles and the quick choke snort as the prop died and the dust by our shack at the airfield rose and fell in the different same place, not mattering, and him, Rarden, strolling out with that big smile on his face. *And Jasper,* he'd say to me, *she is so fine. I never met a woman like that before.* Me thinking that he probably had, but that because I was thinking of what kind of Mary Magdalin woman I thought she was and not what he thought she was. Fueling, and him up again, in love and flying, which is what he did, like some men walk or run, or go into business. He fell in love and flew. He just drank on the side.

It was Rarden taught me to fly. Nobody could see a nigger in the air. But me. I could see it and wanted it so bad I could chew it like gristle and toted gas and loaded chemicals for it and don't think nobody would never have let me up but crazy Rarden. *Hey, Jasper,* those low-ground niggers at the cafe say, *Hey, Crow man. Crow. You want to fly,* he said, grinning, ear to ear, those goggles on and dusted so he had to clear them with his finger. *Sho',* I said. And him being from the North, Ohio or some such place, laughed, and then was a cowboy again from someplace else again, misplaced again, like he always was, a square peg in a round hole, laughing, and talking like me, saying *sho' nuf?* Put me in a cockpit and took me up. *Born with wings,* he yelled over the hum rush buzz of air, me already with the stick. And it was true. After leaving that old ground, there wasn't nothing else I ever wanted to do. Like an angel. Couldn't go back to just being some low-count field nigger no more. 'Cause I been to heaven. I seen that light. A *goddamned natural,* he said and made me his partner right on the spot, even though I told him I didn't have no money and couldn't afford to buy no stock, and he just looked at me. It was true he didn't have no idea what I was talking about and didn't want a dime.

Of course, De La Palma owned her and there never was a chance for them. Owned her not like a slave and like a slave, like a rich man owns a Chocktaw Chickasaw probably nigger that nobody else does and maybe can't get a job but that she's good-looking and quiet and was willing or didn't think enough of it not to go down on her back. But you couldn't tell that to Rarden. He'd just snort and take a drink and offer me the bottle and I'd take a swig and pass it back and him not bothering to even swipe the lip with his sleeve. That was the kind of man he was. This after work, fourteen hours of spraying, flying, and flying the thing between us, air, sky, blue, and we both could have used more, and us both sitting in our shack, with our partner name, R & J, for Rarden and Jasper, fresh-painted on the door. Crop dusters just plain too long and so we left it off.

Fine, he'd say about her, *fine.* Dreamy-like.

And me thinking there wasn't no chance in hell and saying that she was Mr. De La Palma's girl like everybody knew and nobody said or wanted to know just how, like the devil owns souls. He even owned Nadine's though everybody said it was Nadine's. But it was his jack that kept the place going. But saying to Rarden, *She's just a plain girl. Just a girl. Ain't got no people, ain't got no home.*

Felicity Jane? You talking about Felicity Jane. And this frowning, whiskey-thinking look at me. This kind a crazy look. He was crazy. And he was sane too.

And I'd say, *Well.* And leave it at that.

Now she lives down over by the Hushpuckashaw River, in a little cabin there, the trestle bridge rising over and above her, still on De La Palma's land, though De La Palma dead and been dead twenty years and never touched her after she turned thirty no ways. I see her sometimes snapping beans into a bright Indian-looking apron. Her gray hair long down her back, like a cape down her back, earned these fifty years since. But we don't talk about him. Though maybe we should, both of us being so old now, over for us, and Rarden being the best and worst thing that ever happened to either one of us. The only real free man, white or black or Indian, crazy or sane, that I ever seen. And for her too. I'm sure of that. Not De La Palma.

* * *

It was both of them that climbed the water tower. Together. Arm over arm, hand over hand, up that Jacob's ladder. To the top. And him toting that candy-apple red red paint and a brush. It was the same brush he used to paint our partner name, R & J. Up and up. Until they were up there standing and laughing and no doubt drinking, because there was that between them too, or not between but *with* them—and still all that way to go back down—but Rarden I know didn't care because he, like any bird, was totally disregardless of heights, and she too, like me, was more natural and alive in the air, and so had no fear of dying that way. Wings. Angels. Crows. Eagles. And I wonder how he saw that in us? What he saw in us? A nigger and a Chickasaw Choctaw half-breed nigger too? What was it about us that he picked out? And how did we fall back to this man and woman's ground again? 'Cept that we were out of place as him. And him from a kind of place like Ohio? But he did pick us. But maybe too it was us picked him. And he took that brush out, and I can see them now, up there, kissing, her breasts filling up that beaded shirt, and her long lightish colt legs under her one skirt, and swiping that brush across that tower in huge arm-sweeping candy-apple red letters, big, FELICITY JANE. The town unable to escape it, obvious now, even to De La Palma.

De La Palma was not one of these Southern sheriffs you see on TV and Rarden didn't hate him, not really, and he, De La Palma, got us more business, more fields—maybe just to increase the odds, more air time, more time for crashing. Give him time. Let God take care of it. He will, you know. But he got the fields for us, and we were thankful. Us flying from dusk 'til dawn to dusk again. Until it was even too much for us, much as I liked to take my turns. So Naomi quit Nadine's and her too now, up. Rotating in and out. That old Jenny whining, humming, thrumming up and up, swooping down, raining pellets to fight that old red vine, that nasty bo' weevil, all them things which creep up on man's cotton. And she was good. More than I. Both of us flying.

All three of us flying high. Money. We had more money than what we knew to do with 'cause Rarden didn't want it, see. He just didn't want it. Or if he took some and used it, it wasn't like he cared about it or was hoarding it. And that was the pure thing or what made it the purest thing, flying. And at night one oil lantern and the shadows playing happy with his face and he was good and the best doing what it was he did and maybe touching Naomi's leg, playing with the fringe of her Indian kind of jacket, beads, and laughing. Drinking. And going up tomorrow. Seven days a week. Asking, *Why should you rest when you're doing what you want to do? Why should anything keep you out of the air? Nothing, man,* I'd say, I'm saying. *Nothing.*

From there, the water tower, God's perch, the whole town laid out like something you could read, like something you could understand, like a map maybe: FELICITY JANE and the silver rail tracks north-pulsing glints of sunshine, and the little block town, and then two-lane 46 highway, and quilt fields like red, brown, green, greener, greenest swatches of cloth and pieced together with the stitching border of trees. And the trestle bridge which was an old one, in fact used to swivel to let steamboats through but not any more, crossing the Hushpuckashaw River and just high enough. Just. Barely just. And like a final test of knowing your craft coming down up humping the reaching oaks and then slick slide like a fair ride and scooting down close to the water, taking the slow curve bend and then there suddenly the bridge and just enough to clear the wheels, *sppppiiiittttzzzzz,* dragging the current, the sound of zipping fishing line trawled by a fast boat, and the wings on either side inches from the bricks and your legs warm weak and weary wonderful like after loving and hand gentle fine and squeaking out and another curve, and a kind of hop back on the stick, ballsy barnstorming, and up over leaning back and the fingers of that gravity tickling you out, upside down, rolling all the way over and loop once sliding long back over the field and out, safe and screaming the best thing you ever done. I seen him do it a hundred times. I done it three. Naomi done it every time she got the chance. And him in the back sometimes too, just riding, drinking, both hands in the air, trusting her.

Free. That's all any of us can hope for. And Rarden was. No strings. Flying. Making love. Drinking. Up and up. The only free man, white or black or anything, that I ever made the acquaintance of. Knew the real value of time and money—which is nothing unless it's to buy and have the afternoon and evening to drink whiskey—and was willing to pass on the gift of flight, or let you know if you had it, to touch you with the chance, which was enough and all anybody can ask for, didn't want to hang on to it for himself. Because Rarden was what he was. No explanations for that. And I can't explain why, because that would be like saying why something fly and something else don't. When it flies it's good enough. Fly it.

But Naomi. FELICITY JANE. Choctaw. Chickasaw. Nigger. Probably white. But she grew up black, or as good or bad as black. Outside of town. On De La Palma's place, and that's where De La Palma found her. Raised her really when, I'm sure, he saw her potential for beauty. And she was beautiful in that way of mixing which had come out somehow right and the good strong features of four separate peoples, giving her something nobody else—something nobody else woulda even chosen given the choice—but she had it. Silent as an Indian and as thoughtful. She would laugh, those nights spent in our shack drinking and talking flying which was the only thing to talk, R & J & FJ now on the door—he couldn't call her just Felicity or just Jane and never Naomi and she didn't even seem to mind or even care what he called her, not in a bad way, but like an Indian, as if she was who she was and a name didn't catch her no ways, like naming the "wind"—but her laugh was just a smile, thin-lipped, real, but reserved, and it was only when flying that I saw her really break it out, sparkling, beautiful.

But I'm thinking something about the end, why she killed him. Because De La Palma owned her? Owned her as much as the land, the soil and earth what made her and so could never be free from that? Or that she was free enough for a moment to free him, the best and kindest way, and a hell of a thing too? And so I am thinking about being free. What is it about being set free? What is it about setting someone free? Making me think, again, now all these past fifty years, *And what does free mean?*

She was up, her turn, out spraying, and we were sitting in our partner shack, the smell of gasoline, and Poast 316, and lime too, and the radio going on K96, playing, feet up, whiskey between us, the hot taste of fertilizer and dust still in my mouth from my own flight, almost lunchtime. When then a choke and gurgle spit sputter and out the door us already scanning the sky for the Jenny and then saw her worbling in too low to clear the power and telephone wires and then *No!* and the wheels snagged, caught, growl and snatched out of the air like swiping a fly, yanked out of the air, swung down around it, wrapped in the wire, buzzing, crackle, *BANG!* of the transformer and sizzling electricity, popping, and us both running, the plane hung from the wires by its tail like a condemned man from the rope, like a giant trophy fish, engine dead, and Naomi there slung down, arms out, and Rarden saved her, chinned up onto the propellor, shimmied up to the cockpit and pulled her out, unconscious, and lowered her down, and no sooner all of us on the ground when the wires snapped and the Jenny crumpled, nose first, into the ground.

That was the end of R & J & FJ. We had money but not enough for another plane. Rarden even went to De La Palma. De La Palma said he wished he could help us. He *wished* he could.

* * *

An angel on the ground, though maybe still an angel, is lacking. She no longer has that something which makes her special. An eagle on the ground ain't no longer no eagle. A crow even less a crow. The water tower now as high as Rarden could go in the flat delta and he went there all the time. He was drunk and he was there all the time, and if people had been afraid of him when he was flying, they were downright terrified of him now. He was gone, they'd say at the barbershop and at the hardware store and on the sidewalks and say *I told you so, I told you,* and shake their heads. Everyone just waiting for part two to see what he would do. *I'll bet he'll go back north,* they'd say, and *I'll bet he'll blow his head off,* some would laugh, and some just, *Goddamn,* and maybe chuckle that De La Palma had Naomi back, which was, like I said, a thing no one knew for sure but knew too. Because even during the day you could see him up there, tiny as a dot at the top of that ladder, and his feets dangling over the side. His FELICITY JANE painted behind him in candy-apple red. And at night he slept there, and I would climb up hand over hand up that ladder and would sit and drink with him. He wouldn't say nothing, and I wouldn't say nothing back neither. Just sitting up there and swiping the Old Crow back and forth. The bridge you could see from there where we sat, but it wasn't nothing no more. It was just a bridge. No longer a test. *The* test of his art. Our craft. I had done it only three times, but those three times were the best three things I had ever done or have done, or I feel safe to say, will ever do in this life. There was still the swatches of land. But it wasn't the same. We were squirrels high up in a single tree where once we had been birds. So drunk I can't even say, so that I woke with the sun kicking my head, Rarden sitting on the edge, the empty bottle caught between his knees. I picked up my aching noggin and said, *Shit, man. Shit.* Shaking. And he turned and looked at me up and down like he didn't have no idea who I was and I had just got there anyhow.

* * *

But me imagining those nights her with him, in the air again, her on his lap on a Saturday night with her pretty buckskin skirt hiked up to her waist, I can imagine, flying, her handling the stick, him the rudders, together like that, together, and the other way too, and taking the bridge, like that, right like that, fitted, heads back, yelling all they worth. Just sitting there and imagining that. Always imagining them like that. Still. Her. This kind of love. After everything.

Naomi went back to Nadine's and Nadine took her back because De La Palma asked her to, and I went back into the fields—stalled long as I could, drinking on the water tower and pleading we get out of that place, go someplace else, work up the stake for another Jenny—but then had to climb back down, put my feet on solid ground and hitch up into that tractor, snatching glimpses of the blue from under my cowshed, slow crawling down them long rows. And that was the first time I ever saw Rarden angry —though I seen him drunk and shouting or into a silence plenty of times—when Naomi took back that job. He busted up our partner shack. Trashed it. Made kinlin of the chairs, hatched the table. Smashed the lantern, and then he set it all afire. We were just sitting there and drinking and talking nothing back and forth when he just stood up and swung down that first chair, and I said *Goddamn!* splinters going everywhere. But his eyes was wild with whiskey, and I don't think he even heard me. He grabbed up the lantern and crashed it to the floor. Me just sitting there in the almost dark and thinking *what the fuck?* and watching and not even really believing what was happening yet. Until he went for the ax and buried it into the table, so that I had to jump back to get missed and yelled, *God-damn-it, man! You crazy!* But he wasn't listening. Rarden wasn't even there. I grabbed him by the shoulders to stop him, and that's when he turned on me, didn't say nothing, just rushed me backwards screaming into the wall. We hit and fell and then he had me against the stove and his fists and teeths coming from every which where so that it felt like there was a whole gang of him. And me throwing one or two, but bigger and heavier and somehow coming out rolling up on top and punching him good so that I couldn't stop until I stopped him and he was just laying there gasping like a bellied fish and I got up off him and his blood and mine too on my hands wiping my bloody nose and left saying, *Goddamnit, Rarden. Just goddamnit man*. And shaking my head.

And that was the same night she killed him. In self-defense, the *Herald* said. Rape attempt was understood, because they wrote it so you couldn't understand it in no other way. So while that fire was eating our partner shack, me laying on the cool dirt between two rows of waist-high cotton, thinking about what I had just done and touching my ribs and licking at the gash of my knuckles and watching them flames lick up that night, that fire breathing our shack all the way down to the smoldering hell ground, he, Rarden, had dragged himself up, busted lip and nose and blackening eye that I imagine and all, thinking how I hit him and couldn't stop hitting him, and was at Nadine's drinking. And I hear that he called her a whore, and gnashing my teeth to think of it, for *him*, Rarden, to say that about her—hanging at the end of his own rope. People sitting in the booths there heard that and the fact that he was at Nadine's was in the *Herald*. And her working there and sure nobody going to stop anyone from calling her a whore or anything else for that matter. Him the only one, and it was him calling her that. I imagine that he even grabbed her between her slim thighs, treating her like what she was and what he had spent hisself proving she wasn't. This while the flames ate our shack and I lay hidden between the cotton, nursing my ribs, my busted jaw, the jags of light catching the crowd of people's mouths who had come out to watch in *ooohs* and *aaaahs*. Naomi working back at Nadine's and me back on the spring seat of that tractor, up under that cowshed. And I can see Naomi's face too when he called her that, *whore*, bashed, imagine, coming from the only person she would've taken offense to it from, but him saying it, and her doing it all for him too, though she should've known he couldn't never see it that way, *whore,* so that in the end she had to take his hand from out under her skirt and lay down her apron on the counter and lead him like that out the door.

They were found naked, on the trestle, in the middle, where underneath there was the ancient turnstile to raise the sides. Rarden was naked and shot dead nine times. And I can't help but shudder at that quiet awful time she had taken to reload the revolver and start again—the six slow smacked shots and that silence as she emptied the chambers and reloaded shell by shell and started in again, pulling the trigger three more times, waiting for the slap of each bullet to ricochet away between the riverbanks before she shot him again. Found her naked, her feet dangling over the side, staring into the moon-wrinkled water which she had skimmed so wildly, carefully, screaming, on Rarden's lap, the pistol, one of De La Palma's, which it was said, he had given to her to protect herself when he had gotten her back her job at Nadine's, still caught in her two hands. There was also whiskey involved. And from there, I've since checked, you can see the water tower, even at night, with a good moon, bright.

Now, after fifty years, she sits on the front porch of her cabin, under the trestle, and snaps beans. Her hair gray and long down her back. The children, my grandchildren—I have grandchildren now and a wife of forty-five years—think she's crazy, the Old Indian Lady they call her, a witch, and race by, as good as any graveyard. We never really talk. We have never talked about him since. I don't think we ever talked much even before, but then we didn't have to. There was the sky, the air, flying, joining us all three. People still talk about that crazy Yankee and his Jenny from Ohio. But we don't. There was a time when I was in the air. I could fly. I got farther than most people, white or black. But not any more. On the ground again, I am any nigger, any joe, bob, harry, frank. Any man. Any woman. Any slave. Slave to the small things I know and have never let myself escape. And even my own kids, my grandkids, don't believe I was once free. And my one witness, Naomi, who could tell them it was true, is grounded under the old trestle. And when I bounce by her on my tractor every morning or every evening on my way back to the shop, she looks up from her snapping beans and our eyes meet and we nod or I stop and ask her about her gardenias or say how humid it is out, but we don't talk about him. We never talk about him or that night, and I never want to. Me, I just want to remember him the way things was. The best thing I ever done. But maybe still asking myself as I swing the big 3640 into a day of cotton, *What is free?* It being maybe easier to say what's not free. That after fifty years.

Clyde Edgerton

CHANGING NAMES

(from *The Southern Review*)

She had been going to Preacher Gordon for counseling a good two months when the car wreck happened and killed the little boy. She had been a member of the church for almost a year. I guess she found out she needed some counseling—first with her divorce and child custody and all that. Then she took up with that Ralph Bales right after she joined the church, and then married him, but couldn't get him to come to church, though Mary Bowden said she'd seen them go shopping together. Mary lives next door. He's not a bad-looking man. And she's sweet in a way, but a little flighty, and don't keep herself up like she should. And I do wish she'd wear a little less makeup, but you know how the styles are.

It's good that she was going to see Preacher Gordon on a regular basis when the wreck happened because it was natural for her to keep the visits up regular, just to come on over and see him on her next scheduled visit. He has a full schedule on Monday mornings—and Thursday nights too, which a lot of people don't know about. He has to do it because of so many people working now, full-time, in the day. Women. Harold, close that blind so the sun won't get in Miss Laura's eyes. . . . There, that's better. We can more or less tell who's coming to see him because he'll drop in on the circle meeting and say something like, Gwendlyn

Thomas might could use a little visit from somebody, and we'll know that Gwendlyn has been in to see him about some worry of hers, and one of us will drop in to visit her that week. There are ones he don't mention, too. He knows which ones to mention. If he mentioned the wrong one, then they could be scared off by having one of us come by because they'd figure out that Preacher Gordon had told. But as it is, the ones he tells us about need a visit so bad they don't care whether he's told or not.

Anyway, we was stopped at the intersection of the Expressway and—what road is that, Harold?—when she come barreling through there.

Redmill Road.

Redmill Road, no more than a minute before the wreck, when she come barreling through there with that little boy in the backseat. He was leaning way up forward with his hands on the back of the front seat, sort of holding on. He didn't have a shirt on and you could see dirt rings around his neck. She was trying to make the light. If we hadn't been turning to go to the mall we would have come up on the wreck sure as the world.

He was dead before he hit the ground—flew fifty-one feet.

Well, Miss Laura don't want to be hearing about that, Harold.

Took off both ears.

Harold.

She just had one broke rib and a bump on her head. That's all.

Harold, I don't think—

That's what Drew said.

Well, the thing about it is nobody knew what was going on behind the scenes about the tombstone business until Preacher Gordon sort of, I guess, verified the facts behind it all. Told Jim Tate, and then too, Mary, next door to her, kind of pieced it all together. See, after her divorce and being left with that child, she started coming to church and at the same time going with that Ralph Bales. He spent the night over there several times, so I hear. He's got one of them camouflaged trucks.

He's the one that moves houses.

Yes, not the other Ralph Bales. Not Tommy's son. This one never amounted to much—the house-mover Ralph—except he was good to that boy, so said Mary. But I don't think he's much of a house mover. When do you see a house getting moved around here? Of course, I guess he travels around doing it, and you're just not that aware of it.

Anyway, about the tombstone thing. The boy's name was John Moody Jr., after her first husband. But she had such a rough time of it with John senior and all, and being as she was about to marry Ralph, she promised Ralph that as soon as they got married she would change the boy's name to Ralph Bales Jr. Legally. The first thing Preacher Gordon thought about when she told him was how the boy felt about it because he said he—Preacher Gordon—thought changing the little boy's name was a kind of critical thing to do unless the boy was one hundred percent in favor of it. So he got her to bring the boy in. She did, and he said he *wanted* his name changed. Preacher Gordon counseled him a little bit and the boy said he wanted his name changed because Ralph took him hunting and to ball games and his real daddy never did. Mary said Ralph and the boy would get up and leave before light and be gone all day, hunting or fishing. Ralph's got a camouflaged boat, too. Preacher Gordon said he thought there might be some legal problem with calling somebody a junior after somebody who was their stepfather, but of course he never got around to checking into that, and I don't know what the law might be on that. Do you, Harold?

I think you can name them whatever you want to.

After the burial service—he won't but eight or nine, poor thing—Ralph and her had started walking back to the family car when he looked on the little nameplate that they had stuck in the ground, for the grave diggers, I guess, and he pulled her over there and started giving her down the country. That's what Celia Durham told Mary. Can you imagine that—at a funeral? I was too far in back of the crowd to hear anything, but I did see him holding her by the arm and pointing down to the ground, talking about something. I thought it had something to do with the flowers and didn't pay that much attention to it. You didn't either, did you, Harold?

I wadn't there.

That's right. You stayed home. But Mary did have to call the sheriff out there to their house to break up a fight no more than a week after the funeral, said they fought across the backyard and into the garage—like dogs. Idn't that awful? They were fighting about the name—about what name was going to go on the tombstone, Mary said.

That's when she started to see Preacher Gordon sometimes more than once a week. I saw her going in out there—once it was twice in the same day—and you know Ralph went with her at least once that I know of. At the time, I didn't know whether to say anything to Preacher Gordon or not, you know, about whether I ought to visit her or not. She has a couple of friends in the church—that Watkins girl, and Sheila Peterson stands and talks to her sometimes—so I didn't say anything.

Well, right many people got interested in what the tombstone would say on it. Claremont done it. And they are slow. It was a footstone, and dark. Dark gray. Claremont's the only ones that use the real dark stones. People had gotten interested enough, you know, to want to see what was written on the stone. What name they used. Well, there it was: John Moody Jr., with the dates. Then it wadn't more than two days later when here comes Mary telling me there's another tombstone out there in place of the first one. A light pink one, a little smaller than the first one. When me and Harold drove out there to take a look, there was two people there I hadn't ever seen. They were pretending they weren't there to see the new tombstone, but I could tell they were. Course we didn't get out of the car—you could drive right up to it and read it without getting out. It said Ralph Bales Jr., with the dates. I imagine those other people were from IBM, where she works. Surely she's talked about it to some of them. Mary said he hauled that thing out there in his truck hisself. I

can't imagine what he did with the other one. When I saw that
name, Ralph Bales Jr., I knew it won't right. I could feel it. That
boy ought to be named after his blood daddy, I thought, no matter what his blood daddy had done. Preacher Gordon said John
senior had beat the boy and his mama right bad at one time or
another, and that's why she left him in the first place. And then,
too, the boy hisself said he wanted his name changed. But he
won't but eight or nine, and those are all the wrong reasons to
change your name.

What difference does it make?

Harold. How can you say that?

Six—half a dozen.

Your name is your name, Harold. That's like playing with
somebody's blood type. Could you have changed the name of a
one of your children?

That's different. Different circumstances.

Well, it's not. I can't imagine. I just saw on television, Miss
Laura, that there's something like seven times more child abuse
than there was ten years ago. . . . Ma'am? What did she say,
Harold?

She said, Where were they going?

Where was who going? Where was who going, Miss Laura?
. . . Oh, the little boy and his mama. When they had the wreck,
you mean. Well, I don't know as anybody knows. She was in a
hurry is all I could tell. Mary did say she'd just had a argument
with Ralph and had pulled that boy out of the house by his arm.
Then barreling through that intersection going too fast, and that
boy sitting up on the front of the backseat with his shirt off and
dirt rings around his neck. If he'd been wearing a seat belt, that
might have saved his life. Of course, the car could have caught
on fire and both of them could have burned up if they'd been
wearing their seat belts.

She was wearing hers.

Oh, I didn't know that.

That's what Drew said.

Well, anyway, I've never heard anything up to it. She's quit coming to church and to see Preacher Gordon and that house that Ralph was moving, out on Lake Collier Road, has been sitting there on them blocks with that truck hooked to it for . . . how long, Harold?

About a month.

About a month. And to top it all, now he's left her. Mary said his truck and boat has been gone since Tuesday night. Course you know she'll change the tombstone now, especially with him gone.

What's that, Miss Laura? . . . What? What did she say, Harold?

She said she wanted a pink tombstone, too.

You tell Faye, Miss Laura. You tell Faye. She'll see that you get one.

Maybe she can get that boy's—after it's changed again.

Harold!

Well, all they'd have to do is turn it over and put her name on top.

Harold.

Ain't that right, Miss Laura. You wouldn't mind having a used tombstone, would you?

Har—

Look, she's laughing.

It's not funny. I do hope they change that boy's name again, though, back to his real name. Speaking of that, me and Harold got to pick out our tombstones one of these days. It's something you can't do too early. But we got to get on home now. We been sitting here over an hour. It's good to see you sitting up again, Miss Laura. You tell Faye we come by to see you. Harold, go out to the car and get that box of candy. We forgot it.

Harold is just a joker, Miss Laura. Don't you pay no attention to him. . . . What? . . . No, Harold is in electronics. He's got an electronics shop. You know that, Miss Laura. No, he don't make tombstones. It was Parker Brothers made that tombstone, the pink one. They're the only one does pink ones. Here, here comes Harold with a little something for you, and you keep that smile on your face, and keep sitting up—Preacher Gordon ought to be by sometime this afternoon.

Bob Shacochis

LES FEMMES CREOLES

(from *Hayden's Ferry Review*)

The two old Miss Parkers lived in bed, for the Negroes had taken away all their clothes: they were nearly starved. This happened in 1923, a year before the occupation, which was meant to set everything right, ended. They lay together in an upper-story room at Derby Hill, in the ornate mahogany bed of their parents, its headboard decorated with ormolu. On the same prickly feather mattress too where they had been born, six years apart, in the estate house built by their father in another century, those days when musicians came from New Orleans to play in the ballroom on Boxing Day, the servants were rewarded with hams, and their mother wore dresses that were heavy to carry, absurdly unsuitable to the climate, and took a year or more to arrive from seamstresses in London.

Out any of the three banks of windows in the room where the sisters now reigned, the unpeaceful contours and eruptions of land daily grew more wild across the once-industrious plantation. They spent hours in a state of enraptured emptiness, watching shadows parade off the hills and stall in the destitute fields of guinea grass, muster along the horizon of mangrove to drown in the sea once filled with ships waiting to load coffee, syrup, and cotton.

Outside the south row of windows grew an immense gnip

tree, laden with fruit. Birds would flock in it, overcrowding the branches, and make quite a disharmonious racket at the crack of dawn, and Mary Elizabeth—M.E., or Emmy since birth—who was afraid of birds, would throw the last of her costume jewelry to chase off grackles that landed on the sill. Margaret Gloriana prayed for the birds to cock their iridescent heads at her sister, to have the pleasure of seeing the hoard of cheap necklaces and embarrassing rings pitched out the window. Fare-thee-well to that whore's brooch, she would cheer—to herself, of course, since she didn't want to hurt Emmy's feelings. So much wretched tin and six-penny glass. There went that awful tiara, the tarnished pendants, the gilt-painted earrings—how they made Margaret Gloriana's hands tremble for the few real objects they had replaced, the treasures they had been forced to sell one by one to the Syrian in his vile shop, inhaling his turpentine odor.

Yesterday, or perhaps the day before—the sisters were not at all interested in counting—Mary Elizabeth had stood in one of the south windows, her wizened body visible like a stick drawing underneath her muslin nightgown, and leaned out to pick a cluster of gnips for breakfast.

"Sir, sir," Margaret Gloriana had heard her sister calling matter-of-factly to someone below. Emmy had seen a barefoot old black man dodging behind the base of the tree. He was wearing dress pants, a white shirt that was too big, a black necktie that was too short, and a bowler hat with crescents cut through the dusty dome to keep his head from heating up. What's more, he had been sketching a *vévé* in the dirt with his walking stick.

"Sir," Emmy said, waving. "Behind the tree. I saw you." She implored him to gather her bird ammunition and toss it back into the room.

Margaret Gloriana sprang out of bed, forgetting both her age and her nakedness. Throughout her life she had preferred to sleep with nothing on against the cool linens, and so when all was lost she was left without even a nightshirt to cover herself. "Who could you be talking to?" she wondered out loud, wrapping her-

self in the single sheet they shared. Everyone they knew was dead
or gone away. Everyone they didn't know was unkind. She came
up behind her sister, who was flapping like a scarecrow, went to
the next window over, and squinted her sharp blue eyes at the
figure below, who had stepped halfway out from behind the gnip
tree to marvel at them.

"Who are you?" she demanded to be told, and then decided
since she was speaking to a man out in the yard, it was more practical to use outside language. "What you want, jack-o, snoopin'
about? Who give you permission to draw *vévé* in we dirt?"

With a jolted expression, the man below looked at the two
crones, from the ethereal Mary Elizabeth to the shroud-bound
Margaret Gloriana, the long white braid of her hair dangling
over the sill like a hangman's rope. One spirit beckoned him forward, one scolded him like a fierce archangel—the windows of
temptation and retribution. In the excitement, Margaret Gloriana forgot that she wore no clothes; she opened her hands to
brace herself and the sheet slipped to the floor. The old man's
eyes enlarged even with the brim of his hat, his knees had dog-
shake, he took a nervous step backward to learn if this was what
they were waiting for to kill him, and then he scuttered off into
the bush, convinced he had seen twin harpies, a very ungodly
apparition.

"White people ain' need no wanga magic," Margaret Gloriana
shouted as he fled. "No island spells." He was the first soul to
come poke around since the last family of servants had disappeared one rainy midnight, hauling what remained in the house,
and the first man to have a good square wake-up-Maggie-it's-
Christmas-morning look at her body, such as it was, since her
days of childhood. Well, she felt giddily unashamed about it, and
now that she was shouting, she had the impulse to shout more,
to shout something scandalously satisfying.

"Backra bubbies on sale today!"

She felt the blood rising in her mossy cheeks, fermentation
in her delicate stomach. She tried again, exhilarated by the ad-

vance she had willingly made toward shandyism and disgrace. She craned out the window, her emaciated backside thrust toward Emmy, her breasts like a mauga dog's swinging in the air.

"A fart fill your sail, you Guinee rogue!" she cried out, making a bony fist, and collapsed back into the room, alarmed at how extraordinarily good it felt to raise her voice, to say something nasty and speak in the rough island dialect she had heard all her life.

"*Margaret Gloriana!*" Emmy, blushed and tittering, had stooped for the sheet. She spread her arms, opened like linen wings to receive her sister. They promenaded side by side back to the bed. "Where are your principles! You sound like a *filibustier!*"

"Oh, get on," Margaret said, unconcerned. She propped herself with their one pillow, pulled out her braid, set it on her chest, and began to unwind it. It was her favorite, most gratifying act, brushing the length of her pale brittle hair, blowing the broken strands off her fingertips to the floor. She had a desire for a glass of ginger wine, or sherry, which she had never tasted.

"I sound just like Father, that's who."

"Thank you, I don't need to be reminded," Emmy sniffed. "Still, it's very shocking to hear it from you."

"You will live your life," Margaret Gloriana sermonized, "and I will live mine."

Emmy slid down flat and wiggled her stiff toes, imagining she was a fish at the bottom of a mustard yellow lake, which was the color left in plaster patches on the walls of the room. She tried to remember her father ever saying anything nice or gallant or uplifting to anybody. He had once traded a young female servant for a sow, the price determined by matching the girl's weight against that of the pig's. Of course, the pig was worth more. She went through the ordeal of sitting back upright, weary from being at the bottom, the austere and lonely bottom, of a yellow lake.

"Do me now, Maggie dear," she said, touching the hawksbill shell of the brush which, with their enamel chamber pot and two cracked Worcester cups, was the extent of their common wealth.

"You have such pretty hair," Margaret Gloriana said, stroking her sister's silvery, ever-slackening curls.

"Oh, but it's not as pretty as yours." The two old Miss Parkers had been saying so to each other since the beginning of time.

After several hours of tying and untying two threads she had unraveled from the hem of the sheet, the younger sister, Mary Elizabeth, announced her momentous news.

"Don't be upset," she forewarned. "I have a lover."

"You do?" Margaret Gloriana, who had been staring at a blue beetle on the ceiling, sat straight up. "How can you?" Out of respect for her sister's sensitive circumstance, she looked merely doubtful, although her reaction could have been far more dramatic.

"Why, yes, I do," said Emmy, intransigent, feeling revitalized with confidence now that her secret was out in the open. "He has a gold tooth."

The present vacancy of life expanded out of focus. Margaret Gloriana folded her weightless hands and thought for a minute before she spoke again. "You have given yourself back to Christ Our Lord," she concluded, famous at Derby Hill for her uninspired good sense. "I thought you'd gotten over that ages ago. When they burned the church."

"I did," Emmy agreed. "What good is it to love someone if you can't even go to his house and have lovely conversations with his guests? I don't see the point."

Margaret Gloriana shifted restlessly, her shoulder blades scraping against the headboard, and made a second guess. "Is it Papa? Didn't he have a gold tooth?"

"He had eight or nine, I think." Emmy shrugged with her awkward matchstick arms. "No, it isn't him. How could it be? I always, always hated Papa. Why should I love him now that he's dead? What is there to love about the dead, except that they're not in your way? What strange ideas you have."

"Well then," Margaret Gloriana snapped. "Who is it, who can it be? There's nobody."

"He's coming." Emmy's eyes had an unsettling starry luster to them, entirely inappropriate for a woman her age. "You'll see."

Margaret Gloriana looked incredulous, wheezed—she couldn't help it. The sound created a brassy vibration in the hollow expanse of the room. Her sister was a ninny, always had been, anyone could see, disrupting their fragile serenity, threatening their sistership with youthful fantasies.

"And when he comes, what will you do with him, you old moth?"

As much as they had seen of life, they had not seen much of men. They were not beauties, but they were not without their feminine merits either. Even so, year after year, they were condemned never to be more to any man's life than their father's maiden daughters, and the island itself conspired with this destiny. Once, on the Queen's birthday, they had both danced the quadrille with a Captain Selcroft, ashore off one of the trading ships, but their father spoiled it by belligerently insisting he be told which one Selcroft intended to marry; and when the Captain balked, challenged him to an affair of honor; and when the Captain refused to raise a pistol on the grounds that the daughters, as fair as they might be, weren't ladies enough to die for—an opinion to which *pere* Parker brutally conceded—challenged him to a horse race, which Selcroft accepted, but finished the loser with a broken neck. Only a Napoleon was foolish enough to fetch away an island girl.

"When he comes, then I shall die . . . and happily," Emmy confessed. She crossed her forearms over the washboard of her ribs as though she were practicing to be stuffed in a hole. "Not a day sooner."

But how unfair, thought Margaret Gloriana, who by virtue of being the elder felt she had every right to die first. Besides, Mary Elizabeth would appreciate the upper hand, late as it was to come to her, and who in the world would tend to her corpse and save her spirit from wandering about if not Emmy.

"What shall you die of, then?"

"Is it at all true what they say, that you can die of love?" Emmy whispered in ghostly repose, her hands clasped over her flaccid bosom. "That would be the least I could do for love, after all this time. Wouldn't you think?"

Margaret Gloriana groused for a bit, unimpressed. "You always want everything perfect," she said.

They were without oil lamps or candles but it didn't matter. When the sun, only minutes from setting, dropped into the western windows in the late afternoon, the glare was a powerful soporific; it absorbed their reservoir of strength, disordered their thoughts, and put them almost instantly to sleep: the deepest, most forlorn, most uninhabited sleep they had ever experienced. They were also in the habit of waking hours later, simultaneously, like a pair of zombies, in the middle of the night. Then they would use the chamber pot and patter back to bed, nestled together but trying not to move, listening to the gunfire in the mountains while they waited for their wistfulness to turn to a second, more benevolent sleep. For years (they didn't know how many exactly) the island had been occupied by foreign troops (they didn't know whose, really) and a resistance movement had organized against the outsiders (they weren't actually sure why) but they did know that the men only fought after dark, which the sisters thought cowardly and of a fiendish design. Eventually they would close their eyes again, the translucent lids lowering shut, and enjoy separate but identical dreams: the *vévé* the old black man had scratched in the dirt under the gnip tree, a crosshatched heart pierced by two swords. Now it was being inscribed by Captain Selcroft.

Not the following day but not long after, perhaps a day or perhaps two, Mary Elizabeth was kneeling on the sill of a south window, her insubstantial waist encircled by Margaret Gloriana while she stretched as far as she could—not very far because she was characteristically timid and her sister was making her do it anyway, so her heart wasn't in it—stretching to reach a second group of ripe gnips, the first and closest already eaten in weeks past. Birds dashed from branch to branch with dizzying speed, mocking her. She leaned a few more inches, then for no apparent reason and without warning, Emmy blasted the fresh morning air with one of her girlish screams. Margaret Gloriana hugged tighter—all their lives they had been lean healthy women, not weak (though Maggie was tall), and now they each weighed no more than a basket of sorrel blossoms. She tried to pull Emmy back in but couldn't; her sister spread herself out like a cobweb in the window, opening her knees and grabbing hold of the shutters and vines. "Are you falling?" Margaret Gloriana asked. "You don't seem to be."

Emmy quit resisting and floated in her sister's arms. Margaret Gloriana helped her down quickly from the sill, afraid she was being stung to death by jack spaniars or assaulted by the birds. Once she was on her feet again, Emmy, her face feverish, her jaw quivering, took one guilty glancing look at Margaret Gloriana and burst into tears. She gestured toward the south as if she were shooing mosquitoes.

"There's a man on horseback coming," she wailed miserably.

The older sister rushed to the window. "Where?" There was nothing much wrong with her sight, but she could see no man on horseback near or far.

"He's a white man," blubbered Emmy.

"Impossible," Margaret Gloriana clucked. "Inconceivable. You're making-believe again." She peered into the green-tangled distance where disciplined groves had once stood, as sweet to the eye as rose gardens. Nothing was out there anymore but a spiteful jungle re-creating itself. Not a chicken or peacock or guinea fowl, not a goat or black-bellied sheep, not an ox or cow, a donkey or a horse, and certainly not a backra man, which would be terribly disconcerting, for neither of them had seen or spoken to a white man in years, and they would sooner transform themselves into *crapauds* than prepare for a civilized visit. It was an indecent idea.

"Stop bawling," Margaret Gloriana said, leading her sister back to bed. "It's very tiresome to hear you go on like this. No one's coming." She cuddled her sister to her breast and rocked gently, as she had so many times in the past. Who would come this far into the abandoned countryside to gape at two old women with flesh like salt cod and not a stitch to wear? Who even knew they were alive, and why should anyone care, and if they cared, what business was it of theirs, she'd like to know.

"My lover," lamented Emmy, reading her sister's mind, a skill she had been explicitly forbidden to use long ago. "If only I had some violet water."

"Oh dear, let's not start up with that." Were they even alive? Maybe someone would come and tell them if they were one way or another.

"Or a gown. Or just a ribbon for my hair."

Not much was wrong with the old sisters' hearing either, and they were both startled by the muffled impish laugh of a whinny, still miles away on the serpentine path that traversed down palisades, dipped into ravines, wove through vaulted tunnels of ceiba trees, vanished across irrigation canals grown solid with lily pads —yet close enough to make their hearts flutter. Emmy felt her sister's long nails dig into her shoulders and she squirmed to the other side of the bed.

"I told you," Emmy despaired. "Dear God Almighty Jesus, what shall I wear?" She begged her sister to go back to the window to see how near the rider had come.

"No, I can't bear it." Margaret Gloriana rasped her disavowal of whatever might happen next. She began to shudder and pulled the sheet up to her chin. "I don't want to see a white man. You go."

But Emmy herself was too distraught to move except to yank her own side of the sheet up to her face, so they lay there quaking, their dehydrated skin turned clammy. The horse whinnied again, much nearer, then after a while snorted, nearer still, and not a minute later the day—which had been like so many others and not worth complaining about, because what had been done was irreparable—was being praised in a booming voice that seemed to cause a rumble in the stone foundation of the house.

"Good day, good day, good day!"

"I'm fainting," said Emmy in a barely audible sigh.

"So am I," answered Margaret Gloriana. "He's your lover. Tell him to go away."

There was a knocking—though not at the door, for the servants had sprung its hinges and taken it too.

"Hello, halloo, *bonjour,* anybody home?"

"He has a powerful voice," noted Emmy.

"He sounds to me like a *cinquantaine,*" Margaret Gloriana replied, hissing. She had no precise idea of what a *cinquantaine* actually was, only that it was her father's most relished label for whomever he didn't like. He had been a man delighted with the abundance of his enemies—Irish rebels, Gallic Protestants and Papists, Scottish Covenanters, Quakers, Puritans, and all manner of psychotics, convicts, and deportees, not to mention the Dutch, the Portagee, Jacobin French, and barbarous Spaniards. The intruder down below would likely be representing one or more of these diabolic traditions.

"A hairpin," murmured Emmy, "a teaspoon of scented powder."

"If he comes in the house he'll murder us," said Margaret Gloriana. "That's what kind of white men show their face these days."

He came in the house, stamping his boots on the fractured terrazzo, crunching a path through broken table legs and chicken bones and the busted machinery of clocks. They listened to him playing football with coconut husks, they heard the tintinnabulation of porcelain and pottery, shattered on a night of inscrutable liberation. What made them all the more apprehensive was his dreadful whistling, a low-pitched melody like none they had ever imagined, a sinister bold and bumpy rhythm. When he reached the wooden floorboards of the dining hall he became an earthquake, and when a foot thundered down on the first step of the main staircase, and then the second thundered down on the next step, and so on to the top of the landing, the two Miss Parkers whipped the sheet over their heads and lay petrified, immobile as plaster saints. Throughout the halls and passages the repercussions amplified to apocalyptic proportion; he clomped from room to room like a nosy Goliath until at last he clomped into theirs and halted at the foot of the bed. The whistling ceased, but the atmosphere still rang with his noise.

"Are you alive?" he inquired politely.

He repeated the question in Spanish, which confirmed Margaret Gloriana's cutthroat fears, and then in French, which made Emmy shiver imperceptibly in anticipation, because she had always known the French to wear such provocative hats. Receiving no response, the man began to pull ever so cautiously at the sheet, inching it down farther and farther until he saw one grizzled and one flossy mop of hair, pinkish scalps, the glossy crowns of two foreheads, liver-spotted and additionally marred by the scarlet dappling of sun-made cancers. He took a steadying breath and continued: a double set of eyebrows astonishing for their coal-black thickness, and then, regrettably, the pure but lifeless eyes, wonder-stricken by the beyond. His face saddened, he drew his hand back from the sheet and crossed himself, muttering in a language neither sister could understand but which sounded groans and smacks. He went to a window and sagged against its peeling frame, staring out at the vast and savage terrain.

Contained within the slightest exhalation of breath, a sound not different from the natural silence of the house, Mary Elizabeth spoke to her sister.

"He's wonderful."

Margaret Gloriana puffed back, an insufflation as soft as blowing into a baby's ear. "He's much too young—and thin."

"He's very handsome."

"He has a nose like a Jew."

They did not think it odd or offensive that the young man had a carbine strapped across his back, for on the island men had always carried guns, even to the dinner table, and they did not perceive that his soiled gray blouse and stained flannel pants were in fact a uniform. But through the weave of the sheet, Margaret Gloriana, at least, could taste the bitterness of cordite that enveloped him, and smell the familiar sorrow of blood, and knew without having to ask that he had come fresh from battle. Emmy would have registered this evidence too, for her senses were equally refined by solitude as her sister's, but she was drifting, overwhelmed, pursuing vague memories of passion through the museum of her heart.

The young deserter went from window to window, surveying the dense panorama, and assured himself he had not been followed. He wished he had discovered the two old women alive and prosperous, quick to offer him a plate of lamb and pudding, and he would sit, assuming they owned a chair, and confess the peculiar fate that had befallen him and they, poor withered figs, saturated with long experience distilled to wisdom of the world, would advise him what to do. They would tell him how to undo what history had done to him: how he, a Flemish village boy who aspired to play in the most renowned beer gardens and cabarets of Europe, lubricating the dreams of the masses with new and dangerous music, how he, who until yesterday had masqueraded as the heroic Charlie Andrews, might recross the ocean and repatriate himself to the ravaged continent as his civilian self, the Liege *savant* by the name of Josef Krunder, who since the age of three could play the "Marseillaise" or any of a dozen anthems on whatever instrument he was handed. He, Josef Krunder, who was Charlie Andrews risen to first lieutenant's rank, a member of a great army that had been victorious in a great war, now doomed by an invisible momentum to tidy up jungles and deserts, islands with names no one ever heard.

On the other hand, he had participated in splendid adventures, and increased his repertoire of popular songs tenfold—but enough was enough.

Throughout the exotic diaspora of sinners where he had campaigned, he had viewed uncountable dead, the majority of them flayed and mutilated, and he had stumbled upon more than a few old women like these in the bed, but none so intimately. They were like forsaken goddesses who had outlasted their value, dispossessed by their celebrants and allowed to spoil, unworshipped, suspended in purgatory between a fallen world and one as yet unborn. He returned across the room to replace the sheet as he had found it, taking a last gaze into the soul of their eyes, inanimate as miniature pale-blue doll parasols. Swept by profound homesickness—what, after all, had become of his own mother—he marched out of the bedroom, downstairs, and then outside into the heat, from a cistern splashed water on his face and neck and began to police the grounds in search of a shovel, obligated by a Christian upbringing to bury the hags before he rode on to the sea.

After a time he gave up the hunt, having discovered nothing in the dilapidated outbuildings of any use save a hoe blade with its shaft broken and a cutlass filed as sleek as a rapier. Back to the house he went, through a rear entrance that passed him into a library strewn with excreta and goose feathers, its remaining volumes flowering a slick vivid mold, and he thought to himself that he would say a prayer over the stiffs and leave it at that. Belated last rites. But the day had progressed too far for traveling hostile territory, and he reasoned he should stop the night until the moon rose, and then go on. His village superstitions, however, argued against such a plan: pass the evening with two dead women and get attached to whatever curse lingered over the violated estate. Yet to think of the world this way, so vulnerable to mystery, was no longer possible for Josef Krunder Charlie Andrews. His conscience chided him, he was taunted by the imperatives of manhood, and so he resolved to stay—and to quicken the time he would offer a requiem, so that the dead might look down from heaven and know they had not been, for once, forgotten.

In the final hour of daylight, the sisters as unconscious as logs, he ascended to the sun-swept upstairs room outfitted like a junk dealer. From the ubiquitous trash of devastation, he had combed three galvanized pails with their bottoms partially rusted out, a length of cedar planking hanging by its last nail from one of the sheds, a half-burnt spindle from a ladder-back chair, and from his saddle an army-issued wool blanket and a paraffin plug of candle. Near the foot of the bed he went to work, set the cedar plank spanning two of the pails, upturned the third as a stool cushioned by folding his blanket into a pad. Out the windows, the evening's stridulation of crickets and frogs began to saw at the tranquility of twilight. He lit the candle and took his seat, gripped the charred point of the spindle, and with it reproduced a crude outline of a keyboard upon the surface of the cedar plank, minus the highest and lowest scales for want of space. He flexed his hands, practiced several finger exercises, limbering the knuckles, and called the notes in his head but to his surprise they came as sterile letters, not tones, until he pictured the clefs like a charge of helmeted troops, advancing through the scales from bass to treble.

His countercharge, the requiem. He was ready to perform.

"*Eternal rest grant upon them, O Lord,*" he sang in a tenor's voice. His spidery hands crept along the board in a solemn cadence, the calluses tweaked by splinters, fingertips blackened by char. His amateurish preoccupation with striking the correct keys; a panic as the formal sequence of the mass temporarily faded from memory—these shortcomings slowly dissolved and he was transported by the literal resurrection, impoverished as it was, of music. As his instincts revived and intensified, he concentrated less on the act itself and more on abstract appreciation, oneness, union. He smiled mournfully upon his subjects, aware that they and they alone could hear the divine orchestration that resonated with such compassion within the chamber of his mind, but as he approached the *Dies Irae*, he was spontaneously delivered back to his youth into the slicing scrubbed hands of his choirmaster father, a bloody bastard he was, and he inhaled again the frankincense of suffocation of the church, and felt its smothering robes on his shoulders. His hands slammed clumsily on the plank, he glowered at the two desiccated crones and their whiffy mattress, his eyes raked their loathsome morbid shapes. And as he played on, his nails indenting the wood, he realized something was different—wrong—about the arrangement of the corpses. He squinted through the dim and shifting illumination, his voice rose until he was bellowing in Latin. The noise outside the windows churned like the engines of a mighty factory. Was he mad, or had the geometry of their bones been reformulated? Then he had it: When he had first looked down upon them earlier in the day, they were aligned in bed like two fallen fence posts in a snowy field. Now they had thaumaturgically branched. Now their parallel arms formed a chevron. They were holding hands.

"The hell with this, ladies," Charlie Josef sang, and with a flourish of vaudevillian chords, bridged over to a ragtime dirge, putting himself in a sweat. Then he gave the two possums love songs, folk songs, drinking songs, ballads from operettas, every music-hall ditty that came to mind, songs in Flemish and Celtic, Finnish and German, torch songs, war songs, minstrel songs and shanties, verse upon verse, chorus and refrain, one after another on into the night until his mouth was paste and his throat nostalgically raw, the candle extinguished to a frozen puddle and the room flooded with satin mists of moonlight.

With throbbing fingers and stiffness in his knees, his thighs cramped from riding all last night down from the mountains, he got to his feet, refastened his rifle over his shoulder, and approached the head of the bed. Tenderly, he turned back the corner of the sheet, exposing Mary Elizabeth's smitten expression, and bent over.

"How far is the coast, madame?"

"Two leagues southwest," peeped Emmy to the relief of Margaret Gloriana, who was sure her sister had fulfilled her own premonition by dying hours ago when she had released her water into the mattress, and her hand had gone limp and cool. Still, she didn't think it necessary to converse with the man in French, like a *soubrette*. He leaned over and turned the opposite corner of the sheet, but Margaret Gloriana clung to inexpression, refuting any notion of her continued existence.

"Can I do something for you, *Gran-mere?*"

Emmy asked that he send her a pair of black crepe drawers, if he'd be so kind.

She remained in an ecstatic trance for days, effervescing upon occasion, uttering endearments at the birds, fragmented lyrics, frivolities about gold teeth (which she hadn't verified) and artistic temperament, until Margaret Gloriana was disgusted with her pretense, the latest of many perpetrated by her younger sister since they were children. She contrived a list of mortal sins the singer had most likely committed in his young life, but Emmy wouldn't listen, and so in frustration over losing her company, she fought fire with fire and declared that she too had a lover.

In Emmy's eyes, the cloudy bliss instantly clarified, her nostrils dilated with the restorative vapors of rivalry. "Why, I don't believe it," she protested. "I would be so happy for you, but I don't believe it at all."

"Yes," Margaret Gloriana held firm, although she herself didn't believe a word that rolled from her mouth, "and he will come very very soon."

"How do you know? Can't you tell him there's no hurry?"

Emmy felt her sister meant to punish her for luring the singer to Derby Hill with her yearning. Ever since his nocturnal concert, all Margaret could do was malign his innocent talents, point to the smudged board across the pails (which she dare not touch) as if it were a pagan altar, diminish the gift he had endowed to her memory. He sang such devilish things, Margaret Gloriana accused daily. Oh, they were so much fun, Emmy would defend. His intention was to rob all that was left in the house, and that could only be their eternal spirits, her older sister retorted. But that was fine with Emmy; she said he was welcome to hers.

"I know because the shooting has stopped at night." The end of the conflict seemed to have occurred the evening before the white man appeared to beguile them with evil crooning. "The war is over," Margaret Gloriana improvised. "He has done his duty valiantly. He is free. I won't say another word about it."

They lay together at a standstill for several more days, fatigued by the smallest exchange of civilities encouraged by this new tension. They sucked on the creamy orange pulp of gnips, sipped cistern water from cracked cups, and tried to speak of other less selfish things. Of their mother, for instance, who became ill when they were twelve and six and returned to her homeland for treatment. They could not remember the illness she suffered, but the treatment administered apparently had great healing power, for it cured her of being a colonist's wife.

"She sent for us and sent for us," recalled Emmy.

"But she died."

"Father wouldn't agree."

"But he did. We couldn't leave, though, unless she came to claim us."

"She never came."

"She couldn't. He would have hacked her to pieces."

"Would you have gone?"

Their remembrance of their mother consistently ended with this uncomfortable question, each of them shy to answer for fear of distressing the other, and they would move on to other events.

"The November hurricane was the worst day of my life."

"It killed Alexander Brumfield." Emmy threw a gnip seed at a trio of grackles on the sill.

"You were too young to remember."

"I remember. The servants picked cuttlefish out of the trees."

"Alexander was cut right in half. Something flew in the air and hit him, but it went so fast no one saw what it was."

"Alexander was going to marry you."

"You can't remember, you were only three."

"I was four. The fishermen never came home, but their boats did. I remember we made coffins from them."

The sisters conjured up the scouring stones along the river bank, the eddies of moss-green water. The stones were flipped like pancakes during an earthquake and ruined for laundering for at least another century, their smooth lye-bleached surfaces, burnished by so much cotton, replaced by slime-coated coarse undersides. The same catastrophe had rocked the Virgin Mary from her chapel pedestal, breaking the statue into three pieces and releasing an egg snake that had lived in the hollow of the casting. Their father had it caught, and kept in a grass basket on a table in the parlor, and only white men were permitted to look at it. The sisters saw the workers in the fields fanned out like a line of ragged infantry, bent to the ground in a torturous advance, as if searching all day for a dropped coin. And the painter from Italy who resembled, in their opinion, a Biblical shepherd. The servant women were rendered too merry and independent by his brush, with faces like voluptuous moons, and no one purchased the canvasses. They reminisced about the itinerant professor, his smokehouse pungency; his thin frock coat, his mustard shirt with too few buttons, the gray trousers with a black stripe down the outer seams; his green flat-sided carpenter's pencil; his purse a soda-cracker tin with a rope strap, stuffed with papers. He left them untutored except through mimicry, scattered lines from *Othello* and *The Tempest*—"Hell is empty, and all the devils are here" and "Do that good mischief which may make this island thine own forever"—and schooled them in the details and habits of foreigners, a class that excluded no one. They remembered the dentist in the capital who repaired their teeth with caulking compound; the charcoal-makers who cooked entire trees like pigs in the soil; the vomit smell of grinding houses and the caramel smell of boiling houses; the taste of the baked spheres of cheeses, stuffed with prawns, sweetbreads, and pigeons; tamarind butter, sunbonnets, and whale oil lamps; the vulgar little monkeys that would shit on the veranda; the parrots, now extinct, and the carnival flamboyance of their plumage. The campfires of the laborers, the ululations of their legends. How many empty columns of time had passed since they had admired the handsomeness of their father's *paso finos,* the best of them raced in Jamaica? And before the instrument was outlawed by the last governor, the frantic seductive sound of the *tambu,* drumming from inside the mountains? Neither of them could say how many years it had been since the week-long poisoning epidemic, which first took their father's bulls, then his mastiffs, then the man himself; but they could remember the last drought because of the pink-and-black-petaled strawflowers that bloomed only during periods of exceptional dryness. And they could hear their mother teaching them the alphabet as if they had savored the queer vinegary edge of her breath—she drank red wine—only yesterday:

A is for Albion; B is for Berkshire and Buckingham; C is for the Crown and Cruelty; D is for Devonshire, Drake, Decadence, and the Damned; E is for Eternity, which is the length of any day under this roof.

But the alphabet failed to subvert the sisters. Their mother could not persuade her daughters that they were prisoners in a world confounded by an inexhaustible capacity for sin; she could not teach them not to call it home.

And so he came, as he must given the unwitting prescience of the sisters, the thinning of the veil stretched across the future. He was one of the freedom fighters, a black man come out of the mountains after untold years of struggle. He hung with filthy rags; one leg bled from an undressed wound, and the flesh around his left eye was slack from an invisible injury. There were no more bullets for the rifle he carried, but he didn't need them anyway for he had triumphed over his enemies, over all adversity, and was now untouchable. He limped through the broad shadows of waning moonlight. With eyes most keen after sundown, he inspected the *vévé* at the base of the gnip tree; other signs throughout the yard—the skeleton of a land turtle, an Erebus moth that flew against his cheek—warned him that Derby Hill was haunted. But he knew as well already, it was why he had come, and he praised the gods for this opportunity, this further evidence that he had been chosen, that his trials were divine, that now he must wage peace on the dead as successfully as he had waged war on the living. He had returned to his place of birth.

The two old sisters, in between their first and second sleep, heard the sawboning of the jungle cease and knew he had arrived, passing over the grounds and into the house with no more disturbance than a stray breeze rising off the sea. They listened carefully and for some time heard nothing, nothing distinct other than the tremulous presence of his breathing in the kitchen, until finally there was an anguished cry, and the house echoed with his grieving.

"Why does he weep?" Mary Elizabeth asked in a whisper.

"Oh, how should I know?" Margaret Gloriana said, acutely agitated. She wanted this fellow to come up, present himself with expedience, then go about his business elsewhere. She was feeling especially old and frail tonight, weary of this recent plague of males, tipping the sublime calibration of the scales of sisterhood. Nevertheless, she felt compelled to defend him. "And why shouldn't he weep?" she said. "It's no worse than the other one's singing."

Yet it was worse, much worse, this tragic outpour, and it resounded through the ruin of the house and into the surrounding countryside like the mourning of a nation. "I wouldn't say he's terribly pleased to be here," Emmy observed.

"Quick to judge, quick to apologize." Her sister lowered herself off her elbows.

There was a natural rhythm to his baritone keening; before long the sisters had accustomed themselves to its aqueous surges, its failing ebbs, and were lulled back into their twin dreams of Captain Selcroft. They woke at dawn to the same sobs, which had lost none of their vigor. All through the day the man's marathon sorrow continued unabated, afflicting the two old Miss Parkers with its depth of wretchedness and preempting their sisterly discussions, but as the sun balled its light and simmered down toward the western windows, the crying stopped and Emmy, who was first to see him enter the bedroom, made a ravenous gasp for air as if she had been submerged underwater and had almost drowned. Thus alerted, Margaret Gloriana sat up in bed and, mortified by what she saw, just as quickly slumped back down.

"That's not who you think it is!" she blurted out.

"Mother of God," said Emmy, "you're in love with a darkie." So much of the time through the years there had been scant else to do but look in the opposite direction, not merely away from the tribulations of the blacks, but from the extravagances of the whites as well, and half the world was too full of wonder, the other half constricted by manners and taboos, to have extra room for temptation. And so Mary Elizabeth marveled at how impetuous her sister had become at the end of her life.

Margaret Gloriana, however, was hardly capable of speaking. "Absolutely not," she croaked without her customary authority. "That's his servant." But she knew this was no more true than her original announcement, that this feral being poised inside the door was no more another man's servant than he was or could be her swain, real or imagined, if at all a man himself, and yet despite his lycanthropic eyes and beard, and the mien of a beast who feasted on human virtues, from the sound of it he had wept as other men do, with a crushed heart, a long-suffering spirit, and a lust for the infancy of pain. In this regard his humanity was more outspokenly noble than their father's ever had been, their father who had lived a closet of avarice and moral certainty and had died roaring hatred for all peoples, including his own kind. Still, Margaret Gloriana surmised, she had stupidly, childishly, summoned a nemesis, the only lover that would ever come for either sister—the brilliant solitaire, their death.

As for the black maroon, whose name was Alvaro Toussaint Parker—no blood relation but the surname of a slave brand inherited from his ancestors—he took one freezing look at the sisters, the prominence of their yellowing teeth, the transparent skin varnished around their skulls, the witch's locks, the purpled eyepits, the beaks of nose, and addressed them as if they were indeed already dead, though of a more privileged caste of duppy than the other ghosts he had sought to communicate with during his time in the house. Falling to his knees at their bedside, he spoke to the spirits as a supplicant.

"I might ask you to ask my mother to forgive me," he said.

Straight off, the sisters were too amazed by the formality and dignified tone of his speech to reply. He had mastered their own language, the house language and empire's language, but emitted from so swollen a mouth it struck their ears as a masquerade, a subterfuge. It so spun around Emmy's thoughts that she changed roles and responded in the patois that was or should have been his own, maintaining a most irregular social symmetry.

"Hear now, Moses, who you muddah?" she squeaked and, aghast, clapped her hand over her mouth.

Margaret Gloriana yawned, willing herself to remain composed, yet she began to feel drowsy. "Why don't you go on your way and ask her yourself?" she suggested. She blinked uncontrollably and yawned a second time.

"My mother was Lydalia Parker, laundress," Alvaro Toussaint Parker answered the first sister. Throughout the past infelicitous hours he had spent in the house, that's all he had done: asked his mother directly for forgiveness for betraying his eight brothers and four cousins by conspiring with the occupation troops, because you can persuade yourself of many crimes when you know you cannot win, nor your cause prevail, and so he had led his comrades into ambush. All night and all day he had offered contrition, beseeched his mother for absolution. Instead of acknowledging him, she would not come away from her scouring stones at the river, where she slapped massa's wet linens against the whitened boulders, kneading them like dough with her muscular arms, singing hymns of resurrection. He felt he would go mad begging her to come to her feet and comfort him, her youngest son, in his grim passage of leadership.

"Lydalia Parker, laundress," he droned balefully, "Lydalia Parker, mother of her country."

Lydalia's family *was* big, I recall, thought Emmy as she sank into unconsciousness. He bowed his leaf-flecked head to wait for the dead to deliver his penance, craving pardon so that he might resume his self-appointed mission without malediction. He remained kneeling, full of remorse; the sisters fondly remembered the laundress Lydalia Parker but had ceded the power to speak; the western windows blazed like doors thrown open to a hellish furnace. Blood-red glorioles irradiated the phantoms in the bed; Alvaro raised his eyes and saw the spirits reduce glimmer by shrinking glimmer back into nothingness of inert flesh. In the deluded mind of Alvaro Toussaint Parker, their departure was a merciless disconnection. The *loas* had rejected his plea, they would not enter as his advocate into the netherworld and intervene on his behalf. He bounded to his feet, vowing this was the first and last time he would petition backra spirits for their charity. He noticed the cedar plank on its pails, deciphered its smudges, and Alvaro Toussaint Parker condemned himself for not foreseeing the full and malicious range of plots he was up against. He crawled from the house, on hands and knees, sideways at times like a crab, to search for his mother's grave.

They awakened at their habitual hour, in the middle of the night, not to the distant pops of gunfire, or the chirring of the insects, but this time to the labor of muffled chopping, and they rose together, Ladies Lazarus, and went to stand in the northern windows. There was another, more fluid sound reaching them, like blankets being shaken out, and now they located its source, the high fire on the nearby hillside within the low stone walls of Derby Hill's cemetery. The shape of a man jerked between flame and shadow, lifting an arm, a skull balanced in its hand.

"It's the professor," Emmy said. He had been given to campfire reenactments of *Hamlet*, staged on the dirt between the cluster of servants' huts.

"What's he doing back, do you think?" Margaret Gloriana wondered—out loud or to herself, it no longer mattered.

"I suppose no one told him that everything's different now."

Hand in hand, the sisters wobbled back to bed a last time.

Alvaro Toussaint Parker dropped the skull of his laundress mother into the conflagration, gathered the leathery scales of her skin, the kindling of her bones, and threw them in as well. He withdrew from the plot of his ancestors and slunk farther up the hill to its crest and renewed his digging, sinking the hoe blade with the broken shaft at a furious pace, as far into the rich ground as he could drive it. *Go on,* he heard the sisters urge in their transcended voices, and he struck open the old patriarch's coffin and cast his poison-twisted bones into the flames. *Go on,* the sisters urged through the night, *Go on,* as he persevered, emptying grave after grave, until by dawn he had spent his obsession, tarred by mud and ash and crumbs of dead peoples' clothes, and there was but one grave undisturbed in the cemetery, its marker carved with a sailing ship.

"*Go on,*" exhorted Margaret Gloriana in the black man's ear. "That one too."

"Him especially," said Mary Elizabeth.

With all the strength of those before him who had been bonded to the land, Alvaro Toussaint Parker obeyed this ultimate command and hoed as long as it took to finish the job of enthrallment forever. Then, exhausted, he stumbled to the river, past the scouring stones with their dark sides turned up, stripped the abomination of rags from his body, and washed himself. Energy crackled back from his flesh and he returned to the grounds of the manor house and stood below the gnip tree, adorning himself with peddler's jewels. Naked but for these cast-off ornaments of his destiny, he reentered the shambles of the house and mounted the stairs, wrapped his waist with the threadbare sheet, tore the sleeves from the muslin nightgown and dropped it over his head like a vestment, and descended once more to the outside world to begin his long arduous pilgrimage across the island, to the capital where he would rule his people in the lunatic passions popular to this day, leaving the two old Miss Parkers curled on the mahogany bed of their parents, the windows filled with curious grackles, the *vévé* cleaned away by the advent of the rains, a graveyard readied for the future, the sisters hand in hand with expressions isolated from possibility but as if poised to fall faithfully under the influence of an irrestible attraction.

Molly Best Tinsley

ZOE

(from *Shenandoah*)

She liked to be the first to speak. It wasn't that she wanted to be nice, or put them at ease; it was her way of warning them not to be, of setting the tone she liked best: bemused, even ironic, but formal. She didn't want any of them thinking she was someone to cultivate. Whenever those voices, low and strained, interrupted her life downstairs, whether they came late at night from the front hall or mornings from the kitchen, she slipped into the one-piece camouflage suit she used as a bathrobe, wrapped the belt twice around her slim waist, and ascended to meet her mother's latest. She liked to catch him with breakfast in his mouth, or romance on his mind, and then before he could compose himself, announce, "I am Zoe, her daughter," offering a little bow and a graceful hand, limp as a spray of japonica.

It usually left him stammering, fumbling—this blend of child-like respect and self-possession. If he'd already begun to imagine her mother recharging his life with pleasure and purpose, Zoe's winsome presence made such visions more intense, then tipped them into unsettling. Though he'd never gone in for kids before, he might find himself thinking at first how agreeable it would be to have a delicate creature like her around, slender, long-legged, with pale freckles across her nose. These days she has her auburn hair bobbed at the ears so it curls up shorter in back above a softly fringed nape. But if he thought for a moment how much the child must know, her poise could seem ominous—all the things *he* didn't know, was hungry to find out, but might not want to hear.

"So what's it like, living with her?" one of them asked Zoe once, as if he expected soon to be sharing the experience, to be given exclusive credit for recognizing that her mother was an extraordinary woman. He reminded Zoe of a large rabbit—a confusion of timidity and helpless lust.

"There's never a dull moment," Zoe answered, sweet but nonchalant. "I meet a lot of interesting men." That was stretching things. Most were rabbits.

Often they felt called upon to tell Zoe, "Your mom's a great lady." Did they think Zoe was responsible for raising her mother and not the other way around? Or that she had a choice of mothers? Or that she couldn't guess what they meant, that her mother was something else in bed, that they'd never done it to a Sibelius symphony before?

Since the age of five when her parents split up, Zoe Cameron and her mother, Phyllis Rush, have lived beyond the D.C. Beltway in The Colonies of Virginia, clusters of townhouses subtly tucked into one hundred acres of rolling woods, whose inhabitants readily paid a little more to get aesthetic design and proximity to nature. Set against the ridge of a hill, with cathedral ceilings and an expanse of glass to the south, Zoe's mother's unit welcomes light, draws it in to challenge her work—heavy terra cotta, here and there a dull giant bronze—set off by white walls. Each piece has been given a woman's name, yet they are only parts of women, global buttocks and thighs, pairs of breasts larger than the heads mounted upon them—Leda, Electra, Helen, truncated. They are one reason Zoe stopped bringing home friends, who tended to stare about in stunned silence or whisper words like *gross* and *perverted*. Zoe has learned contempt for kids her own age, who cannot understand true art. Yet she hates her mother's women: fat, naked blobs. The bald definition of nipple or vulva makes her sick. There are more of them on exhibit in the local gallery her mother manages in The Commons. The public tends not to buy them, but Phyllis does enter them in shows and they have won awards, including a purchase prize at the Corcoran. After that, a man from the *Washington Post* came out to photograph Phyllis at home in her skylit studio. Zoe declined to be in any of his shots. He took her mother to dinner in Great Falls. When Zoe came up the next morning to leave for school, he was in the kitchen alone making raisin toast. He offered her a slice, trying to act as if he owned the place, but she drank her sixteen ounces of water as if he weren't there. It was easier than ever to resist that sweet yeasty aroma, tainted as it was by his male pride.

As far as Lucas is concerned, Zoe would give anything to go back and start over again with the moment she arrived home in the early afternoon to find his body sticking out from under the sink. Thinking her mother had finally called someone to fix the dishwasher, Zoe set her wide-brimmed hat down on the table and looked on absently as the body twisted and grunted with its efforts. Her hunger had been stubborn that day, conjuring extravagant food fantasies that almost sabotaged a test in precalculus. But she had conquered temptation, and now what she wanted was plenty of water and maybe a carrot to get through until dinner.

"Let me out of here," came a roar, all of a sudden, followed by bumping sounds and *great god*'s, and the upper part of the man extricated itself from the cabinet. His knuckles were smudged with black, his once-starched shirt was sharply wrinkled, and he rubbed the top of his head ruefully, but when he saw Zoe, his expression flexed in a smile. "Well, look at you," he said. "Don't you look out of this world!" And not expecting such a remark from a repairman, Zoe, who was known to become transfixed by her own image whenever she found it reflected, who that day was wearing one of her favorite suits—broadly padded shoulders over a short slim skirt, a blue that turned her eyes blue—

could not bring herself to disagree, nor think of anything to say back. She did try her ironic geisha bow, but in the same instant noticed the roaches hurrying over the sill of the sink cabinet and out across the kitchen floor in a dark stream.

Before she knew it she had emitted a soft scream, more out of embarrassment than fear. She had certainly seen roaches in the kitchen before, those nights when she gave in to temptation and felt her way up the stairs in the dark. Thinking it was almost like sleepwalking, she was almost not responsible for what she was about to do: forage for food, cookies, bagels, leftover pasta, cinnamon raisin toast drenched in butter. When she turned on the light, there they always were collected on some vertical surface in clusters of imperceptible activity, and she caught her breath in disgust, but went on to get what she had come for.

"They must have a nest under there," the man said, a little out of breath. He was somehow hopping and stooping at the same time, slapping at the creatures with one of his moccasins. "How about giving me a hand here?"

Zoe looked down helplessly at her clothes, her inch-high patent heels.

"How about insecticide, a spray or something?"

"If we have any, it's in there." She pointed to the cabinet from which they kept coming. The floor around him was awash with brown spots. Some had been hit and were finished moving. "Close the door," Zoe cried. When she realized the sense of her suggestion, she repeated it more calmly.

He smacked the door shut, and the stream was cut off. "Good thinking," he said.

She pursed her lips to hide her pleasure. Producing a fly swatter from the closet in the front hall, she commenced ceremoniously to slap at the remaining roaches from the comfortable distance its handle allowed. "Mother," she called.

"She went to the store," the man said, rubbing his bare foot along his pants leg, then replacing his shoe. "I thought I'd keep myself busy until she got back."

That was when Zoe realized he wasn't a plumber and that she had been inexplicably foolish. Her mother, who scorned home maintenance, who refused to spend any time on fixing things when she could be making something new—why would her mother suddenly hire a plumber? "I am Zoe, her daughter," she said, with a final stroke of the swatter, but it was too late.

"I assumed as much," the man said. "From the side you're a dead ringer." He introduced himself: Lucas Washburn. He had light, almost frizzy hair and eyebrows, no cheekbones to speak of, and his nose must have been broken once and never set straight. His skin was fissured from past acne, and his eyes were a flat, changeless gray. He was not handsome, Zoe decided, but there was something about him. His hair was cropped short, his skin evenly tanned, his khaki pants creased. Clean—in spite of his disarray, he seemed oddly, utterly clean.

"I assumed you were the plumber." Zoe pulled the broom out from beside the refrigerator and began with dignity to sweep roach hulls into a pile.

"I can see why. I hear you're down to one bathtub."

Zoe stiffened at the forced intimacy, the hint of sympathy. She normally did not interfere in her mother's affairs, patiently allowing what Phyllis would call nature to take its course. But this man, with his long cheekless face, who had poked around under their sink, discovered their roaches—he was not at all her mother's type, and the sooner he was history, the better. "And it happens to be my bathtub downstairs, which gets pretty inconvenient if you think about it. One of her quote friends pulled the soap holder off the wall in *her* tub and half the tiles came with it, and the guest tub has a leak that drips into the front hall. Actually, the whole house is a total wreck." She finished, and made herself laugh, but in the silence that was his reply, she heard her words echo like a blurted confession, false notes, as if something were playing in the background in a different key. Blasé wasn't working.

"If I had my tools," Lucas said, "we could get this sink to drain, and I could take a look at those tubs. Next time I'll bring my tools."

That is a lot to assume, next time, Zoe thought, and to her surprise, that was what she said.

Lucas nodded solemnly, then turned his back on her and began washing his hands. Should she explain that her mother had very liberal views, that if men and women were allowed to live naturally, without the inhibitions imposed by society, they would choose to spend their nights in each other's beds all the time, different other's beds as the impulse moved them, mornings parting, more often than not, forever? And that was all right with her, Zoe, for it was much worse when a man of her mother's showed up a second time, all twitchy and trembly, and suggested doing something that included her, and her mother, seduced by some transient vision of family, agreed.

"I appreciate the warning," Lucas said, drying his long hands finger by finger. Then he added, "Maybe I've got something in common with those guys in there"—he jerked his head toward the roach settlement—"I'm pretty hard to get rid of."

That night her mother and Lucas fixed strip steaks, steamed artichokes, wild rice. As she often did, Phyllis set up small folding tables on the balcony off the living room in view of the sunset, but Lucas moved the hibachi to the backyard below to comply with the county fire code. ("What fire code?" Phyllis asked. She had never heard of any fire code.) Zoe went downstairs to change into a faded denim jumpsuit, espadrilles. She rolled a fuchsia bandana into a headband and tied her curls down, Indian-style. She freshened the strip of pale blue shadow on her lower lids, all the while aware that Lucas was right beyond the glass door, the drapes that don't quite meet, calling arguments up to her mother in favor of well-done. Phyllis stuck to rare. Her face blank and impersonal, Zoe made a last appraisal in the full-length mirror. She pushed a fist into her sucked-in abdomen. *I hate my stomach,* she thought. You couldn't trust mirrors; they could be designed to make people look thinner. All the ones in stores were deceptive that way.

Lucas sawed off huge blocks of meat and swallowed them almost whole. Her mother plucked her artichoke, petal by petal, dragged each one through her lips slowly, her subtly silvered eyelids drooping with the pleasure. She had a strong jaw, and a wide mouth, with large teeth—but she knew how to recontour her face with light and shade, to make her eyes seem bigger, mysterious. Yes, Zoe had her nose, rising fine and straight from the brow, nostrils flared back, so that if you happened to have a cold or be cold, their moisture was open to view. Zoe had learned to carry her head tilted slightly forward, to make it hard for anyone to see into her nose.

To Lucas' credit he seemed not to be noticing Phyllis' sensual performance. He was expressing his suspicion that her clogged dishwasher and drain stemmed from a failure to scrape dirty dishes thoroughly; a small chicken bone in the trap, for example, was all it took to start an obstruction.

Phyllis threw her head back and laughed. "You sound like my mother," she said.

Lucas wasn't fazed. "You're talking to someone who's trained to eliminate human error." Lucas flew for Pan Am; Phyllis had picked him out of the happy-hour crowd in the lounge at Dulles Airport after dropping off a friend.

Phyllis stroked his closest arm. "That's Mother all over again."

"Another word for it is *accident*."

"It's only a dishwasher," Phyllis said, sullenly, and the fatalist in Zoe settled back with the vaguest sense of loss to watch this man ruin things with her mother long before he could get the bathtubs fixed.

In a steady, almost uninflected voice, he was talking improvements. He could see a brick patio in their backyard, and redwood planters and a hexagonal redwood picnic table. Zoe saw clumsy strategy, tinged with pathos. He frankly admitted he was tired of living on the tenth floor of a condo in Hunting Towers. Between his job and the apartments he unpacked in, he never had his feet on the ground. "It's about time I got my feet on the ground," he said. Phyllis suggested he sprinkle dirt in his socks.

She was being strangely tolerant; maybe he had touched off an attack of what she called her *passion for reality,* when practical dailiness, what everyone else did, became the exotic object of curiosity and desire. Lucas was neither suave nor witty. If you sanded his face, he might be handsome. Zoe guessed he had what her mother would call a good body, though she, Zoe, had trouble looking at a male body long enough to form a complete picture of one. She tended to focus on them piece by piece, and they stayed like that in her mind, a jumble of parts. Her mother often said it was an insult to women the way men let themselves go after a certain age, after they had good incomes. Phyllis herself kept her weight down by smoking and thought women should band together and hold men to the same physical standards everyone held women to.

"Why me?" Phyllis asked Lucas, and seemed genuinely to wonder. "For how many years you've been tied to no place particular and been perfectly happy? Why pick on my place? Maybe I like it this way."

"Look at that," Lucas said, pointing above them at a strip of white streaks and blotches on the cedar stain. "Look at the mess those birds have made of your siding. Starlings. They must have a roost in the eaves. I'd have to take care of that before I'd put in a patio right under their flight lines!"

Phyllis pulled forward a lock of her thick dark hair. "I don't begrudge them that. It's nature." She gave a quick yank, then let the breeze lift an offending gray strand from her fingers.

"Like roaches under the sink."

Zoe held her breath as her mother lit a cigarette. Was he joking or criticizing? Either way he had no right; either way her mother would finally put him in his place. Then why was she stretching, smiling languidly at his rudeness? "Everyone has them," she said, blowing a plume of smoke. "They're a fact of life."

"You don't have to give in totally," Lucas persisted.

"It isn't in me to go around poisoning things."

Her mother's reasonableness was a puzzle to Zoe. *Why him?*

she kept asking herself, until the answer came to her, all at once: it made her a little queasy. It was obviously something to do with sex that gave Lucas this power, this license. Wasn't her mother always declaring that everything came down to that? It must be something sexual he did to her mother or for her, which she, Zoe, for all her determined precocity, had not yet figured out. Then she felt very empty—empty as though she had failed an exam, empty because she didn't want to think of Lucas that way. In the back of her mind, she had been hoping he was different, and she didn't even know she was hoping until he turned out to be the same—just another male, who in the irresistible flux of life must soon disappear. Well, she could care less.

That night Zoe ate. Once dead silence told her Lucas and her mother had settled down, she stole upstairs in the dark, removed from the freezer a half gallon of vanilla ice cream and went back down to her room. She sat on the bed, and gazing at the photos of lithe models she had cut from her magazines, began to spoon ice cream into her mouth. Each mouthful hit her empty stomach like a cold stone. It made her feel a little crazy; she couldn't think straight anymore. She swung between defiance—when she agreed with herself that this was incomparable pleasure, no matter how high the price, this cool, bland sweetness, this private solitude—defiance, and despair. "Eat up," she heard her mother encouraging, as she had all evening, though never showing concern when Zoe didn't. "She eats like the proverbial bird," her mother told Lucas. And then Lucas had said, "Do you know how much a bird eats? One of those starlings, for example? They eat something like four times their body weight in one day."

Ah Lucas, the way he looked at Zoe then, as if he knew that sometimes she forgot she must be thinner. She forgot the terrible burden of stomach and hateful thighs, which kept you from ever being wonderful, and she ate, and having forgotten, she ate more, to forget she forgot. One hand around the damp, softening box of ice cream, in the other the spoon, hands like bird claws, eating like a bird. Her stomach danced madly as if filled with birds. Her whole body felt in motion. She strutted across her own mind, plump-chested, preening; she opened her wings and took off, soared and swooped above the balcony where Lucas, the flier, watched captivated. And then the ice cream was gone, and all that motion froze, like someone caught in the act. She looked down at her denim thighs spreading against the bed; she could barely get both hands around one. Her stomach was monstrous, almost pregnant. She was losing her shape. She would turn into one of those crude female blobs of her mother's. The thought alone was all it took to convulse her, as, eyes closed above the toilet, she imagined all the birds escaping from the cage of her ribs.

Afterwards she would not allow herself to sleep. Awake burned more calories, burned flesh from bones. She held one hand to the hollow of her throat and felt her heart beating fast and hot as a bird's.

This afternoon Zoe found her mother nestled in the wine velvet cushions of the sofa, her legs drawn up under a long Indian cotton skirt, smoking with one hand, sipping maté tea with the other. From the dull puffiness of her mother's eyes, Zoe could tell she had been crying. *It is all right to cry,* Phyllis has always said. *It is a natural response of the body. Holding it back is harmful.* Zoe hates it when her mother cries, hates to see the pain, the rivulets of mascara, the surrender.

"The bus was a little late today," Zoe says, hitching the knees of her linen pants and perching on the chair opposite.

Her mother pulled herself upright, bare soles on the floor, began carefully to shift the position of everything around her— the huge pillows, ashtray, teapot, the extra cup, which she filled and handed to Zoe. "You're not happy," she told her daughter.

"I'm not?" Zoe asked, with a careful laugh.

"Oh, Zoe, you don't have to pretend. But why, when two people love each other, can't at least one of them be happy? You'd think they could pool their resources and work on one of them. Tell me something you want, Zoe, okay?"

"Kids my age just aren't very happy." Her mother was in one of her moods. "We grow out of it. It's no big deal."

"But what would make you happy? We could manage it."

"You must have had a bad day," Zoe said.

Phyllis took a long pull on her cigarette. "For six hours I have tried to work." She didn't exhale but let the smoke seep out as she talked. "I felt like any minute my hands were going to do something no one has ever done before, but they never did. Nothing. I might as well have been kneading bread. At least I'd have something to show for my time."

"Let's go to the mall," Zoe suggested. She and her mother have always had a good time shopping for Zoe's clothes. When Zoe was small, her mother said, it was like having a doll. Now Zoe has her own ideas, and Phyllis, rather than objecting, seems able to guess almost infallibly what they are—sophisticated angular lines, in pastels or white and black, plenty of defining black; Phyllis combs the racks, and brings a steady supply of possibilities into the fitting room for Zoe to try. Phyllis has always shopped for herself alone and piecemeal, at craft fairs, antique markets, Episcopal church rummage sales in Leesburg, Fairfax. She's owned her favorite jacket for over twenty years—brown leather with a sunrise appliquéd in faded patches and strips on the back.

"I'm going back to pots," Phyllis said dramatically. "Tomorrow I'm hooking up the wheel."

"Let's go to the mall." Zoe bounced twice in the chair to demonstrate eagerness. "I need summer things. That would make me happy."

Her mother paused, searched Zoe's face. "Lucas gets in at five," she said finally. "I think he'll be coming right over."

"Lucas?" Why the flare of panic? Zoe had not seen him since the afternoon of the roaches, assumed that, like one of her mother's moods, he had passed.

"That's what he said last week before he left. He had back-to-back European runs. He said he'd be carrying his tools in the trunk of his car." Her mother's voice quavered, as if she were afraid of something, too.

"What did *you* say?"

Her mother went into a prolonged shrug. "I said all right."

"Well, you must like him then," Zoe said dismissively, deciding it was all right with her, at least one of them would be happy.

"I don't know. I don't understand him. I don't know what he's after." She laughed nervously.

"Mother," Zoe said, stressing each syllable. This was no time for either one of them to act innocent.

"Do you know what he said to me? He said, 'Why do you women assume that's all you've got to offer?'" Phyllis shook her hair violently. "We shouldn't be talking like this."

"We always talk like this."

"I know, but . . ."

"Don't be weird, okay? You've got to tell me what's going on." That has been, after all, Zoe's main fare—knowing. "I can handle things."

"I was asking him to spend the night."

"So?" Zoe had handled that countless times. Then all at once question and answer came together in her mind. "He didn't spend the night?" A rush of feeling, worse than any amount of fear, washed away her strength. She fell back into the chair, crushing her linen blazer.

"He said, number one, it wasn't safe anymore and I should know better, and number two, that it didn't matter because he'd promised himself the next time he met a woman he liked he would wait to sleep with her for six months." Her mother spoke haltingly, as though his reasoning mortified her.

"He said he liked you anyway?"

"He said he'd been through enough relationships that began with great sex. He can't afford another."

Zoe pulled herself up straight again. "Did you tell him what you think, about tapping into the flow of nature, and creating the sensuous present?"

"I can't remember," her mother said faintly, then all at once roared angrily through her teeth. "Forget him," she said, bounding up, jabbing each foot into a thong. "Let's go. He's too damned controlled. Forget him."

"I don't mind staying here and waiting to see if he shows up." Zoe's voice was playing tricks on her, first whispering and then suddenly wanting to shout. "It would be nice to have the plumbing work."

Lucas arrived around seven, looking as if he'd never thought for a moment that he wouldn't. He was wearing fresh khakis and a white knit shirt, with the last of four neck buttons open. He had stopped somewhere to rent a giant ladder, which he had tied onto the ski rack of his perfectly restored Karman Ghia. If there was awkwardness in the rather formal greetings he received from mother and daughter in the front hall, he didn't seem to notice; he was more interested in introducing the two of them to his plumber's pliers, assorted wrenches, a drain snake, a staple gun, and a roll of six-inch-wide screening. He was ready to work.

"You must be hungry," Phyllis said. "I've got pastrami, Swiss cheese. A wonderful melon. Aren't you too tired for this? I mean, what time is it for you? It must be after midnight. You ought to sleep. I can make up the couch," she added quickly.

He wasn't ready to sleep. He'd spent all that time in the air dreaming of feet-on-the-ground work, making mental lists of things to do. He had promised to return the ladder the next morning, and the sun was already dropping into the trees in back. "First things first," he said, unlashing the ladder from his car. He took one end, Phyllis and Zoe the other, and he led them back into the house, down the front hall, miraculously through the living room, without bumping a life-sized bronze of staunchly planted legs and hips—the Arch of Triumph, he had dubbed it last week. Out on the balcony, he passed his end over the rail and took over theirs.

He dug the ladder firmly into the grass below, then produced a shoelace from his pocket and tied one end around the staple gun, the other around a belt loop. He slipped the roll of screen up his arm, swung a leg onto the ladder, and descended. When he reached the ground, he stamped his feet a few times as if to get used to it. "Come on down," he called back to them.

Zoe had never been on a ladder before—the whole thing made her think of burning buildings, great escapes—she scrambled over the edge, linen pants, Capezios and all, and breathing deep against the slight sway, carefully eased herself from rung to rung. She was afraid of losing it if she looked down, so turned her eyes on her mother's face, where she found the blank patient expression of someone lying low.

"I think I'll use the stairs," her mother said, and disappeared. By the time she slid open the glass door, Lucas had extended the ladder twice to the impossible height of three stories. "It's simple physics," he had told Zoe, waving away her offer to steady the bottom. "It can't go anywhere." He had one foot on the first rung.

"Wait a minute, wait a minute," Phyllis said.

Lucas froze, eyes front, hands in midair.

"What are you going to do?"

"I am going to staple this stuff over the vents in the soffit, to keep the birds from getting up under your eaves and building nests and shitting on your siding." It took great control for him to speak that slowly, clearly.

"And you have to do it right now? I mean, it must be two in the morning."

Lucas looked at his watch and then back at Phyllis, stared at her as if he were having trouble translating her language. He didn't want to sleep, he didn't want to stop and wait for sleep to overtake him, he wanted to push himself until he dropped—at least that was what Zoe recognized.

Phyllis clenched her jaw, swallowed visibly. "I don't know whether I'm being pushed around or cared for."

"Give it a while," Lucas said, "and you ought to be able to tell the difference." Unblinking, he watched her, as she appeared to consider this. Then her shoulders fell forward.

"I'll be inside," she said.

Lucas was on the ladder, his feet over Zoe's head, when she realized that she must love him. She wasn't sure why—maybe because he didn't belong to her mother, maybe because there was something so definite about him, but it wasn't a boyfriend sort of love. He didn't have to return it; in fact she would rather he didn't. He just had to stay there, in her life, and let her watch him while he fixed things, and she would privately love him. The ladder flexed in toward the house.

"You sure this will hold you?" she called up to him. "What if the three pieces came apart?"

"I checked everything out," he called from the higher rungs. "But thanks for your concern."

She pursed her mouth. He was pressing the strip of screen against the eaves with the fingertips of one hand. With the other he tried to bring the staple gun into range, but he couldn't get it there: the shoelace was too short. He cursed and then tugged again, but only managed to hike his pants up on the right side where he'd tied it. The ladder shuddered, and Zoe clutched it for all she was worth.

Then resolutely, Lucas climbed up a rung, and then another, until his head and shoulders ran out of ladder, the tips of which had come to rest just below the gutters. He wrapped his legs around the top rungs, twisted his right hip toward the house, and blindly felt the screen into place, firing the staple gun along its edges, clunk, clunk. He wavered precariously at each recoil. She gaped up at him in wonder, and not just his body at that odd foreshortening angle, but his whole heroic being seemed clear to her, shining. She was still afraid he would fall, but just as sure that there was a way to fall, a way to land so you didn't get hurt, and Lucas would know what it was.

In a few minutes he was down, and without pausing to comment or change the arrangement with the inadequate shoelace, had moved the ladder and mounted it again. He did this three times, four. And Zoe remained dutifully at its foot, face upturned, holding him in place with her eyes.

At first she thought her ears had begun to ring from craning her neck so long. She covered and uncovered them—the noise was outside, she had never heard it start, and now it had grown in volume to something shrill and unpleasant. Beyond the cluster of townhouses to the south, a long cloud of black birds hung in the pale violet sky. They were their own fixed path, funneling in from the invisible distance, spreading to rest in the saved trees at the base of the back slope. The shrieking came from the trees; when you looked closely among the leaves, it was as if each branch was thick with black fruit. Zoe had never seen anything like it.

When Lucas came down to move the ladder for the last time, she said, "They don't like what we're doing." It did seem their shrieking was directed at the two of them. "Maybe they think you've caught one of their friends up there behind the screen," Zoe said, to be amusing, but Lucas said it was just what starlings did, gather for the night in communal roosts. They had probably been there every night since early spring, carrying on, making a mess. She had just never noticed it.

"I guess I'd rather sleep up under our eaves where I could get comfortable than have to balance all night on a tree branch," said Zoe.

"Starlings are the roaches of the bird world," Lucas called down meaningfully as he climbed one last time. A few minutes later he was finished, sliding the ladder back to carrying size with loud clanks.

"Could you see whether they've built any nests yet up there?" Zoe asked.

"Didn't look," Lucas said.

"Probably they haven't yet." She gazed skeptically at the streaks and blotches on the siding.

"Hard to say. It is that time of year. You know," Lucas went on, "being a pilot, there's no love lost between myself and birds. I could tell you a story or two about the accidents they've caused, hitting propellors, getting sucked into jet engines, gumming up the works. A couple months ago out of Kennedy a bunch of gulls sailed right up into one of my engines two minutes after takeoff."

"That's weird. What happened to them?"

"The point isn't what happened to them. The way a jet turbine works, it's got these finely balanced blades. A bird carcass gets in there and the engine chokes up." Zoe made a little gagging sound of revulsion. "Look," Lucas said, "that engine was ruined. I had to fly out over the Atlantic and dump 100,000 pounds of fuel before that jumbo was light enough to land minus an engine. That's good money down the drain, not to mention the danger. When you look at it that way, it's them or us."

Zoe could tell that she was being tested. She wasn't supposed to waste sympathy on the gulls, act squeamish at their fate. That was all right. She could see that a jumbo jet was more important than a handful of birds. Lucas was realistic. How much he knew about certain things—clear, definite knowledge. She searched her mind for something comparably definite to say, something to suggest she was in agreement with him on the issue of birds. But all that came to mind in that driving clamor of bird screams was a jumble of her mother's pronouncements, bitter and nebulous as a mouthful of smoke.

Lucas has showered in Zoe's tub and crashed on the sofa, which Phyllis fixed up for him. There was nothing for mother and daughter to do then but retire early to their own rooms upstairs and downstairs, leaving him the middle. Was it because Lucas was watching that Zoe hugged her mother before they parted, something she never did willingly, unless for a camera? And why her mother's body seemed so sadly appealing to her arms—her mother's odd scorched smell, so suddenly sweet—Zoe didn't know.

Zoe won't be able to eat tonight because she doesn't dare try to sneak by Lucas. That is all right. She would much rather know he is stationed there at the center of the house, a guardian of order. Stomach clenched around its treasured pain, she lies awake thinking about this man—his determination on the ladder, when he thanked her for her concern. She goes over and over these moments in her mind, savoring them. She imagines that she has emptied herself in order to be filled more purely and perfectly by his image. When she closes her eyes, he is all she sees, poised at the foot of the ladder, then at different stages of his ascent. *Give it a while,* he keeps telling her, and she knows that he does what he does because he cares.

He has climbed far above her now, and the ladder keeps lengthening. He is climbing far beyond the roof of the house, so far she can hardly see him. Her stomach begins to ache with worry. Then the dreadful noise begins—she knows even while it is dim and distant, it is dreadful. She tries to call a warning to Lucas, but he is too high to hear, and soon the noise is deafening, and the sky darkens with enemy starlings. Lucas is engulfed by a black cloud of them; Zoe screams as loud as she can, but nothing can be heard over that noise. Then as she looks up, something comes sliding down the ladder, something shapeless, shrunken lands at her feet. She wakes up in terror, the noise still in her ears.

She must calm herself. She is awake now. She is safe inside. There are no birds, they are all asleep in the trees, balancing somehow on their branches without falling.

But that noise still shrieks in her ears, and she must make sure. She turns on the light and stumbles to the window, pulls the drape aside, tries to peer beyond the glass, through the reflection of her own room, her own body, all arms and legs, wrapped in a large men's T-shirt. She is awake now, yet it seems the noise has filled her room, and she drags open the glass door to let it out. The night air flows in, chills her into alertness. The noise inside dissipates, met as it is by another sound from above, beyond the screen, softer, but as shrill and relentless, the sort of sound, like crickets, or running water, you could confuse with silence unless you had been warned it was there.

Ron Robinson

WHERE WE LAND

(from *Phoenix*)

I.

Althea Deerinwater Baty scoots her hard-backed chair up close to the dining room window and leans toward the thin pane of glass. Her cheeks touch the pink blossoms of the angel-winged begonias that line the sill and become a veil, allowing her to gaze unseen at the yard next door and beyond to Ash Street. On this August morning in Oklahoma City, Althea cannot see the sun. Her view of it is obstructed by buildings, a filmy and humid haze, and the eaves of her own house. Nevertheless, it reaches her. Its heat is drawn through her window and magnified, warms her face.

When she first moved into this house sixty-three years ago, it was on the edge of town. But even that closeness to others had been uncomfortable. There was little room for a garden and with stores only three miles away she had felt little need of one. Now Ash Street was in the middle of the city and her house in the veritable shadow of a hospital one block away. Over the years she had learned to live with it all—sleeping through the night barely conscious of sirens, of seeing neighbors come and go as if Ash Street were itself some residential boarding house, of absorbing into herself the identity of being a widow at age thirty-four and the unnaturalness of burying children. One mainstay had been

Zoe Lindstrom and her flowers next door, but a month ago Zoe walked past Althea's house, around the corner and up to the hospital's emergency room and never returned. Now she was under the ground and her perennials were uprooted and Althea feared there might be nothing more to look at outside than there was inside.

Then the night before, as she woke from an evening nap, a young man moved into Zoe's house. It had taken him less than an hour to carry in all his possessions. Two weeks before, Zoe's daughter had emptied the house and offered it for rent. Only a week ago a man in a pickup full of branches and trash came to trim back Zoe's lilacs to half their size, and, with stems wrapped around his gloved hands, he had twisted up both weeds and the mums from the brick-lined bed that stretched the length of Zoe's driveway.

The young man had a dog. An odd fact that Althea had often considered was that as the town turned into a city and spread around her, much as a flood parts around a boulder before finally rising above it, so too did Ash Street seem invaded, seem occupied, by cats. The dogs began to disappear soon after the children in the block were grown and gone. The only ones she'd seen of late were poodles and terriers and other small breeds, the kind that lived mostly indoors anyway. Althea herself had outlived three cats, and she figured the only reason her son hadn't recently dumped another on her was this time he didn't expect the cat to go first.

The young man had worked on his dog's new home before he went inside to unpack and arrange his own things. Althea watched him in the twilight, hastily stringing wire across a narrow open space between their houses, connecting his newly-created fence to her own rusted wobbly one. She noticed the dog kept its distance and watched, too. It was part collie and part something else.

And so this morning she looks outside and sees the dog curled asleep in a sunny spot on the driveway behind her new neighbor's blue car. It is resting in the heat coming off the concrete just as she herself basks in the warmed-up air next to the window. That spot must be the dog's usual place to sleep, she thinks. Which means they must have moved to Ash from somewhere in the country. She remembers her own long nights of restlessness after she had married Tom Baty when she was twenty—at an age and in a time and place when being twenty and not married meant you were under pressure to prove yourself not a burden to your family, or so she had felt—and he had taken her from the familiar woods of the Cookson Hills off to the flatland of this place and to a better life, where, he proudly told her during the train ride, ten thousand people had settled in one night. The land rush. That it had occurred a decade before he was born was obviously one of the regrets of his short life. That he then proceeded to be killed a scant fourteen years later and she, in turn, was to live out the brunt of her life as much alone and dependent on her one surviving child as if she had remained an old maid in the hills was a twist of fate for which she still sometimes blamed Tom. What made her restless in those early days was the silence of the nights in the city, here where she had expected to face the noise and traffic of people who set their day's work by something other than the sun. At night in the country there had been plenty of sound—of insects and tree frogs and coyotes—but there it was all continuous and comforting. She had been able to lose herself in it. Everything out there kept its distance and was, as she'd often been reminded, more afraid of her than she could be of it. But the nights in the city, even on the edge of town, had long stretches of quiet in which she just waited for something to happen.

She hears the front door slam next door and sees the dog rise to its feet, even before she sees the man stride into the yard that without Zoe's usual care has browned under the August sun. He squats, holds out a hand curved into a fist as if offering something and the dog springs to him, moving across the grass in three quick thrusts—only to have the man rise, grab it by the collar, and swat its rump.

Seconds later Althea sees them reappear in the back yard. He holds the dog with one hand and touches the fence with his other, following the bent wire until he reaches the new gap in the strands. Then he pauses, looks up behind him to the nearby hospital, its top and helicopter pad visible from Ash, and then glances at his wristwatch and to the dog now sniffing the wire, as if picking up its own trail. He goes into his house and comes back with a chain, clamps it to the dog's collar and loops it around a gas meter on the far side from Althea's window. The dog is confined there in thick brush. Right where Zoe grew her honeysuckle.

Soon the man leaves the house and walks along the sidewalk past Althea's house. He wears black slacks, a striped tie, and a short white medical jacket with a red patch on one sleeve showing some design she cannot discern. What sort of machine, she wonders, does he run?

She pushes her chair back to its place beside the dining table and goes back to the kitchen to rinse her coffee cup, fill it with tap water, and swallow first her pill for her blood pressure and then the one that has gold in it that's to alleviate her arthritis. And she wonders why she and Zoe never became friends. It's not a question she has only discovered after Zoe's death, but for most of the forty years that Carl and Zoe lived next door she wondered it too, waiting for what she felt would be inevitable, but didn't happen. They had not gone shopping together, nor even for walks about the neighborhood when they could have done so without much alarm. And yet, if not friends, they still were close, even if it was from necessity alone and the fact that it was expected, simply a sign of the times. They met daily outside, by the fence, and talked of children and flowers and other things soon forgotten but that had passed the time and kept up the conversation. Althea figured the relationship did not progress because the Lindstroms did not move in until a few years after Tom was killed, that Zoe did not want to start something that would leave out her own husband. This assumption further hardened her anger at Tom's death, which came from a fall while he was working on a new building downtown. When, at a full ten years younger than Althea, Zoe had died in the hospital, it surprised Althea more so than had Tom's death, which everyone had lamented as occurring in his prime. But she had always expected his death, had had dreams of tornadoes sweeping him off the sides of buildings. And though she mourned him, for he at least knew her past and shared a brief history with her, she realized that she had always felt herself living with him on borrowed time, that it had been her fate to live alone and was only an oversight on someone's part that Tom had been allowed to spirit her away. When Carl Lindstrom had ended his long demise from cancer a year ago, Althea renewed her hopes that, out of a shared grief this time, Zoe would become her friend and, as happens, they would become the kind of old lady couple that intertwine their lives out of a desperation, a conviction that they will not be helpless alone. Zoe's grief, however, had consumed her, and even before her death the neglect of her flowers and her yard had showed it.

In the afternoon Althea is attracted back to her window. There is a commotion of twigs and leaves. The dog has turned around in the brush and old vines and has tangled the chain in the branches and its own hind legs. Leaning forward, straining, it looks like a statue of a pointer you might see out in front of a large estate. Althea has gazed periodically at the dog all during the morning and has not once seen it even test the limits of the chain. Now, under the dog's pressure, the chain's clamp bends open upon the metal ring of the collar and the dog falls free. Its path returning to the front yard is straight and easy. It only makes another hole in the loose wire of the young man's homemade fence.

Althea again peers through the begonias to watch the dog venture out into the street. It sticks its nose into the Scotts' zinnias. It circles their trash can on the curb. Their cat takes sudden refuge atop the Buick.

In the evening her new neighbor works on his fence. Which

means, Althea tells herself, that at least he, too, doesn't want to keep it chained. He hammers wooden stakes into the hard ground in front of the fence, using the kind of stakes that used to be made for growing tomatoes, and then from stake to stake he strings a second fence with even more wire, makes it tighter, with smaller squares. The dog paces in front of the work, then lies beside it, its tail striking a low strand, its head raised and turned in Althea's direction.

Each night she waits for her son to call from his home in the suburbs. Just to chat, he always says, but she knows it for what it is, a death watch. He will retire in another year and has begun his own anxious pondering. Sometimes she lets her phone ring for several minutes before answering. "I was out for a walk," she says and listens to his lecture. She feels she can no more teach him about getting ready to die than she could about where to live. She had always talked up the virtues of country life and had harbored the dream that one of her children would move to open places and take her along. Hadn't she read, and seen for herself, that this was an age where no one stayed put? But her children treated her stories as fairy tales and cast them aside when they grew up, when they were on their own and could go anywhere they pleased. Two of them were already dead—breast cancer from smoking took one, a heart attack from drinking too much took the other—and now the third expected it. She knew such things could happen any place, but she still felt guilty for bearing children in town.

Ten years ago she had quit reading the newspaper. Her son thought it was on account of her eyesight. She stopped watching television, and he thought it must be her hearing. Why correct him? What her son could not know, nor imagine, was how she had begun concentrating all her senses. To see and hear and feel more than ever. A mockingbird rocking on a limb in the mulberry. The berries ripening in the branches that scratched against the side of the house. The screams in the playground at the end of Ash. Even the grind of the teeter-totter. And her fingers, which constantly tingled, had become so sensitive she held her coffee cup to her lips with a tea towel. She would learn to live outside her body, she told herself, then dying would be nothing.

This night, as she waits for her son's call, she eats a butter-and-tomato sandwich, pleased with its coolness against her gums. She is also pleased to see the young man playing with his dog. They criss-cross the back yard. He yells, feints right and left, always jumps away at the last second, getting out of reach of the dog's paws. He stops, winded, sits on his porch step and pets the dog.

Althea is winded, too, just from watching.

2.

She wakes at six. She knows if you are old in Oklahoma and sleep late in August then you may never wake, for it is the cool morning winds that start the heart beating. If she waits even another hour the humidity will be heavy in the air and will sink upon her dreams. She'll never know what hit her. So she rises at once, and the memory of the dog next door rises with her.

It is in the front yard again.

"Hoo boy, here we go," she says.

Althea fixes her coffee and sits by the window to look at what had been a recently fortified fence. Now one of the stakes leans backward and the top of the wire fence is bent into the shape of a *V*.

When the man discovers the dog loose this time, he just chains it to the clothesline pole in the middle of the back yard, well away from any brush. He loops the chain around the bottom of the pole until it isn't long enough to reach any fence.

There the dog stays. Althea hears the man come home for a few minutes sometime around noon, but he leaves things the way they are.

"It's over now," she says and goes to bed.

When she wakes later she remains in bed. The long nap does

not refresh her, but leaves her stiff and as if drugged. The oscil-
lating fan blows her gown in waves across her legs and lap.

Then through her fog she hears someone shout. She goes
to the dining room window and looks first into her neighbor's
empty back yard, a foolish reaction she later tells herself, and then
gazes to the front where the man carries the dog hard against his
white jacket.

Studying the back yard, she sees the only way the dog could
have managed the escape. Once again it had turned in circles,
wrapping the chain around the pole until no slack remained, then
it had jumped and pulled until the clamp broke.

That night, and for the next few weeks—each afternoon and
night—the dog found a new spot to jump over, squeeze through,
or dig under. At times it would dig so deep by the fence that
Althea could only see its tail wagging above the hole. And each
morning and evening the young man used more cement blocks
and more boards to reinforce the fence. He built it higher and
stronger. Soon it blocked part of Althea's view into the back yard.

He can't leave the dog chained, she thinks, and he can't let it
run free. Not in the city he can't.

3.

One evening he brings home a long chain with links more than
an inch thick. A running chain. This way the dog would have
the whole of the yard to roam while still connected to the pole.
He wraps silver duct tape around the clamp to prevent its prying
apart and, just in case, he works well into the night on his much-
maligned fence. Althea lies in bed and listens to him work, can
see him with her mind's eye, the way he hammers those stakes,
pulls tight the wire, stacks the cement blocks even higher. She
decides it won't work. It's a bad compromise. Nothing can trick
that dog. You can never let them out in the first place if you later
want to keep them in. She wonders how long he can go on.

When she wakes on the next day it is still dark. September has crept up on her once again. A west wind coming from the Panhandle rattles her bedroom window. She tells herself there'll be dust in the air this day.

She sits at the dining room table and pulls a shawl around her shoulders to wait for daybreak. There's nothing to see until then. Outside now there's only the wind, steady and rhythmic. She takes aspirin with her coffee and dozes off to the sound of the things blown by the wind.

When she raises her head off her crossed arms she sees by the clock that only ten minutes have elapsed, though the sky is lighter and it feels to her as if another whole night has passed. She gazes into her neighbor's front yard looking for the dog, but before she focuses on Ash Street she glimpses a dark shape moving against the outside of the fence and she knows what it is.

There the dog swings, bumping against the boards and wire it has jumped over. The chain has caught on a stake and the dog's hind legs barely touch the ground. They jerk each time the front paws and head touch the fence. As if it were trying to jump back over, she thinks, as if having realized too late where it really belongs.

Althea stands and watches and waits—for the dog to jump back over, though she knows that isn't possible; for it to slip through its collar and walk away; for the man to appear. Things out there have always gone on without her, it seems, but this time nothing happens. Soon she gets a strong, unfamiliar feeling that something is waiting on her.

She knows what to do. It is a simple job of undoing the clamp from the collar. But by the time she leaves her house, takes each slow step down the porch, and makes her way around the corner to the new fence, she has already been enveloped by the chill wind penetrating her loose gown and she feels exposed, embarrassed, helpless. She knows she is probably too late and keeps her gaze averted from that of the dog's. She does not want to touch the dog, when for weeks all she could imagine was what it would be like to pet it, have it lying heavily on her feet in bed at night.

She touches the metal clamp and as she does so her fingers,

numbed from the cold, brush against the stiff wet hairs on the dog's neck that feel as if it has been sweating, swelling. There is no room to work her fingers around the collar and there is too much force on the clamp for her to pry it open.

In anger she forgets herself and just wraps her arms around the dog, hugs it, tries to lift it back to the top where it can roll on to the other side. Instead it slumps lower, sliding out of her arms, its weight gradually bending the stake that impales the chain. The hind legs fold and its rump rests in the grass. With the dog's neck still stretched, pointing up, and with the front paws hanging in the air, it looks like any dog that's just been told to sit, to beg.

Althea wants to holler for help, but she doesn't feel the strength. Her own breathing has become rapid, shallow. And who else but her, she thinks, would be up at this early hour? So she leaves the dog and hurries to her neighbor's front door. She tells herself to calm down so she can speak.

She knocks loudly and alternates the fists she uses on the screen door so the pain in her knuckles and wrists will be evenly spread, diminished. As she waits, she practices what she will say. But when the door opens and she faces the man, who wears only cut-off blue jeans and a look of consternation and fright, her prepared words vanish. They are replaced by a sense of vanity she never knew she had. The sudden consciousness of herself—her sagging brown skin, vacant mouth, and closely cropped black hair—make her feel ashamed before this man. She forgets for a moment why she is here.

"I'm your neighbor," she says. She holds onto the knob of the screen door.

"Are you all right?" he asks.

"Yes," she says. "Fine."

"Do you need something? Has something happened?"

"No," she says. "Yes."

"Do you want to come in?" he asks. "Come on in."

He grabs the door knob on his side.

"Your dog," she says, letting go of the door then and stepping back. "He's on the fence."

He passes by her and she doesn't try to keep up with him or follow. There's nothing she can do. She goes straight back home and gets in bed and covers up.

Her body aches in every place. Muscles cramp in every limb. She tries to concentrate on each of her senses, tries to escape the pain as she's been practicing to do, but the land of her imagination just disappears, her mind can't even start to overcome the matter welling up within her, filling her spaces. No longer is her heart a thing separate, a muscle fixed in one certain locale, shielded by bone, its presence easily forgotten, detected only by stillness and by probing for an artery. Now its contractions, this pulsing from her temples to her toes, coming way too quickly, is all there is of her, of Althea Deerinwater Baty, who has never been so much alive, so much at home.

Larry Brown

SLEEP

(from *The Carolina Quarterly*)

My wife hears the noises and she wakes me in the night. The dream I've been having is not a good one. There is a huge black cow with long white horns chasing me, its breath right on my neck. I don't know what it means, but I'm frightened when I awake. Her hand is gripping my arm. She is holding her breath, almost.

Sometimes I sleep well and sometimes I don't. My wife hardly ever sleeps at all. Oh, she takes little naps in the daytime, but you can stand back and watch her, and you'll see what she goes through. She moans, and twists, and shakes her head no no no.

Long ago we'd go on picnics, take Sunday drives in the car. Long before that, we parked in cars and moved our hands over each other. Now all we do is try to sleep, seems like.

It's dark in the room, but I can see a little. I move my arm and my elbow makes a tiny pop. I'm thinking coffee, orange juice, two over easy. But I'm a long way away from that. And then I know she's hearing the noises once more.

"They're down there again," she says.

I don't even nod my head. I don't want to get up. It's useless anyway, and I just do it for her, and I never get through doing it. I'm warm under the covers, and the world apart from the two of us under here is cold. I think maybe if I pretend to be asleep, she'll give it up. So I lie quietly for a few moments, breathing in and out. I gave us a new electric blanket for our anniversary. The thermostat clicks on and off, with a small reassuring sound, keeping us warm. I think about hash browns, and toast, and shit on a shingle. I think about cold places I've been in. It's wonderful to do that, and then feel the warm spaces between my toes.

"Get up," she says.

Once I was trapped in a blizzard in Kansas. I was traveling, and a snowstorm came through, and the snow was so furious I drove my car right off the road into a deep ditch. I couldn't even see the highway from where I was, and I foolishly decided to stay in the car, run the heater, and wait for help. I had almost a full tank of gas. The snow started covering my vehicle. I had no overshoes, no gloves. All I had was a car coat. The windshield was like the inside of an igloo, except for a small hole where I ran the defroster. I ran out of gas after nine hours of idling. Then the cold closed in. I think about that time, and feel my nice warm pajamas.

"You getting up?" she says.

I'm playing that I'm still asleep, that I haven't heard her wake me. I'm drifting back off, scrambling eggs, warming up the leftover T-bone in the microwave, looking for the sugar bowl and the milk. The dog has the paper in his mouth.

"Did you hear me?" she says.

I hear her. She knows I hear her. I hear her every night, and it never fails to discourage me. Sometimes this getting up and down seems to go on forever. I've even considered separate beds. But so far we've just gone on like we nearly always have.

I suppose there's nothing to do but get up. But if only she knew how bad I don't want to.

"*Louis*. For God's sake. Will you get up?"

Another time I was stationed at a small base on the North Carolina coast. We had to pull guard duty at night. After a four-hour shift my feet would be blocks of ice. It would take two hours of rubbing them with my socks off, and drinking coffee, to get them back to normal. The wind came off the ocean in the winter, and it cut right through your clothes. I had that once, and now I have this. The thermostat clicks. It's doing its small, steady job, regulating the temperature of two human bodies. What a wonderful invention. I'm mixing batter and pouring it on the griddle. Bacon is sizzling in its own grease, shrinking, turning brown, bubbling all along the edges. What lovely bacon, what pretty pancakes. I'll eat and eat.

"Are you going to get up or not?"

I sigh. I think that if I was her and she was me, I wouldn't make her do this. But I don't know that for a fact. How did we know years ago we'd turn out like this? We sleep about a third of our lives and look what all we miss. But sometimes the things we see in our sleep are more horrible and magical than anything we can imagine. People come after you and try to kill you, cars go backward down the highway at seventy miles an hour with you inside and you're standing up on the brake. Sometimes you even get a little.

I lie still in the darkness and without looking around, can see the mound of covers next to me with a gray lump of hair sticking out. She is still, too. I think maybe she's forgotten about the things downstairs. I think maybe if I just keep quiet she'll drift back off to sleep. I try that for a while. The gas heater is throwing the shadow of its grille onto the ceiling and it's leaping around. Through the black window I can see the cold stars in the sky. People are probably getting up somewhere, putting on their housecoats, yawning in their fists, plugging in their Mr. Coffees.

Once I was in the army with a boy from Montana and he got me to go home with him. His parents had a large ranch in the mountains, and they took me in like another son. I'd never seen country like that Big Sky country. Everywhere you looked, all you could see was sky and mountains, and in the winter it snowed. We fed his father's cows out of a truck, throwing hay out in the snow, and boy those cows were glad to get it. They'd come running up as soon as they heard the truck. But I felt sorry for them, having to live outside in the snow and all, like deer. Once in a while we'd find a little calf that had frozen to death, frozen actually to the ground. I would be sad when that happened, thinking about it not ever getting to see the springtime.

I lie still under the covers in my warm bed and wonder what ever became of that boy.

Then she begins. It's always soft, and she never raises her voice. But she's dogcussing me, really putting some venom into it, the same old awful words over and over, until it hurts my ears to hear them. I know she won't stop until I get up, but I hate to feel that cold floor on my feet. She's moved my house shoes again, and I don't want to crawl under the bed looking for them. Spiders are under there, and balls of dust, and maybe even traps set for mice. I don't ever look under there, because I don't want to see what I might.

I tell myself that it's just like diving into cold water. I'll only feel the shock for a second, and that the way to do it is all at once. So I throw the covers back and I stand up. She stops talking to me. I find the flashlight on the stand beside the bed, where I leave it every night. Who needs a broken leg going down the stairs?

It's cold in the hall. I shine the flashlight on the rug, and on my gun cabinet, and for a moment I think I'll go and make coffee in the kitchen, and sit there listening to it brew, and drink a cup of it and smoke a few cigarettes. But it seems an odd time of the night to do a thing like that. The thought passes, and I go down the stairs.

I open the door to the kitchen. Of course there's nothing in there. I shut the door hard so she can hear it. I cross the dining room, lighting my way, looking at her china in the cabinet, at the white tablecloth on the table and the dust on it, and I open the door to the living room. There's nothing in there but furniture, the fireplace, some candy in a dish. I slam the door so she can hear that, too. I'm thinking of all the dreams I could be having right now, uninterrupted. It's too late for Carson, too late for Letterman, too late for Arsenio. They've all gone to bed by now.

I stand downstairs and listen to my house. I cut the light off to hear better. The silence has a noise of its own that it makes. I move to the window and push the curtains aside, but nobody's out there on the streets. It's cold out there. I'm glad I'm in here, and not out there. Still.

I sit in a chair for a little while, tapping the flashlight gently on my knee. I find my cigarettes in the pocket of my robe, and I smoke one. I don't want it, it's just a habit. It kills three or four minutes. And after that, it's been long enough. I find an ashtray with my flashlight, and put out the cigarette. I'm still thinking about that coffee. I even look in the direction of the kitchen. But finally I go ahead and climb the stairs.

I put my hand over the bulb of the flashlight when I get near the bed. I move in my own little circle of light with quiet feet. I keep my hand over it when I move it near her face. I don't want to wake her up if she's asleep. My hand looks red in the light, and my skin looks thin. I don't know how we got so old.

Her eyes are closed. She has her hands folded together, palms flat, like a child with her head resting on them. I don't know what to do with her any more. Maybe tomorrow night she won't hear the things downstairs. Maybe tomorrow night they'll be up in the attic. It's hard to tell.

I turn the flashlight off and set it back on the table beside the bed. I might need it again before the night's over. I don't want to be up stumbling around in the dark.

"Mama had three kittens," she says, and I listen. Her voice is soft, remarkably clear, like a person reciting a poem. I wait for the rest of it, but it never comes. I'm lucky, this time, I guess.

I sit on the side of the bed. I don't want to get under the covers just yet. I want to hear the house quiet again, and the silence is so loud that it's almost overpowering. Finally I lie down and pull the covers up over my head. The warmth is still there. I move toward her, looking for I don't know what. I think of a trip I took to Alaska a long time ago, when I was a young man. There were sled dogs, and plenty of snow, and polar bears fishing among cakes of ice for seals. I wonder how they can live in that cold water. But I figure it's just what you get used to. I close my eyes, and I wait.

Donna Trussell

FISHBONE

(from *TriQuarterly*)

The other girls from my senior class were off at college or working. Not me. I stayed alone in my room and played The Game of Life. Mama didn't like it.

"Wanda, are you on drugs?" she said.

I shook my head. I spun the plastic wheel—it made a ratchet sound—and moved the blue car two spaces, up on a hill. The great thing about The Game of Life was all the plastic hills and valleys. No other game had such realism.

"You need a change," Mama said. "You're going to Meemaw's."

My bus was leaving early the next morning, so I had to pack in a hurry. But I took the time to put a matchbook in my purse. I don't smoke, but I thought it might come in handy if I needed to send a message to the bus driver: Hijacker, ninth row, submachine gun under his coat.

The sky was overcast, and it was a slow, pale trip. The only rest stop was in Centerville, where I got a fish sandwich at the Eat It and Beat It.

Meemaw was waiting for me at the station. She smelled of cold cream and lilacs.

Ed grabbed my suitcase. "Yo," he said.

"Yo," I said back.

Ed's pickup was full of old *Soldier of Fortunes*. I rested my feet on top of a picture of a tank. Meemaw's life sure had changed since she married Ed.

"My little girl," she said. She patted my knee the way a kid flattens Play-doh.

"She's not your girl," Ed said. "She's your granddaughter."

"She *is* my little girl."

A chain link fence now surrounded Meemaw's garden. "Keeps dogs out," she said. The fence made her farm look even less farmish than it had, with its green shack for a barn and refrigerator toppled on its side out back and giant new house modeled after the governor's mansion.

Meemaw fussed over me at supper: Wanda, can I get you some more roast, would you like another helping of butter beans, how about some corn bread?

Ed had three cups of coffee with supper. He poured the coffee into his saucer and blew on it. I asked him why he drank his coffee that way.

He didn't answer. Finally Meemaw said, "To cool it down."

Ed's cup and saucer were monogrammed in gold. My plate too.

"Meemaw, where's your dishes?" I asked. "The ones with purple ribbons and grapes?"

"Well, we have Ed's china now."

He slurped his coffee, staring straight ahead. He might as well have been talking to the curtains when he said, "I'm glad you're here, Wanda, because I've been wanting to ask you something. All day I've been wondering—who paid the hospital when you had that baby? The taxpayers?"

I smashed a butter bean with my fork. "Excuse me," I said and went outside.

I looked out across the pine trees, dark green. I used to believe trees had people inside them. I wished some god would change me into a tree. That wouldn't be a bad life—sun, rain, birds. Kids looking for pine cones. Me shaking my branches for them.

The peat moss in the garden was warm. I lay down and pulled a watermelon close.

After a while Meemaw came out and sat down near my head, in the snapdragons and cucumbers. Meemaw planted vegetables and flowers together, except for the gladiolas, off by themselves. Pink, peach, yellow, white—a million baby shoes, shifting in the wind.

She smoothed my hair and talked about exercise and how important it was.

"Meemaw, what happened to your strawberries?"

"Birds. But that's all right. Plenty for the birds too."

Every morning we'd go out to pull weeds, and she'd tell me uplifting stories about people she knew. Trials they'd had. A young man wanted to commit suicide because law school was so hard. Once a week his mother wrote him letters full of encouraging words.

"What kind of encouraging words?"

"Oh, 'Don't give up.' That sort of thing."

When he graduated he found out she'd been dead for a month. She'd known she was dying, and had written the last letters ahead of time.

Meemaw knew lots of stories about people who "took the path of least resistance" and ended up sick or poor. I got back at her by asking personal questions.

"Meemaw, have you ever had an orgasm?"

Yes, she said. Once. "I was glad to know what it is that causes so much of human behavior." She smiled and handed me a bunch of gladiolas.

Afternoons I stayed in my room. Mama wouldn't let me bring The Game of Life. I lay on the bed a lot. The light fixture had leaves and berries molded in the glass. Once I wrapped my arms around the chest of drawers and put my head down on the cool marble top.

Meemaw would call me to supper. There wasn't much discussion at the table. If anyone said anything, it was Ed talking to

Meemaw or Meemaw talking to me. Except for once, when I went to the stove to get some salt. Ed told me I'd done it all wrong. "You don't bring the *plate* to the salt. You bring the *salt* to the plate."

After supper Meemaw and I went down to the barn. She milked Sissy. I fed the chickens. I'd throw a handful of feed and they'd move in at eighty miles an hour.

Ed never came with us. He hates Sissy, Meemaw told me. "He's jealous."

"Jealous of a cow?"

"Why, of course. I spend so much of my time with her."

Evenings Ed watched *Walking Tall* on his VCR. Or he went inside his toolshed. He never worked on anything. He looked at catalogs and ordered tools, and when they came he hung them on the walls. He read books about the end of the world: the whole state of Colorado was going to turn into Jello, and people will drown. "You've got five years to live, young lady," he told me. "*Five years.*"

He had guns—a whole caseful. Once I saw him polishing them when I was standing in the hall by his study.

"What do you think you're doing?" he said.

I walked away. He shut the door.

One day when I was watching Meemaw through a little diamond shape made of my thumbs and two fingers, Ed said, "You planning on sitting on your butt all summer?"

"I haven't thought about it."

"Start thinking."

Meemaw knew a man in town who was looking for help. She knew everybody in town.

"It's a photography studio," Meemaw said.

"I don't know anything about photography."

"He's willing to train someone. It's a nice place. There's another studio in town, but everybody says Mr. Lamont's is the one that puts on the finishing touch."

She made the phone call. Ed was smiling behind his magazine.
I *knew* he was.

I drove Meemaw's old Fairmont into town. First Ed showed
me all the things I had to do to it, because "service stations don't
do a damned thing anymore." He showed me the oil stick and the
radiator. He told me to check the windshield-wiper blades once a
week. He was just about to make me measure the air in the tires
when I said I'd be late for my interview if I didn't get going.

Mr. Lamont wore glasses and a pair of green doubleknit pants
that were stretched about as far as they could go.

"Wanda, you put here that your last job was back in December.
What have you been doing since then?"

"Nothing."

"Nothing?"

"Nothing you'd want to know about."

"But I would like to know."

"O.K. I was in love with this guy. We were going to get married, but then we didn't. And then I had a baby boy."

"Oh."

"He's been adopted."

"I see." Mr. Lamont tried to look neutral, but I could see little
bursts of energy flying from the corners of his mouth.

"I can't pay minimum wage," he said.

"Whatever." I might as well be here, I thought, as out on the
farm with Ed.

After supper Ed gave me a lecture about jobs and responsibility
and attitude. People don't think, they just don't *think*. World War
III is coming, and no one's prepared. All the goddamned niggers
will try to steal their chickens.

"But I'm ready for them," he said. "I've been stocking up on
hollow points. They blow a hole in a man as big as a barrel."
He punched his fist in the air. Meemaw sort of jumped, but she
didn't say anything. She clanked the dishes and sang "Rock of
Ages" a little louder.

I went to bed with the pamphlet Mr. Lamont gave me, *The*

Fine Art of Printing Black and White. The paper is very sensitive, it said.

The next day Mr. Lamont showed me the safelight switch. "See that gouge? I did that so I could feel for it in the dark."

He did a test strip. "Agitate every few seconds," he said, rocking the developer tray.

He let me print a picture of a kid holding a trophy. "Make it light," he said. "The newspaper adds contrast. Look how this one came out." He showed me a clipping of a bunch of Shriners. They looked like they had some kind of skin disease.

After a week I got the hang of it, and Mr. Lamont left me in charge of black and white. I liked the darkroom. No phones. No people, except for the faces that slowly developed before me. Women and their fiancés. Sometimes the man stood behind the woman and put both arms around her waist.

Jimmy used to do that.

He held me like that at the senior picnic. It was windy. Big rocks nailed down the corners of each tablecloth. Blue gingham. The white tablecloths had to be returned because the principal thought they'd remind the students of bedsheets. Jimmy and I laughed; we'd been making love for weeks. We got careless, in the tall grasses by Cedar Creek Lake. Night birds called across the water.

When I was two weeks late, I told him. He looked away. There's a clinic, he said, in Dallas. I covered his lips with my fingers.

At Western Auto they said they'd take him on, weekends and nights. At the Sonic, too, for the morning shift. Jimmy and I looked at an apartment on Burning Tree Drive, southwest of town. A one-bedroom. He stared at the ceiling. Jimmy? I said.

Goodbye, goodbye, I told the mirror long before I really said it.

I read every book I could find about babies and their tadpole bodies. I gave up Coke and barbecue potato chips. My breasts swelled. I felt great. Hormones, the doctor said.

At first my baby was just a rose petal, sleeping, floating. At eight months I played him records, Mama's *South Pacific* and Daddy's "Seventy-six Trombones." I stood right next to the stereo, and he talked to me with thumps of his feet.

You want to feel him kick? I asked. Mama shook her head and kept on ironing. Daddy left the room.

I didn't get a baby shower. Mama told everyone I was putting it up for adoption. "It," she called him. I made up different names for him. Fishbone, one week. Logarithm, the next.

Mama bought me a thin gold wedding band to wear to the hospital. Girls don't do that anymore, I told her. Some girls even keep their babies, these days.

Not here in Grand Saline, she said. Not girls from good families.

My little Fishbone got so big two nurses had to help push him out. Breathe, they said. Pant hard.

Please let me hold him, I said. *Please.*

Now, Wanda, Mama said. You know what's best.

He cried. Then he slipped away, down the hall. The room caved in on me, with its green walls and white light. Mama held me down, saying, We've been through this. We decided.

At the nurse's station Jimmy left me a get-well card. Good luck, he wrote. That's all.

Mama took me home to a chocolate cake, and we never talked about Fishbone again. She never mentioned Jimmy's name.

Sometimes now, before driving home to Meemaw, I stopped at the trailer court at the edge of town. I watched people. A woman would frown and I'd think: that's me heating up a bottle for Fishbone and the formula got too hot. A man takes off his cowboy boots and props his feet on the coffee table. A woman tucks herself next to him. He kisses her hair, her neck.

I remembered love. I remembered it all. Now I felt thick and dull, something to be tossed away in the basement.

* * *

"How's the passport picture coming?" Mr. Lamont asked, knocking on my door.

"Don't come in. Paper exposed."

"That man going to New Guinea is back."

The man had worried about his eyes. I've got what they call raccoon eyes, he'd said, is there any way you can lighten it up around the eyes?

He looked disappointed when I gave him the picture. "I know you did the best you could," he said. He smiled. He didn't look like a criminal when he smiled.

When I got home, Meemaw was cutting up chicken wire and putting it over holes in the coop. Making it "snake proof," she said. I took over the cutting. I'd never used wire cutters before. Everything is just paper in their path.

"It's so bare in the chicken coop," I said. "Why don't you put down an old blanket or something?"

"You know, Wanda, I did that very thing one time, when I had a batch of baby chicks. I put down a carpet scrap, so they'd be warm. And they died. Every single one! I was just heartbroken. And do you know what I found out? They'd eaten the carpet."

"How'd you find that out?"

"I did an autopsy."

"Ooooo, Meemaw! How awful."

She shrugged. "Nothing awful about it. I wanted to know."

"I could never be a doctor," I said.

I read somewhere that these psychologists asked a bunch of surgeons why they became doctors, and they all said they wanted to help people. And then they did psychological tests on them and found out they were part sadists. They liked knives.

"How about a photographer?" Meemaw said. "I hear they teach photography in college now. I would pay for you to go."

I rolled up the leftover chicken wire and put it away in the barn. Meemaw came in after me.

"Time to milk Sissy, isn't it?" I said. I went to get the milk pail.

"What do you want to do with your life, Wanda?"

"You promised not to ask me that anymore."

She laughed and patted me on the back. "Yes, I did." She set the pail under Sissy, and then turned to face me again. "But what *are* you going to do?"

"I don't know, Meemaw."

Lately I'd been thinking about the homeless on TV, and how they live. I live in the gutter, I could say. It has a nice ring to it.

"Wanda, I once read a book where the first page had a quotation from the Bible. I thought it was the most beautiful of any Bible verse I'd ever read. It said the Lord will restore unto you the years the locusts have eaten."

She paused. When I didn't say anything, she waved her arms, saying, "Isn't that beautiful?"

"Uh huh."

The barn door swung open. Ed.

"How many times do I have to tell you not to leave the wheelbarrow out? It's been sitting there in the garden since morning."

"I told her it was O.K.," Meemaw said. "It doesn't hurt anything."

"The hell it doesn't. If you leave it out, it rusts. If it rusts, you have to buy a new one."

"I don't think it'll rust for ten years at least."

"Either you use the tools or they use you. That's all I have to say about it."

He stomped off.

Meemaw rubbed my arm. "Don't worry about it. Ed's just upset because yesterday you left his mail in the glove compartment instead of bringing it in to him. He's afraid somebody could have stolen his pension check."

"Who would steal it out here in the middle of nowhere? Who'd even know it's there?"

Meemaw went back to milking Sissy. I always thought milking a cow would be fun, till I tried it. The milk comes out in tiny streams, about the size of dental floss. It takes forever.

"You know how Ed is."

"Yeah, I know. Why did you marry him, anyway?"

"He needed me."

"But why not marry someone you needed?"

"I don't need anybody. I just need to be needed. They say money is the root of all evil, but I say selfishness is. Selfishness, and lack of exercise."

That got her started.

"Sweetie," she said, "I once read about a mental hospital for rich movie stars. It costs a powerful lot of money to go there. And you know what the doctors make those ladies do? Run in circles. Why, one movie star had to cut wood for two hours."

I thought about that on the way back to the house, but I couldn't see how cutting wood would make a difference.

That night I wrote a letter to Jimmy: "I hope you like it at college. Do you ever think about our baby? Whenever I take a shower, I think I hear him crying. Do you have this problem?"

I signed it, "Your friend, Wanda," and sent the letter in care of his parents.

"Let sleeping dogs lie," Mama wrote. "Think of the future. Pastor Dobbins will be needing a new receptionist at the church, and he told me he's willing to interview you. It's very big of him, considering."

I dropped the letter into the pigpen. The next day I could only see one corner, and after that it was gone.

I did Dwayne Zook, his sister Tracy Zook, and then I was finally done with the high school annual pictures. Mr. Lamont asked me to sit at the front desk to answer the phone and give people their proofs.

"Lovely," they'd say. Or, "Your boss surely does a fine job." Mr. Lamont told me to answer everything with: "He had a lot to work with." There was this one girl, though, who looked like Ted Koppel. I didn't know what to say to her.

We had lots of brides, even in August. I patted their faces dry and gave them crushed ice to eat. I spread their dresses in perfect circles around their feet.

One day Mr. Lamont asked if I'd like to come into his darkroom to see how he did color.

"It looks like pink," he said, "but we call it magenta." He held up another filter. "What would you call that?"

"Turquoise?"

"Cyan," he said.

"Sigh-ann."

He let me do one, a baby sitting with its mother on the grass. The picture turned out too yellow, so I did another one.

"Perfect," he said. "You learn real quick."

"Thanks."

We goofed off the rest of the day. He showed me some wedding pictures that were never picked up. "A real shame," he said. "That's the best shot of the getaway car I've ever done."

He started going down to Food Heaven to get lunch for both of us. We'd eat Crescent City Melts and talk. He teased me about Ed, asking if it was true that he got kicked in the head by a mule when he was a kid.

"Does he really have two Cadillacs?"

"Three. They just sit out back. He drives his pickup truck everywhere."

Sometimes Mr. Lamont would come into my darkroom. He'd check on my supply of stop bath or Panalure. Then he'd lean in the corner and watch me work. He never touched me. We'd just stand there in the cool darkness.

He told me about his mother and why he couldn't leave her. "Cataracts," he said. "I read to her."

I told him about the book I got at the library, *The Songwriter's Book of Rhymes*. Also-ran rhymed with Peter Pan, Marianne, caravan, Yucatan, lumberman, and about two hundred other words.

In *Discovering Your America* every state was pale pink, green, or yellow. Nebraska had tiny bundles of wheat in one corner, and New Mexico had Indian headdresses. That night I dreamed I was high above Texas, watching the whole pink state come alive. Oil wells gushed. Fish flopped high in the air. Little men in hard hats danced around.

"I don't want to go to photography school," I told Meemaw the next morning. "I want to buy a car and drive to West Texas. Or maybe California."

"You can't do that," Meemaw said. "A young girl, alone."

"Why not?"

"It's just not done."

"Why can't *I* be the first to do it?"

"Oh, Wanda."

Meemaw believes in Good and Evil. She doesn't understand how lonely people are. Anyone who tried to hurt me, I would talk to him. I would listen to his tales of old hotels and wide-hipped women who left him.

On my seventy-seventh day at Meemaw's I came home and found Ed filling up the lawnmower.

"It's about time you earned your keep," he said.

"What about supper?"

"Forget supper. You're going to mow the lawn."

"Oh, is that so?"

"Yes, ma'am, you betcha that's so." He sat down on a lawn chair. "Get started."

A vat of green Jello swallowed him up, chair and all.

While I mowed, I thought of another fate for him—a giant cheese grater with arms and legs. Ed ran and ran, and then stumbled. The cheese grater stood over him and laughed as Ed tried to crawl away.

I didn't get to the big finale because the lawnmower made a crunching sound and stopped. Ed came running over, asking how come I didn't comb the yard first, how come I couldn't do anything right? "You're as lazy as a Mexican housecat."

His red, puffy face pushed into mine. In the folds of his skin I could see the luxury Meemaw had given him, her flowers and food and love. He just lapped it up.

He followed me into the house. Young people! Welfare! Good-for-nothings!

"You're a fine one to talk," I said, turning to face him. "I've never seen you lift a finger around here."

He moved towards me, and then stopped. He was so close I could see his eyes roll up into his head, and his eyelids quiver. The room was silent. I heard the hands on the clock move.

"You ungrateful bitch," he said. "Your grandmother thinks you're different, but I told her. I told her what you are."

It got dark while he told me what I was. He must have been rehearsing. I heard words I knew he got out of a dictionary. Meemaw twirled yarn and cried.

He got my suitcase and threw it at my feet.

"Get out. Now." He turned to Meemaw. "If she's here when I come back, I'll send for my things."

He slammed the door. His truck roared out, spitting gravel into the night.

"He's a child," Meemaw said. "A grown-up child, and I can't do anything about it." She held my face in her hands. "My little girl. My sweetie. What are we going to do?"

She put my head on her shoulder. We stood there, rocking.

"I named my baby Fishbone," I said. "Did you know that?" She shushed me and patted my back.

He'd be eight months old now. In twenty years he'll come looking for me. We'll have iced tea and wonder how to act. I wanted you, I'll tell him, but I was young. I didn't know I was strong.

"There's a bus to Grand Saline in the morning," Meemaw said. "I'll call your mother."

We rode a taxi into town. Meemaw got me a room at the motel. She brushed my hair and put me in bed.

"You can go home now, Meemaw."

"Yes, I suppose I can."

She wouldn't leave until I pretended I was asleep. But I couldn't sleep at all. I found a *Weekly World News* under the bed. I read every story in it. Then the ads, about releasing the secret power within you and True Ranches for sale and the Laffs Ahoy Klown Kollege in Daytona Beach.

At five a.m. I went for a walk. The air was cool and clear as October. I breathed deep.

Waffle Emporium was open. Something about dawn at a coffee shop gets to me. Pink tabletops, and people too sleepy to talk. New things around the corner. Carlsbad Caverns. White Sands.

I thought about what I was going to do next. I had eight hundred dollars inside my shoes. I could go anywhere. San Francisco, to work at the Believe It or Not Museum. Or Miami—I could take care of dolphins. I thought about Indian reservations. Gas stations in the desert. Snake farms. The owner would be named Chuck, probably, or Buzz.

I walked to the bus station and read the destination board. I said each city twice, to see how it felt on my tongue.

Rick Bass

THE HISTORY OF RODNEY

(from *Ploughshares*)

I t rains in Rodney, in the winter. But we have history; even for Mississippi, we have that. There's a sweet olive tree that grows all the way up to the third story, where Elizabeth's sun porch is. Butterflies swarm in the front yard, in the summers, drunk on the smell of the tree; but in the winter, it rains. The other people in the town of Rodney are the daughters, sons, and grandchildren of slaves. They own Rodney now.

This old house I am renting costs fifty dollars a month. Electricity sizzles and arcs from the fuse box on the back porch, spills out and tumbles to the ground in little bouncing blue sparks. The house has thirty-five rooms, some of which are rotting—one has a tree growing up through the floor—and the ceilings are all high, though not as high as the trees outside.

Here in the ghost town of Rodney there is a pig, a murderer, that lives under my house, and she has killed several dogs. The pig had twenty piglets this winter, and like the bad toughs in a western, they own the town. When we hear or see them coming, we run, to get out of the street. We could kill them, shoot them down on the center of the dusty lane that used to be a street, but we don't: we're waiting for them to fatten up on their mother's milk.

We're waiting for Preacher to come back, too. He's Daisy's boyfriend, and he's been gone for forty years.

Loose peafowl scream in the night, back in the trees, and it is like the jungle. The river that used to run past Rodney—the Mississippi—shifted course exactly one hundred years ago, and isn't here anymore.

It happened overnight: the bend downstream, the earthen bulge of an oxbow, broke somewhere, sometime in the night, breaking like a human's heart, and the water rushed through. Instead of making its slow, lazy descent through the swamp— northern water, coming down from Minnesota—it pressed, like sex, and broke through.

I've been reading about Rodney, in the old newspapers, and talking to Daisy, who lives across the street, and also, I've been sitting under the sweet olive tree trying to imagine it—and I'm sure that in the morning, after it happened, the townspeople blinked and gaped, because there was only a wide sea of mud.

There were boats full of cotton, stranded in the mud; Rodney was the second largest port in the South, second only to New Orleans. And there were fish dying in the mud, and alligators and snakes wriggling out there, and the townspeople stood on the docks and waited around for a day or two, for a rain to come and fill the big river back up, but when the fish began to smell—a great muddy flat place, covered with dead fish; the river had been almost a mile wide—then they had to pack up, and hike into the hills, into the bluffs and jungles above the river, to escape the disease and stench.

When the mud had dried and grown over with beautiful grass, tall grass, they moved back. Some of the men tracked the river, hunting it as if it were a wounded animal, and they found it seven miles away, flowing big and strong, as wide as it had ever been. It was flowing like a person's life, like a woman in love with something. It had just shifted.

Sixteen thousand people lived in Rodney, before and during the Civil War; now there are only about a dozen of us.

Daisy says they only put you away in Whitfield for forty years, for being a chicken-chaser. That was what the social workers saw, on their visit: Preacher chasing chickens down the street, like a crazy man. He was just doing it for fun—he might have been a *little* hungry, says Daisy, but mostly for fun—but they took him away.

Daisy says she's been keeping track on her calendars—and there are old ones tacked over every wall in her house, beginning with the year they hauled Preacher away—and that forty years will be up this fall, and that she's expecting he'll be back after that, that he'll be coming back any day.

Daisy didn't see the river leave, but her mother did. Daisy says that some of the pigs are Union soldiers, that the townspeople barricaded the soldiers in the Presbyterian church one Sunday, boarded all the doors up, and then Daisy's mother turned them all into pigs.

The mother pig is the size of a small Volkswagen; her babies are the color and shape of footballs. They grunt and snort like a stable of horses, at night, beneath Elizabeth's and my house.

Across the street, Daisy has a TV antenna, rising a hundred and fifty feet into the air, up above the trees. Daisy can cure thrush, or tuberculosis, or snakebite, or ulcers, or anything, as long as it does not affect someone she loves. She's powerless, over that part; she's told me so. She cooks sometimes for Elizabeth and me: we buy the food, and give her some money, and she cooks. Sometimes Elizabeth isn't hungry—she'll be lying on the bed up in the sun room, wearing just her underpants and sunglasses, reading a book—and so I'll go over to Daisy's by myself.

We live so far from civilization: the mail comes only once a week, from Natchez. The mailman is frightened of the pigs. Sometimes they chase his jeep, like dogs, up the steep hill, up the gravel road, back out of town. Their squeals of rage are a high, mad sound, but they run out of breath easily.

Daisy never gets mail, and we let her come over and read ours.

"This used to be a big town," she said, the first time she came over to meet us, to introduce herself, and to read our mail. She gestured out to the cotton field behind her house. "A port town. The river used to lay right out there."

"Why did it leave?" Elizabeth asked.

Daisy shook her head, and wouldn't answer.

"Will you take us to the river?" I asked. "Will you show it to us?"

Daisy shook her head again. "Nope," she said, drawing circles in the dust with her toe. "You got to be in *love* to see the river," she said, looking at me, and then at Elizabeth.

"Oh, but we are!" Elizabeth cried, looking at me and taking my arm. "That's why we're here!"

"Well," said Daisy. "Maybe."

Daisy likes to tell us about Preacher; she talks about him all the time. He was twenty; she was nineteen. There was an old Confederate gunboat out in the middle of the cotton field—it's since rusted away to nothing, and the remains have been buried beneath years and years of slime-mud, from winters' floods, springs' hard rains—but the boat was still in fair shape then, and they lived on it, Preacher and Daisy, out in the middle of this field—the field that's still out there, rich and growing green with cotton, hazy in the fall—and they slept in the captain's quarters, on a striped old mattress with no sheets, and they rubbed vanilla on their bodies to keep the bugs from biting, she said.

There were breezes. There were skeletons in some of the other rooms, and skeletons all around the boat, out in the field, sailors that had drowned when the ship burned and sank, a cannon hole in the bow—but they were old skeletons, a Confederate gunboat, and no more harmful than, say, an old cow's skull, or a horse's.

Daisy and Preacher made love, she said, all the time: in the day, in the blazing afternoon out on the deck, in the middle of the field —the boat half-buried in the field, even then, as if sinking, back into time, back into the earth—and then wild at night, all night, with coal-oil lamps burning all around the ship's perimeter, and cries so loud, said Daisy, cries from the boat, that birds roosting down in the swamp took flight into the darkness, confused, circling over the field then and coming back. . . .

"We weren't going to do anything," said Daisy. "All we were going to do was live out on that boat and make love mostly all day. He wasn't hurtin' anybody. We had a garden, and we went fishing. We rode our horses down to the river and had a real boat down there, a little canoe. We went out on the river in it one day and he caught a porpoise. It had come all the way up from the Gulf after a rainstorm, and was confused by the fresh water. It pulled us all over the river for a whole afternoon."

A whole afternoon. I can see the porpoise leaping; I can see Daisy, young, with no wrinkles, and a straw hat. I can see Preacher leaning forward, battling the big fish.

"It got away," said Daisy, "it broke the line." She was sitting on the porch, shelling peas from the garden, remembering. "Oh, we both cried," she said. "Oh, we wanted that fish."

Lazy skies; streaks of red in the west, streaks of blood, of war —this place has a history, it has skeletons, violence, but we are living here quietly, smoothing it over, making it tame again, carefully; it is like walking on ice. Sometimes I imagine I can hear echoes: noises and sounds from a long, long time ago.

"This place is not on the map, right?" Elizabeth will ask. It's a game we play. We're frightened of cities, of other people.

"It might as well not even exist," I'll tell her.

She seems reassured.

The seasons mix and swirl. Except for the rains, and the hard stifling brutality of August, it can be easy to confuse the seasons. Sometimes wild turkeys gobble and fan in the dust in the street, courting, their lusty gobbles awakening us at daylight, a watery, rushing sound; that means it is April, and the floodwaters will not be coming back. But the other seasons get mixed up. The years do, too.

I'm glad Elizabeth and I have found this place. We have not

done well in other places: cities. We can't understand them. Everything seems like it is over so fast, in a city: minutes, hours, days, lives. . . .

Daisy keeps her yard very neat, cuts it with the push mower weekly, and has tulips and roses lining the edges of it. She's got two little beagle pups, also, and they roll and wrestle in the front yard and on her porch. Daisy gives church services in the abandoned Mt. Zion Baptist Church—it used to be on the shores of the river; now it just looks out at a cotton field—and sometimes we go. She's good. Daisy's sister, Maggie, lives in the old ghost town of Rodney, too. She says that she used to have a crush on Preacher; and that when Preacher was a little boy, he used to sleep curled up in a blanket, in a big empty cardboard box, at the top of a long playground slide in the front of the church. The slide is still there, beneath some pecan trees. It's a magnificent slide, such as you find in big city parks, tall and steep and glittering, shiny with use. It's got a little cabin—a booth—at the top, and that's where he used to sleep, says Maggie.

He didn't have any parents. It kept the rain off. Sometimes the two girls would sit up there with him and play cards. They'd take turns sliding down in the box then. They'd watch the white chickens walk past; walking down the dusty street, clucking.

"Maybe he always wanted one for a pet," Maggie says, trying to figure it out.

Forty years!

All for maybe what was just a mistake. Maybe he just wanted one for a pet.

The mother pig catches dogs. She lures them into the swamp. She runs down the center of what used to be Main Street in a funny, high-backed sort of hobbling, as if wounded, with all the little runt pigs running ahead of her, protected—the foolish dogs following, chasing it, slavering at the thought of fresh and easy meat.

Then the pig reaches the woods, and disappears into the heavy leafiness and undergrowth—the dog, or dogs, follow—and then we hear the squalls and yelps of the dog, or dogs, being killed.

Though we've also seen the sow kill dogs in the center of the street, in the middle of the day. She just tramples them, much as a horse would. I'd say she weighs about six or seven hundred pounds, and maybe more. Elizabeth and I carry a rifle when we go for our walks, an old seven-millimeter Mauser slung over Elizabeth's shoulder on a sling, a relic from the First World War, which we never saw, and which never affected Rodney. But if that pig were to charge us one night, the pig would rue that there had been a war. Elizabeth is a crack shot.

"Are the pigs really cursed people?" Elizabeth asks one evening. We're over on Daisy's porch. Maggie is shelling peas. Fireflies are blinking, floating out in the field as if searching for something with lanterns.

"Oh my, yes," says Maggie. "That big one is a general."

"I want to see the river," says Elizabeth, for about the hundredth time, and Daisy and Maggie laugh.

Daisy leans forward and jabs Elizabeth's leg, laughing. "How you know there even *is* a river?" she asks. "How you know we're not foolin' you?"

"I can smell it," Elizabeth says. She places her hand over her heart and closes her eyes. There's a breeze stirring dry leaves out in the road, a breeze stirring Elizabeth's hair, up on the porch, and she keeps her hand over her heart. "I can *feel* it," she says.

No one's laughing, now. We're thinking about the river, about how once it ran right through our town, through the very heart of it, and how we could have had our chance to see it then, had we been around.

For these old people—Daisy, Maggie, Preacher, and the others —to still be hanging on, to still be waiting around to see it again —well, it must have been quite a sight, quite a feeling.

Elizabeth and I put fireflies in empty mayonnaise jars, screw the lids on tightly and punch holes in the tops, and decorate our porch with them at night; or we'll line the bed with them, and then laugh as we love, with their soft blinking green bellies going on and off like soft, harmless firecrackers, or as if they are applauding. It's almost as if we have become Preacher and Daisy. The firefly bottle-lights around us must be like what the coal-oil lamps looked like, lining the sides of their old boat out in the field. Sometimes we shout, too, out into the night.

The bed—it's one of the best things we've ever done, buying it for this old house. It's huge, a four-poster, and looks as if it came straight off the set from *The Bride of Frankenstein*. It has the lace canopy, and is sturdy enough to handle our shaking. We have to climb a set of wooden steps to get into it, and sleeping in it is like going off on some final voyage, each night, so deep is our slumber, so quiet are the woods around us, and what is left of the town.

The last thing I do before we fall into that exhausted, peaceful sleep is to get up and go over to the window and empty the groggy, oxygen-deprived fireflies into the fresh night air. I shake all the bottles, to make sure I get them all out.

They float feebly down into the bushes, blinking wanly; wounded paratroopers, being released back into their real world, the one they own and know. If you keep them in a bottle too long, they will die. They won't blink anymore.

Elizabeth loves to read. She has books stacked on all the shelves of her sun room, up on the third floor, books stacked in one corner all the way to the ceiling. Sometimes I take iced tea up to her, in a pitcher, with lemons and sugar. I don't go in with it; I just peek through the keyhole. She wears a white dress, with lace, in the sun room, when she's reading, if it's not too hot. Her hair's dark, but there by the window, it looks washed in the light, like someone entirely different. It's scary, and intriguing. I knock on the door, to let her know the iced tea is out there, whenever she feels like getting it. Then I hurry down the steps.

After a while, I hear the click of the old door opening, up there, and the sound of her picking up the tray and carrying it in to her table—shutting the door with the back of her foot, I imagine—and she goes back to reading, holding the book with one hand, and fanning herself with a little cardboard fan with the other, still reading. Reading about make-believe people, and other people, other lives!

I'll sit out on the front steps and picture her drinking the tea, and imagine that I can taste its sweetness; the coolness, and refreshment of it.

I sweat too, in the summer, even down below the sweet olive tree, sitting on the steps, but not like she does, in the oven of her upstairs room. There's no air conditioner, no ceiling fan, and late in the afternoon each day, when she takes the white lacy dress off, it is soaking wet, and we rinse it in the sink, and hang it on the porch to dry in the night breezes.

It smells of sweet olive, the next morning, when she puts it on.

Time is standing still. We are digging in and holding our own, and we are making time stand still.

"We were going to have a baby," says Daisy. "We were just about ready to start, when they took him away. We were going to start that week, so that the baby would be born in the summer."

The slow summer. The time when nothing moves forward, when everything pauses, and then stops. It's a good idea.

In August, the cotton is picked. Men come from all over this part of the state. Trucks drive out into the fields. The men pick by hand. They do not leave much behind. It's like a circus. White horses stand out in the cotton, and watch; red tractor-trailers, and blue sky, and then, behind all of it, the trees, and behind that, the river, which we cannot see, but have been told is there.

Leaves clutter the street. They're brown and dried-up, curled, and the street is covered with them, like a carpet. You can hear the pigs rustling in them at night, snuffling for acorns. You can hear Daisy, in the daytime, walking through them.

Then the men are gone, almost all of the cotton is gone, and there are leaves on the roofs of the houses, leaves in our yards. Daisy rakes.

The sweet olive doesn't lose its leaves, but the other trees do.

Maggie and Daisy burn their leaves continuously, in wire baskets out by the side of the old road.

Something about the fall makes us want to go to Daisy's church services. They last about thirty minutes, and mostly she just reads Bible verses, coming straight from her mind, sometimes making a few up, but they all sound right. Then she sings for a while. She's got a good voice.

Sometimes it makes us sad. We sing, too. In the early fall, when everything is changing, the air takes on a stillness, and we feel like singing to liven things up.

It feels real lonely.

They're old slave songs, that Daisy sings, and mostly you just hum, and sway. You can close your eyes. You can forget about leaving the town of Rodney.

The owl calls at night, up in the attic. He's big. There's a hole in the ceiling, and we can hear him scrabbling through it around ten or eleven o'clock each night.

The full moon pokes through the trees, booms through our many dusty windows and lights the rooms. We hear him scrabble out to the banister, and then with a grunt he launches himself, and we hear the flapping of wings, initially, and then silence: he makes no sound, as he flies.

He flies all through the house—third floor, second floor, first —looking for mice. He screams when he spots one. He nearly always catches them.

We've hidden in the corner, in the big kitchen, and have watched. We've seen it happen. Elizabeth was frightened, at first, but she isn't now.

The longer we live down here, the less frightened she is of anything. She is growing braver with age, as if it is a thing that she will be needing more of.

*   *   *

Elizabeth and I want to build something that won't go away. We're not sure how to go about it, but some nights we go running naked in the moonlight, out in the field. There are these old white plugs, nag horses, that roam loose in the cotton fields, and we ride them some nights. We ride across the field, toward where we think the river is—riding through the fog, and through the blinkings of fireflies—but when we get down into the swamp, we get turned around, lost, and are frightened; and we have to turn back.

Daisy's standing out on her porch sometimes when we come galloping back.

"You can't go to it!" she says, laughing in the night. "It's got to come to you!"

She's waiting for Preacher. No cards. No letters. The air hangs still in the fall, after the cotton men leave. The days do not budge.

Afternoons, in the fall, we go pick up pecans in front of the old church. We fix grilled cheeses for supper. Some nights, we share a bottle of wine.

We sit on the porch in the frayed wicker swing, and watch the moon, and can hear Maggie down the street, humming, hoeing weeds in her garden.

The days go by. I think that we will have just exactly enough time to build what Elizabeth and I want to build—to make a thing that will last, and will not leave.

One night I can't sleep. Elizabeth isn't in bed, when I awaken. I look all through the house for her; a slight, illogical panic that grows, with each empty room.

The moon is out; everything is bathed in hard silver. She is sitting out on the back porch, in her white dress, barefooted, with her feet hanging over the edge, swinging them. Out in the yard, the pigs are feeding in the moonlight: the huge mother and the little ones, small dirigibles now, all around her. There's a wind blowing, from the south. I can taste the salt in it from the coast; it is warm. Elizabeth has a book in her lap; she's reading by the light of the moon.

A dog barks, a long way off, and I feel that I should not be watching. So I climb back up the stairs and get into the big bed, and try to sleep.

But I want to hold on to something!

Luther—an old blind man, who lived down the street, and whom we hardly ever saw—has passed on. Elizabeth and I are the only ones with backs strong enough to dig the grave; we bury him in the old cemetery on the bluff. There are gravestones from the 1850s. Gravestones from the war, too, with the letters "C.S.A." on the stone. Some of the people buried there were named Emancipation, while they were alive—it was a common name then. It's soft, rich earth.

We dig the hole without much trouble. I had to build a coffin out of old lumber.

Daisy says words as we fill the hole back up. That rain of earth, shovels of it, covering the box, with him in it. Sometimes in the spring, and in the fall too, rattlesnakes come out of the cane and lie on the gravestones, for their warmth. No one ever goes up to the cemetery, because of the snakes.

The river used to be visible, below the cemetery. Probably one day again it will be.

A few years ago, one of Daisy's half-sisters died, and they buried her up here. It was the first time anyone had been up to the cemetery in a long time—it was all grown over with brambles and vines, and weedy—and there was the skeleton of a deer, impaled upon the iron spikes of the fence that surrounds the graveyard. Dogs, or something, had been chasing it, and it had tried to leap over the high fence, and had gotten caught. There were only bones left. It's still up there, too high for anyone to reach.

The skull seems to be opening its mouth in a scream.

We pile stones over the mound of fresh earth, to keep the pigs from rooting. One time they dragged a man back down into town, after he had been buried. They were fighting over him, dragging him around on the street and grunting.

Mostly, I just want to start over. I'd like one more chance. I feel so old, some days!

Daisy has a cream, a salve, made from some sort of root, which she smears over her eyelids at night. It's supposed to help her fading vision; maybe even bring it back, I don't know.

Whenever she comes over to read our own sparse mail, she mostly just holds it, and runs her hands over it, and doesn't really look at the words. Instead, I think she just imagines what each letter is saying: what history lies behind it, what chain of circumstances.

Daisy and Preacher used to ride horses up onto the bluff overlooking Rodney, riding through the trees, and would then get off their horses and climb up in one of the tallest trees so that they could see the river. They'd sit up there on a branch, says Daisy, and have a picnic, eat sandwiches and feel the river breezes, and feel the tree swaying, and they would just watch the faraway river for the longest time.

Then they would climb down and ride through the woods some more, looking for old battle things—old rusted rifles, bayonets, canteens, and the like. They would sell these things to the museum in Jackson for a dollar each, boxing them up for the mailman, tying them shut with twine, and sending them C.O.D., and there was always enough money to get by on.

Daisy and Preacher would ride their horses down off the bluff and out across the field, out toward the river, after that, and they would go swimming at night; or sometimes they would just sit on the sandbar and watch the stars, and listen to the river sounds. Sometimes a barge would go by. In the night, in the dark, its silhouette would look like a huge gunboat.

There were wild grapes that grew along the riverbank, tart purple Mustang grapes, cool in the night, and they would pick and eat those as they watched the river.

They took him away when he was twenty; they took him away when she was just nineteen.

"It can go just like that," Daisy says, snapping her fingers. "It can go that fast."

The pigs are growing fat for slaughter. Autumn, coming on again, and they're not piglets anymore: they are pigs. One morning a shot awakens us, and we sit up in bed and look out the window.

Daisy is straddling one of the pigs, and is gutting it with a great bladed knife, a knife from a hundred years ago. She pulls the entrails from the pig's stomach and feeds them to her pups. The other pigs have run off into the woods, but they will be back. It's a cool morning, almost cold, and steam is rising from the pig's open chest.

Later in the afternoon, there's the good smell of fresh meat cooking.

Maggie shoots a pig at dusk, for herself, and two of the old men back down on the other side of town get theirs, the next day.

"I don't want any," Elizabeth says one afternoon, after she's slid down the banister. Her eyes are magic, she's shivering and holding herself, dancing up and down, goose-pimply; she's very happy to be so young.

"I feel as if it will *jinx* me," she says. "I mean, those pigs lived under our *house*."

The smell of pork, of bacon, hangs heavy in the town, like the blue haze from cannon fire.

Coyotes, at night, and the peafowl, screaming. Pecans underfoot. A full moon. The gleam of night cotton. We ride around on an old white plug, out in the cotton field. The cotton is ready to be picked. It is a field of warm, blossoming snow, bursting with white, up to our ankles, even when we sit on the horse.

The men will be coming soon to pick the cotton again. It has been four years, since we've been down here, in the town of Rodney.

"I'm happy," Elizabeth says, and squeezes my arms, sitting behind me on the old horse, and she taps the horse's ribs with her heels. The smell of woodsmoke, and overhead, the slight, nasal, far-off cries of geese, going south. The horse plods along in the dust.

Daisy will be starting her church services again, and once more we'll be going. I'm glad that Elizabeth's happy, living down here in the swamp, in such a little one-horse shell of an ex-town. We'll hold hands, and carry our Bible, and walk slowly down the road to Daisy's church. There will be a few slow, lazy fireflies, in the beginning of dusk. We'll go in and sit on the bench, and listen to Daisy rant and howl.

Then the songs and moans will start. The ones about being slaves. I'll shut my eyes and sway, and try not to think of other places.

And then this is what Elizabeth might say: "You'd better love me," she might say—an order, an ultimatum. But she'll be teasing, playing; she'll know that's all we can do, down here.

There'll still be geese, outside, overhead, and a night wind, and stars—noises and feelings about leaving, about moving on—but I think that we can sing louder, and it'll be all right.

We'll not be able to hear them, if we sing loudly enough.

The air will be stuffy and warm in the little church, and for a moment, we might feel dizzy, light-headed—but the songs are what's important, what matters. The songs about being slaves.

There aren't any words. You just close your eyes, and sway.

Maybe Preacher is not coming, and maybe the river is not coming back, either. But I do not say these things to Daisy. She sits out on the porch and waits for him. She remembers when she was our age, and in love with him. She remembers all the things they did; so much time they had, all that time.

She puts bread crumbs out in the middle of the road, stakes

white chickens out in the yard for him, in case he comes in the night. All she really has left is memory, but Elizabeth and I, we are still young, and we live in the old house across the street from her, and we try to learn from her.

The days go by. I think that we will have just exactly enough time to build what Elizabeth and I want to build—to make a thing that will last, and will not leave.

BIOGRAPHICAL NOTES

Tom Bailey was born in his mother's home town of Indianola, Mississippi, and grew up trailing his father, a Marine Corps aviator, around the South. A graduate of Marshall College in West Virginia, he received a master's degree from the Iowa Writers' Workshop and is now completing a novel, which will serve as the creative dissertation for his Ph.D. from the State University of New York at Binghamton.

Rick Bass was born and raised in Texas. After college in Utah, he worked for some years in Mississippi as a geologist, and now makes his home in Montana. His stories have been selected for *Best American Short Stories, O. Henry Prize Stories, Editors' Choices*, and *New Stories from the South* and, in 1989, W.W. Norton, Inc. published his collection, *The Watch*.

Richard Bausch, who teaches in the Writing Program at George Mason University in Fairfax, Virginia, is the author of four novels and two collections of short stories, the most recent of which is *The Fireman's Wife, and Other Stories* (Linden Press/Simon & Schuster 1990). The recipient of fellowships from the Guggenheim Foundation and the National Endowment for the Arts, Mr. Bausch lives in Fauquier County, Virginia, with his wife, Karen, and their five children.

Larry Brown was born in Oxford, Mississippi, and lives in rural Lafayette County with his wife and three children and his dog, Sam. He now writes full-time.

Moira Crone, a native North Carolinian, lives in Louisiana, where she is acting director of the M.F.A. program at Louisiana State Uni-

227

versity. The author of *The Winnebago Mysteries* (stories) and *A Period of Confinement* (a novel), she has received fellowships from the National Endowment for the Arts and The Bunting Institute of Radcliffe College.

Clyde Edgerton, whose most recent novel is *The Floatplane Notebooks* (Algonquin 1988, Ballentine 1989), received a Guggenheim Fellowship in 1989. He lives in Durham, North Carolina, with his wife, Susan Ketchin, and their daughter, Catherine.

Greg Johnson, from Atlanta, Georgia, got his Ph.D. in English at Emory University and now teaches creative writing at Kennesaw College. He is the author of two volumes of literary criticism, and his first collection of stories is *Distant Friends* (Ontario Review Press 1990). He is at work on a novel and a second collection of short stories.

Nanci Kincaid was born in Tallahassee, Florida, and lives now in Tuscaloosa, Alabama, where she is working toward an M.F.A. from the University of Alabama. Her stories have been anthologized in *New Stories from the South* (1988) and *Homecoming: The Family in Southern Fiction* (August House).

Reginald McKnight, whose father was in the Air Force, was born in Fürstenfeldbrück, Germany. Even so, he spent part of his childhood in his father's home state (Texas) and in his mother's (Alabama). He teaches at the University of Pittsburgh and has recently published a first novel, *I Get on the Bus* (Little, Brown 1990). His first collection of stories, *Moustatha's Eclipse* (University of Pittsburgh Press) won the Drew Heinz Award.

Lewis Nordan is the author of two collections of short fiction, *The All-Girl Football Team* and *Welcome to the Arrow-Catcher Fair*, both recently released by Vintage Contemporaries, Random House. He is a native of Itta Bena, Mississippi, and currently teaches at the University of Pittsburgh.

Lance Olsen grew up in Venezuela, New Jersey, and Texas. He spent ten adult years in the South, first as a graduate student at the University of Virginia, then as an assistant professor at the University of Kentucky. He has published one novel—*Live from Earth*—and two studies of postmodern literature. He teaches at the University of Idaho.

Mark Richard was born in Lake Charles, Louisiana, and grew up in Texas, Virginia, and North Carolina. His stories have appeared in *Esquire, Shenandoah, The Quarterly, Antaeus, Grand Street,* and *Harper's.* His first collection, *The Ice at the Bottom of the World,* was published last year by Alfred A. Knopf, Inc.

Ron Robinson lives in Tahlequah, Oklahoma, where he is at work on a novel. He received his M.F.A. in creative writing from Wichita State University, taught at Northeastern State University in Tahlequah, was editor of the *A.I.D. Review,* and is now a fiction editor for the literary journal, *Nimrod.* He received the Oklahoma Literary Award for Fiction in 1987 from the Arts and Humanities Council of Tulsa.

Bob Shacochis, a native of Virginia, won the 1985 American Book Award for his first collection of stories, *Easy in the Islands.* His most recent collection, *The Next New World,* was awarded the Rome Prize for Literature by the American Academy of Arts and Letters. His journalism appears frequently in *Harper's* magazine, where he is a contributing editor. He is at work on a novel set in Virginia and the Caribbean.

Molly Best Tinsley, having grown up in an Air Force family, isn't from anywhere, and, after twenty years in the suburbs of Washington, D.C., must assume home is yet to be discovered. She teaches on the civilian faculty at the U.S. Naval Academy, and her stories have appeared in *Redbook* and numerous quarterlies.

Donna Trussell was born and raised in Texas and lives now in Kansas City. Her stories and poems have appeared in *Poetry, TriQuarterly, The Massachusetts Review, Poetry Northwest,* and other magazines. She won the David Sokolov Scholarship in Fiction to the 1989 Bread Loaf Writers' Conference.

Shannon Ravenel, the editor, was born and raised in the Carolinas —Charlotte, Camden, and Charleston. She served as series editor of *The Best American Short Stories* annual anthology from 1977 to 1990 and edited *The Best American Short Stories of the Eighties* (Houghton Mifflin 1990). She is senior editor of Algonquin Books of Chapel Hill and lives in Chapel Hill, North Carolina, with her husband, Dale Purves, and their two daughters.